COMIXOLOGY ORIGINALS

STOUT CLUB

Dark Horse Books

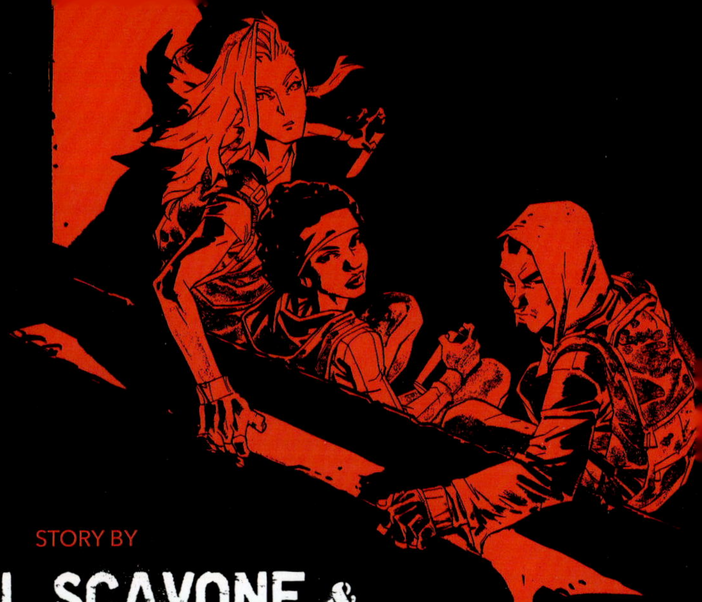

STORY BY
RAFAEL SCAVONE & RAFAEL ALBUQUERQUE

SCRIPT BY
RAFAEL SCAVONE

ART BY
ROGER CRUZ

COLORS BY
CRIS PETER

LETTERS BY
BERNARDO BRICE

COVERS BY
ROGER CRUZ & RAFAEL ALBUQUERQUE

EDITED BY
FELIX HORNE

SPECIAL THANKS
BRYCE GOLD, CHIP MOSHER, DAVID STEINBERGER, EM ERDMAN, PAMELA MULLIN HORVARTH, AND TIA VASILIOU

RED TAG CREATED BY SCAVONE, ALBUQUERQUE, AND CRUZ

Neil Hankerson Executive Vice President • Tom Weddle Chief Financial Officer • Dale LaFountain Chief Information Officer • Tim Wiesch Vice President of Licensing • Vanessa Todd-Holmes Vice President of Production and Scheduling • Mark Bernardi Vice President of Book Trade and Digital Sales • Randy Lahrman Vice President of Product Development and Sales • Cara O'Neil Vice President of Marketing • Ken Lizzi General Counsel • Dave Marshall Editor in Chief • Davey Estrada Editorial Director • Chris Warner Senior Books Editor • Cary Grazzini Director of Specialty Projects • Lia Ribacchi Creative Director • Michael Gombos Senior Director of Licensed Publications • Kari Yadro Director of Custom Programs • Kari Torson Director of International Licensing • Christina Niece Director of Scheduling

Published by Dark Horse Books
A division of Dark Horse Comics LLC
10956 SE Main Street
Milwaukie, OR 97222

First edition: May 2023
Trade paperback ISBN 978-1-50673-097-4

1 3 5 7 9 10 8 6 4 2
Printed in China

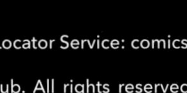

Comic Shop Locator Service: comicshoplocator.com

Red Tag Contents © 2022, 2023 Stout Club. All rights reserved. "Red Tag," its logos, and the likenesses of all characters herein are trademarks of Stout Club, unless otherwise noted. "Stout Club" and the Stout Club logo are trademarks of Stout Club, Inc. "Comixology" and the Comixology logos are registered trademarks of Comixology. Dark Horse Books® and the Dark Horse logo are registered trademarks of Dark Horse Comics LLC. All rights reserved. Dark Horse Comics is a member of Embracer Group. No portion of this publication may be reproduced or transmitted, in any form or by any means, without the express written permission of Stout Club, Comixology, or Dark Horse Comics LLC. Names, characters, places, and incidents featured in this publication either are the product of the author's imagination or are used fictitiously. Any resemblance to actual persons (living or dead), events, institutions, or locales, without satiric intent, is coincidental.

Library of Congress Cataloging-in-Publication Data

Names: Scavone, Rafael, author. | Albuquerque, Rafael, 1981- author,
  artist. | Cruz, Roger, artist. | Peter, Cris, colorist. | Brice,
  Bernardo, letterer.
Title: Red tag / story by Rafael Scavone and Rafael Albuquerque ; script by
  Rafael Scavone ; art by Roger Cruz ; colors by Cris Peter ; letters by
  Bernardo Brice ; covers by Roger Cruz & Rafael Albuquerque.
Description: First edition. | Milwaukie, OR : Dark Horse Books, 2023. |
  "Red Tag created by Scavone, Albuquerque, and Cruz" | Summary: "While
  searching for justice on the streets of São Paulo, Lis. Lu, and Leco -
  three friends bonded by their love for Brazil's unique street art "pixo"
  - find themselves entangled in a life-threatening plot. Dangerous
  people, holdovers from the country's brutal dictatorial past, are
  plotting against the movement for reform in São Paulo, and our three
  heroes may be the only ones who can stop them. RED TAG is a fast-paced
  thriller set in Brazil, starring young characters looking for justice in
  a system built to silencing their voices."-- Provided by publisher.
Identifiers: LCCN 2022054772 | ISBN 9781506730974 (trade paperback)
Subjects: LCSH: Government, Resistance to--Comic books, strips, etc. |
  Street art--Comic books, strips, etc. | São Paulo (Brazil)--Comic
  books, strips, etc. | LCGFT: Thriller comics. | Graphic novels.
Classification: LCC PN6790.B73 S276713 2023 | DDC
  741.5/981--dc23/eng/20221129
LC record available at https://lccn.loc.gov/2022054772

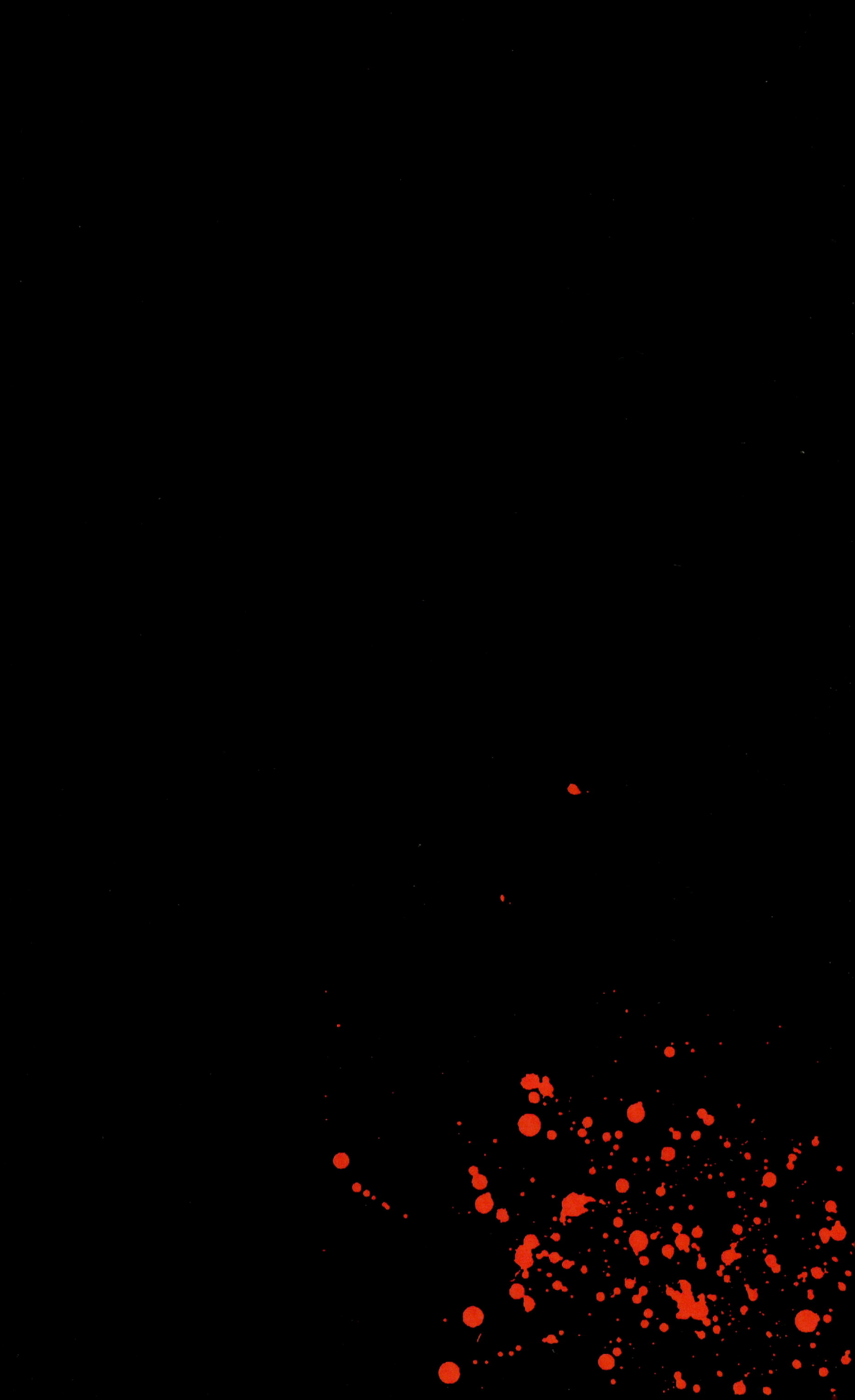

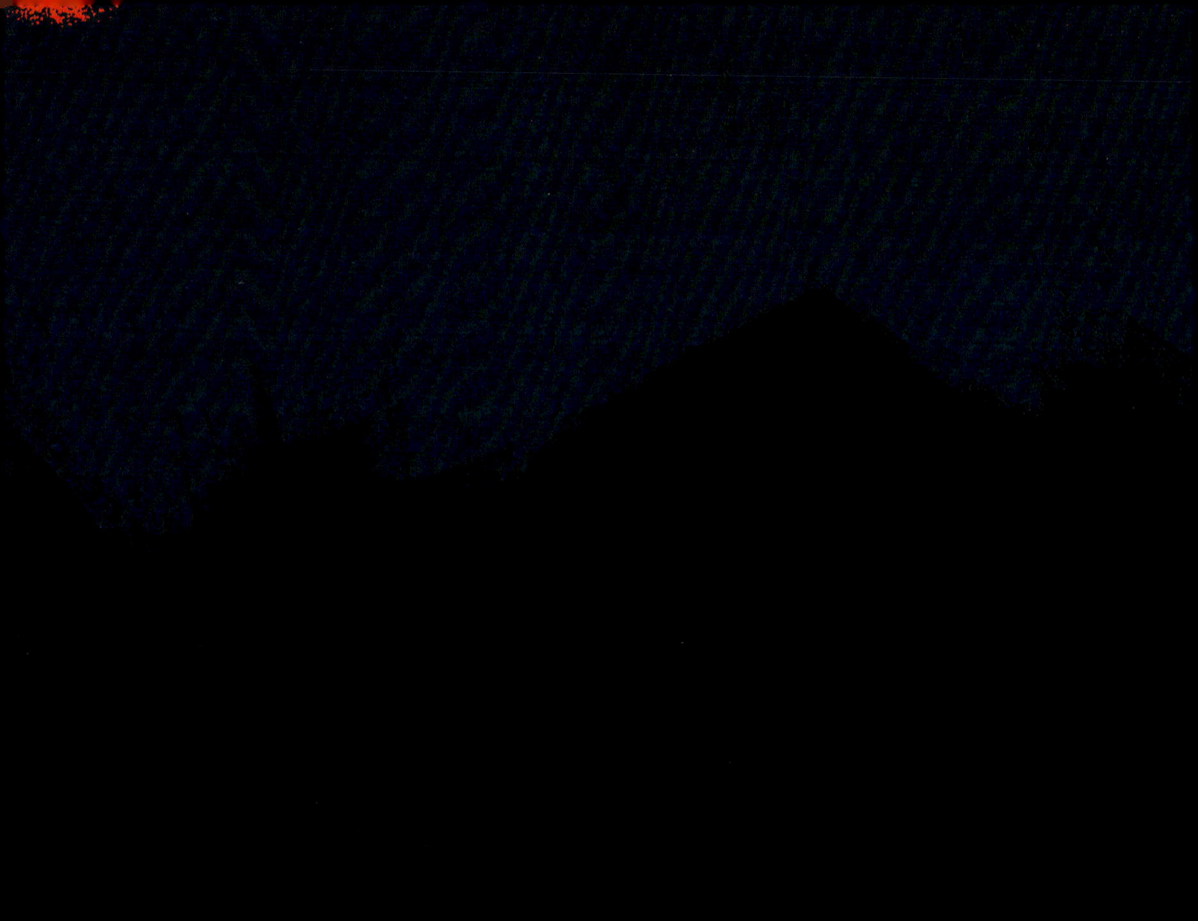

CHAPTER ONE

A DAY FOR THE PREY

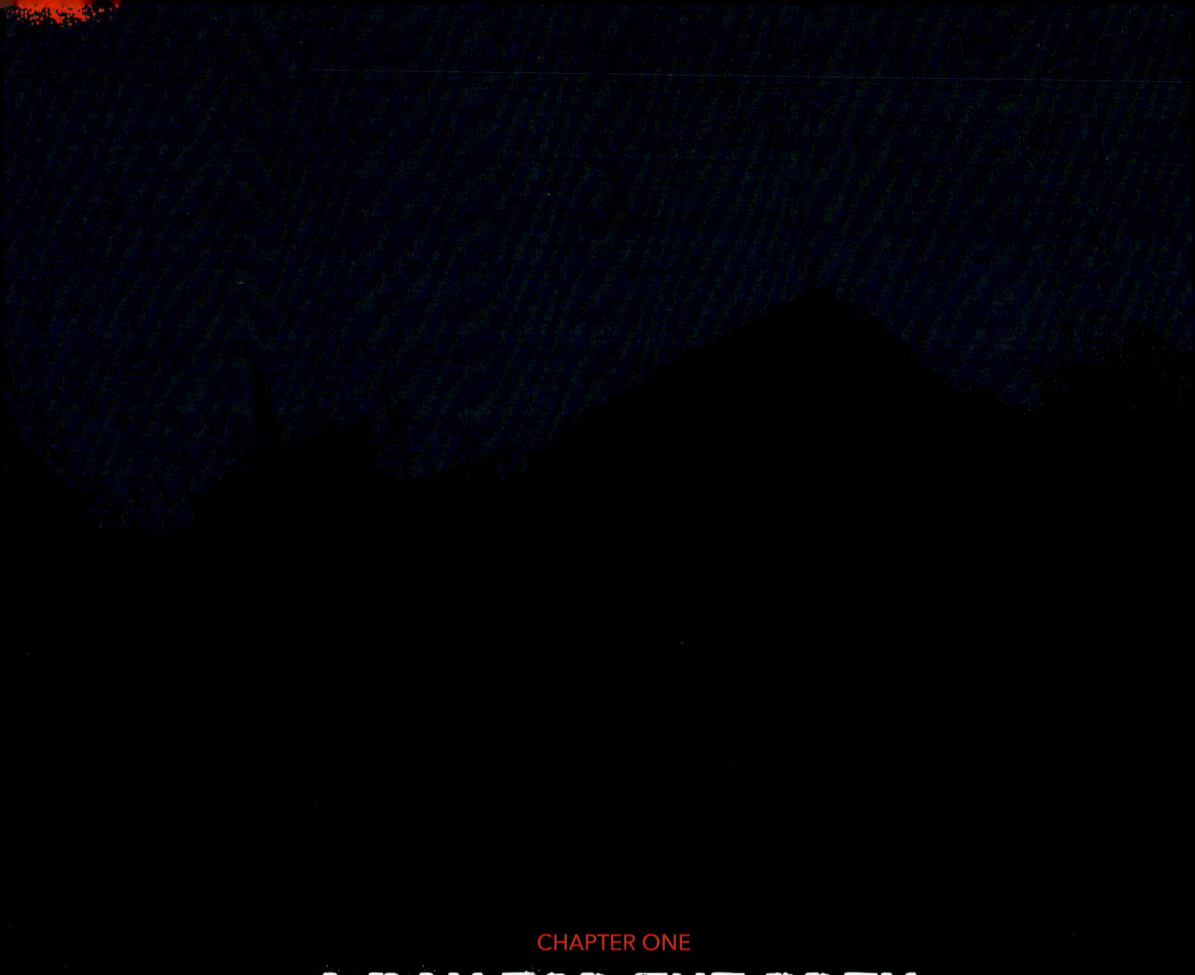

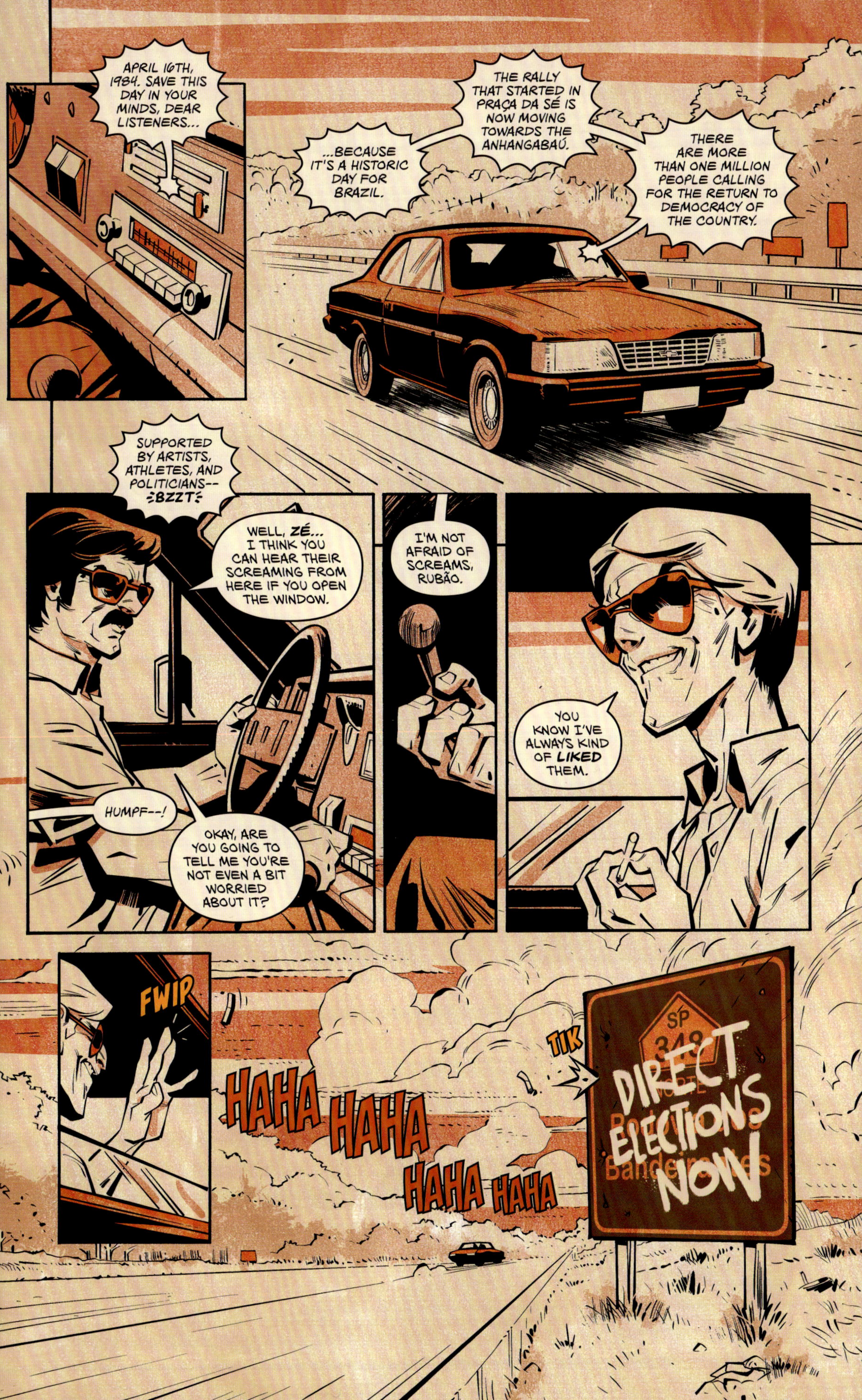
APRIL 16TH, 1984. SAVE THIS DAY IN YOUR MINDS, DEAR LISTENERS...
...BECAUSE IT'S A HISTORIC DAY FOR BRAZIL.
THE RALLY THAT STARTED IN PRAÇA DA SÉ IS NOW MOVING TOWARDS THE ANHANGABAÚ.
THERE ARE MORE THAN ONE MILLION PEOPLE CALLING FOR THE RETURN TO DEMOCRACY OF THE COUNTRY.
SUPPORTED BY ARTISTS, ATHLETES, AND POLITICIANS-- BZZT
WELL, **ZÉ**... I THINK YOU CAN HEAR THEIR SCREAMING FROM HERE IF YOU OPEN THE WINDOW.
HUMPF--!
OKAY, ARE YOU GOING TO TELL ME YOU'RE NOT EVEN A BIT WORRIED ABOUT IT?
I'M NOT AFRAID OF SCREAMS, RUBÃO.
YOU KNOW I'VE ALWAYS KIND OF **LIKED** THEM.
FWIP
HAHA HAHA HAHA HAHA
TIK
SP 348
DIRECT ELECTIONS NOW

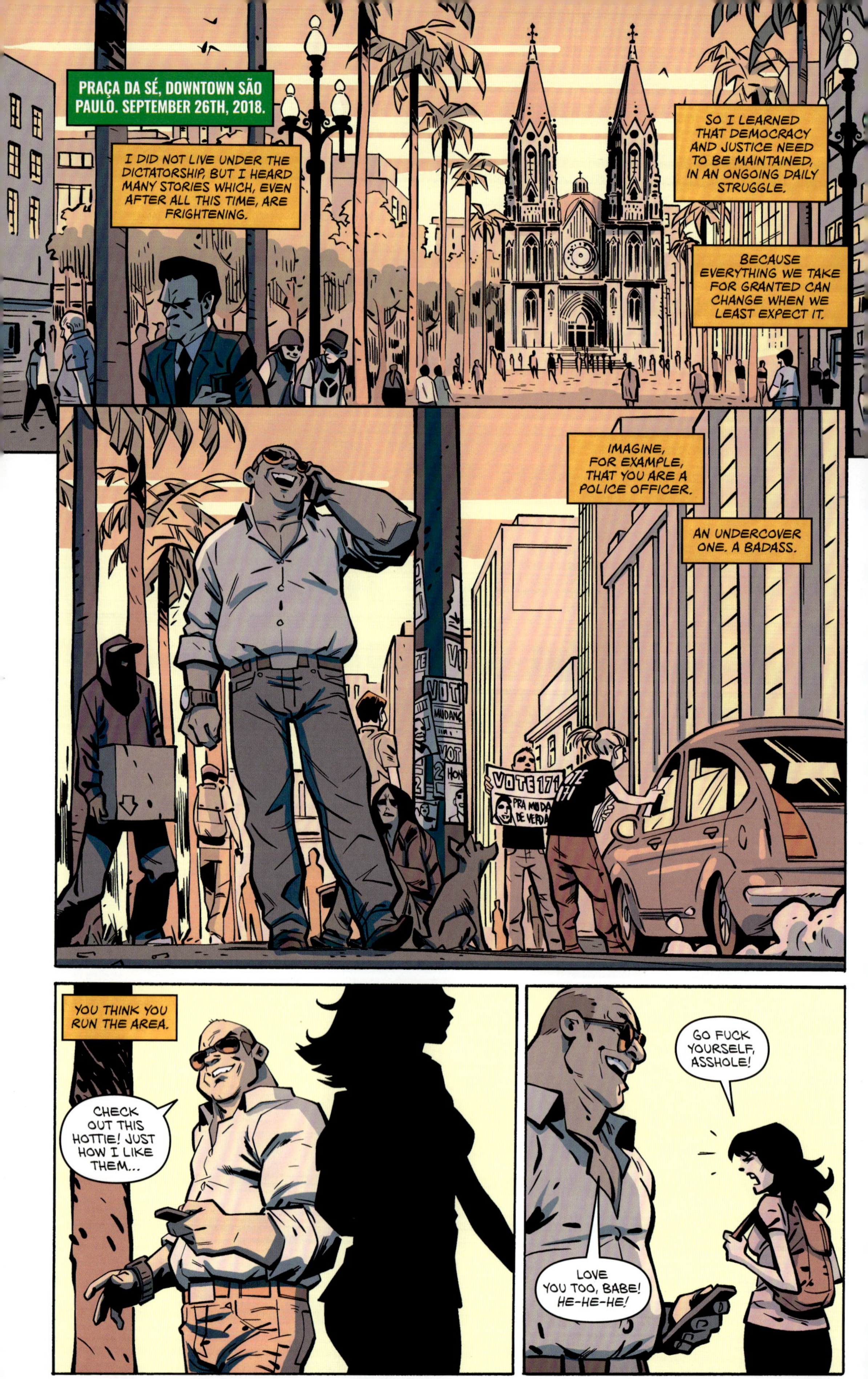
PRAÇA DA SÉ, DOWNTOWN SÃO PAULO. SEPTEMBER 26TH, 2018.
I DID NOT LIVE UNDER THE DICTATORSHIP, BUT I HEARD MANY STORIES WHICH, EVEN AFTER ALL THIS TIME, ARE FRIGHTENING.
SO I LEARNED THAT DEMOCRACY AND JUSTICE NEED TO BE MAINTAINED, IN AN ONGOING DAILY STRUGGLE.
BECAUSE EVERYTHING WE TAKE FOR GRANTED CAN CHANGE WHEN WE LEAST EXPECT IT.
IMAGINE, FOR EXAMPLE, THAT YOU ARE A POLICE OFFICER.
AN UNDERCOVER ONE. A BADASS.
YOU THINK YOU RUN THE AREA.
CHECK OUT THIS HOTTIE! JUST HOW I LIKE THEM...
GO FUCK YOURSELF, ASSHOLE!
LOVE YOU TOO, BABE! HE-HE-HE!

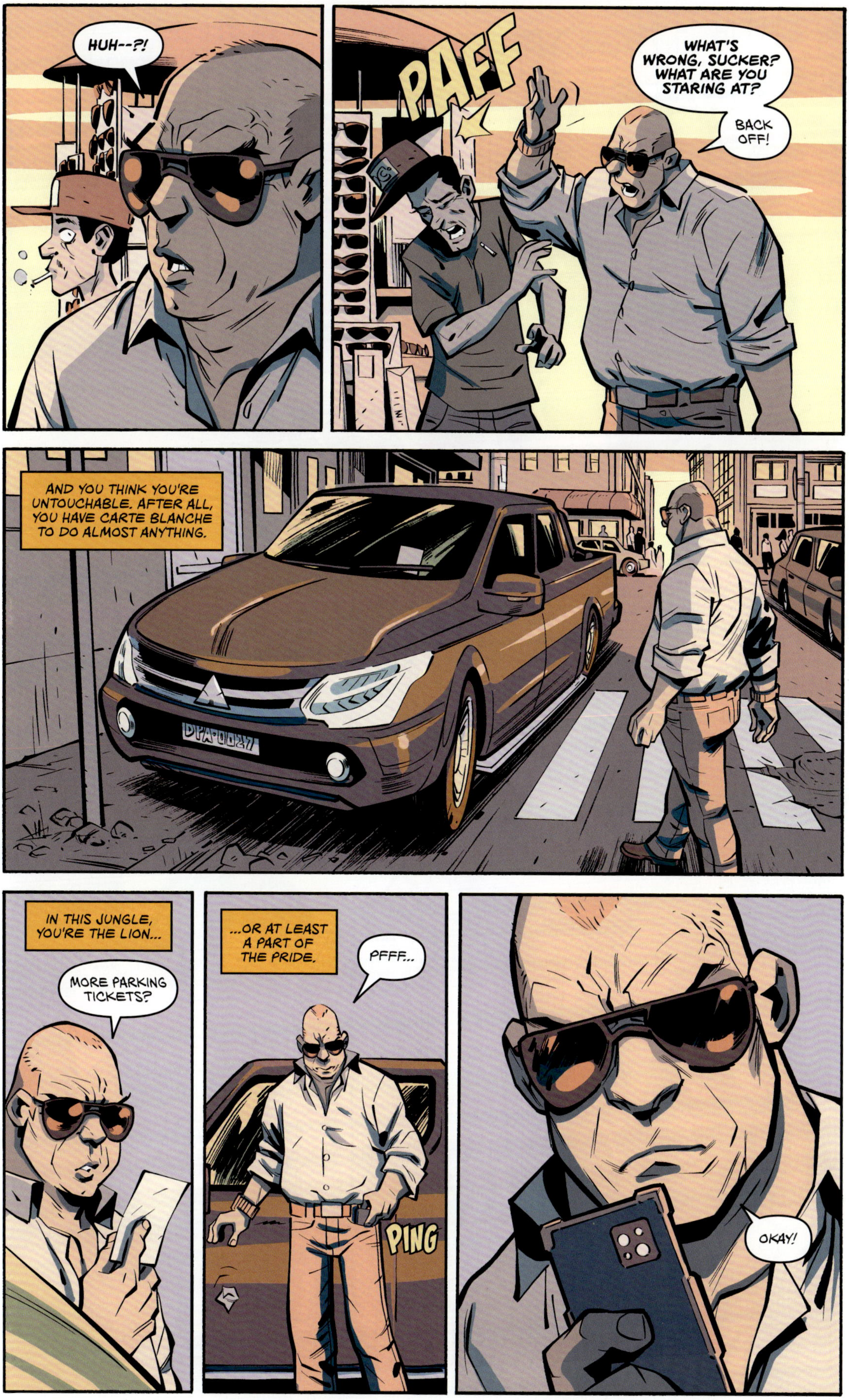
HUH--?!
PAFF
WHAT'S WRONG, SUCKER? WHAT ARE YOU STARING AT?
BACK OFF!
AND YOU THINK YOU'RE UNTOUCHABLE. AFTER ALL, YOU HAVE CARTE BLANCHE TO DO ALMOST ANYTHING.
IN THIS JUNGLE, YOU'RE THE LION...
MORE PARKING TICKETS?
...OR AT LEAST A PART OF THE PRIDE.
PFFF...
PING
OKAY!

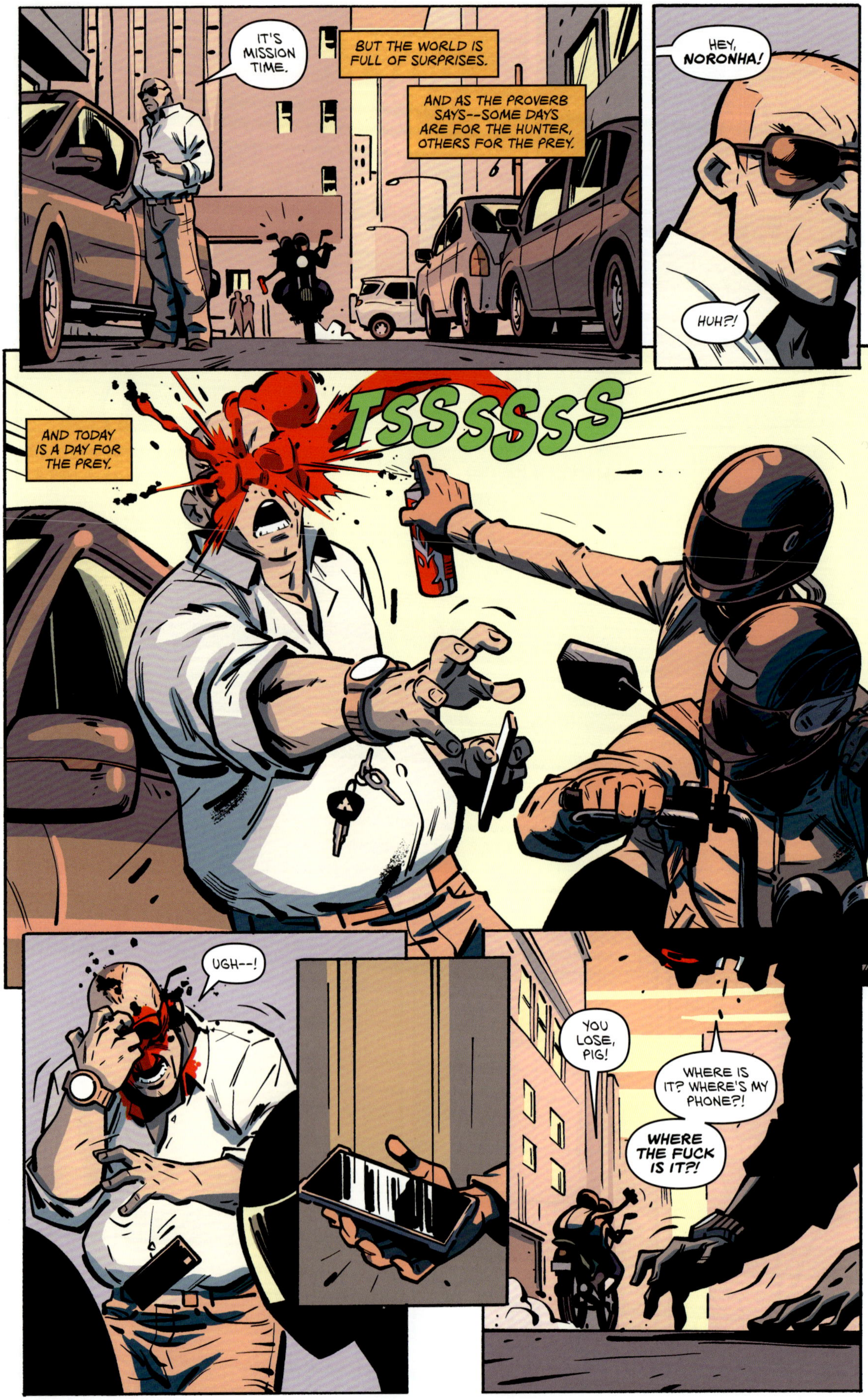
IT'S MISSION TIME.
BUT THE WORLD IS FULL OF SURPRISES.
AND AS THE PROVERB SAYS--SOME DAYS ARE FOR THE HUNTER, OTHERS FOR THE PREY.
HEY, NORONHA!
HUH?!
AND TODAY IS A DAY FOR THE PREY.
TSSSSSS
UGH--!
YOU LOSE, PIG!
WHERE IS IT? WHERE'S MY PHONE?!
WHERE THE FUCK IS IT?!

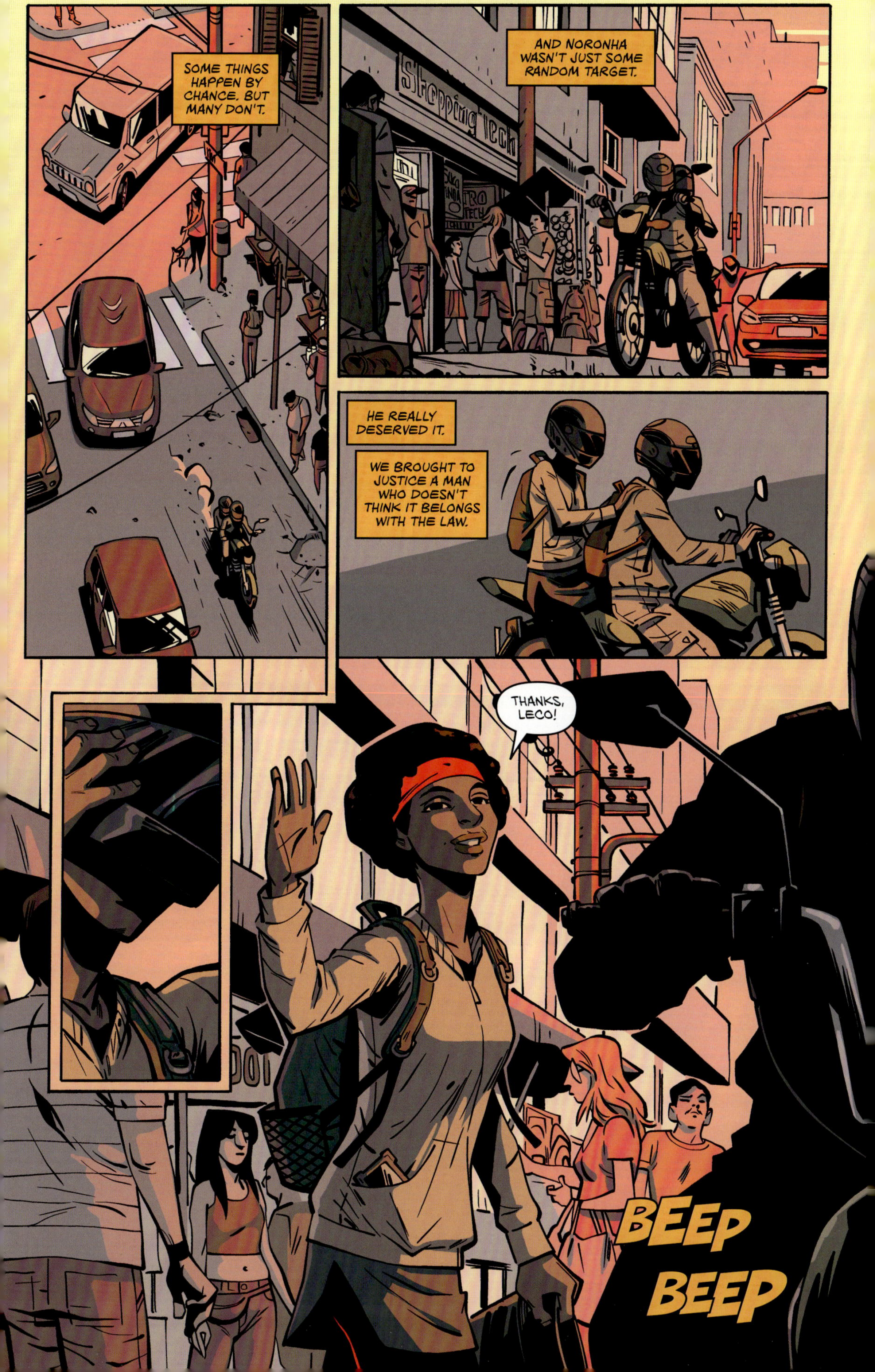
SOME THINGS HAPPEN BY CHANCE. BUT MANY DON'T.
AND NORONHA WASN'T JUST SOME RANDOM TARGET.
HE REALLY DESERVED IT.
WE BROUGHT TO JUSTICE A MAN WHO DOESN'T THINK IT BELONGS WITH THE LAW.
THANKS, LECO!
BEEP
BEEP

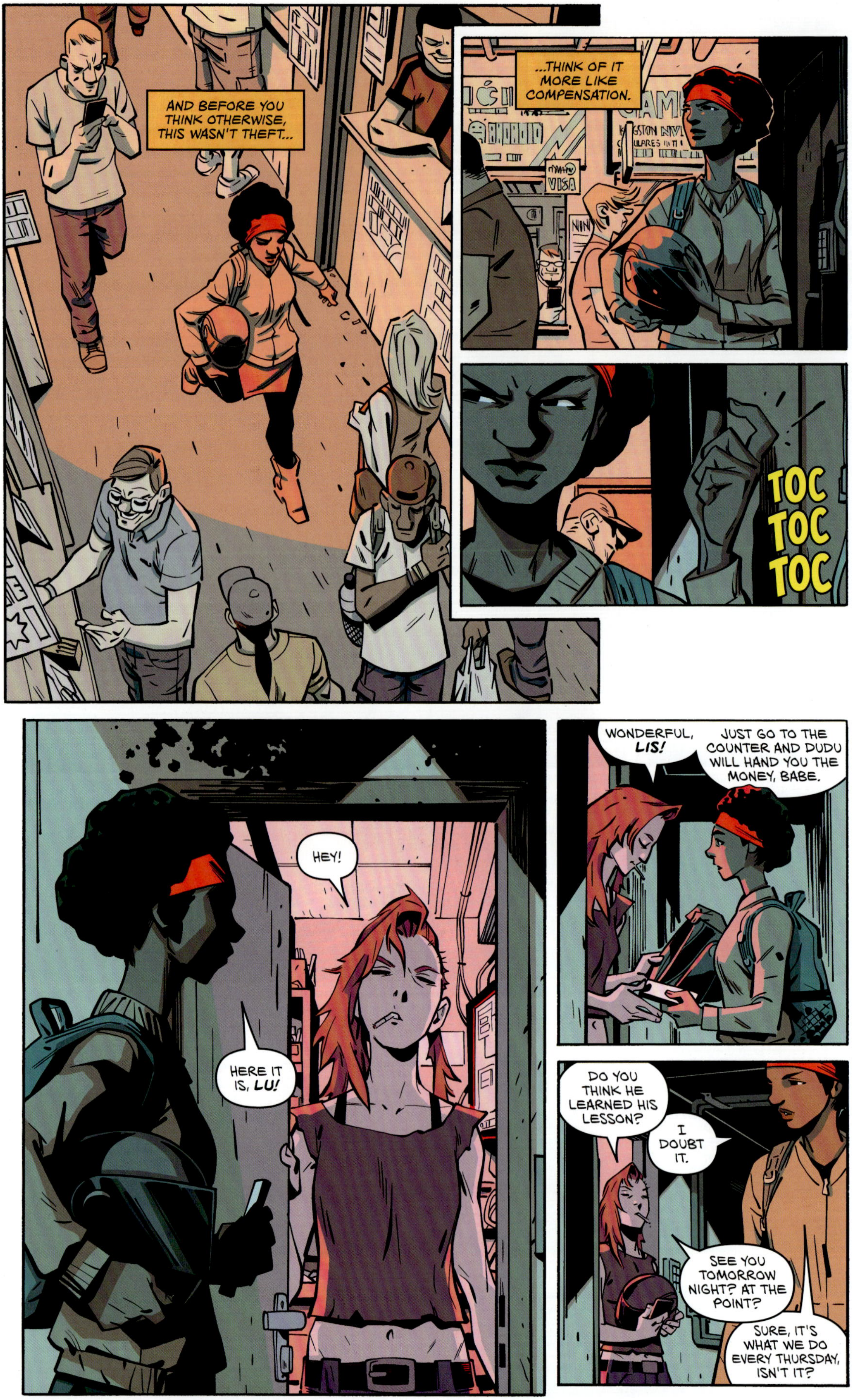
AND BEFORE YOU THINK OTHERWISE, THIS WASN'T THEFT...
...THINK OF IT MORE LIKE COMPENSATION.
VISA
TOC TOC TOC
HEY!
HERE IT IS, LU!
WONDERFUL, LIS!
JUST GO TO THE COUNTER AND DUDU WILL HAND YOU THE MONEY, BABE.
DO YOU THINK HE LEARNED HIS LESSON?
I DOUBT IT.
SEE YOU TOMORROW NIGHT? AT THE POINT?
SURE, IT'S WHAT WE DO EVERY THURSDAY, ISN'T IT?

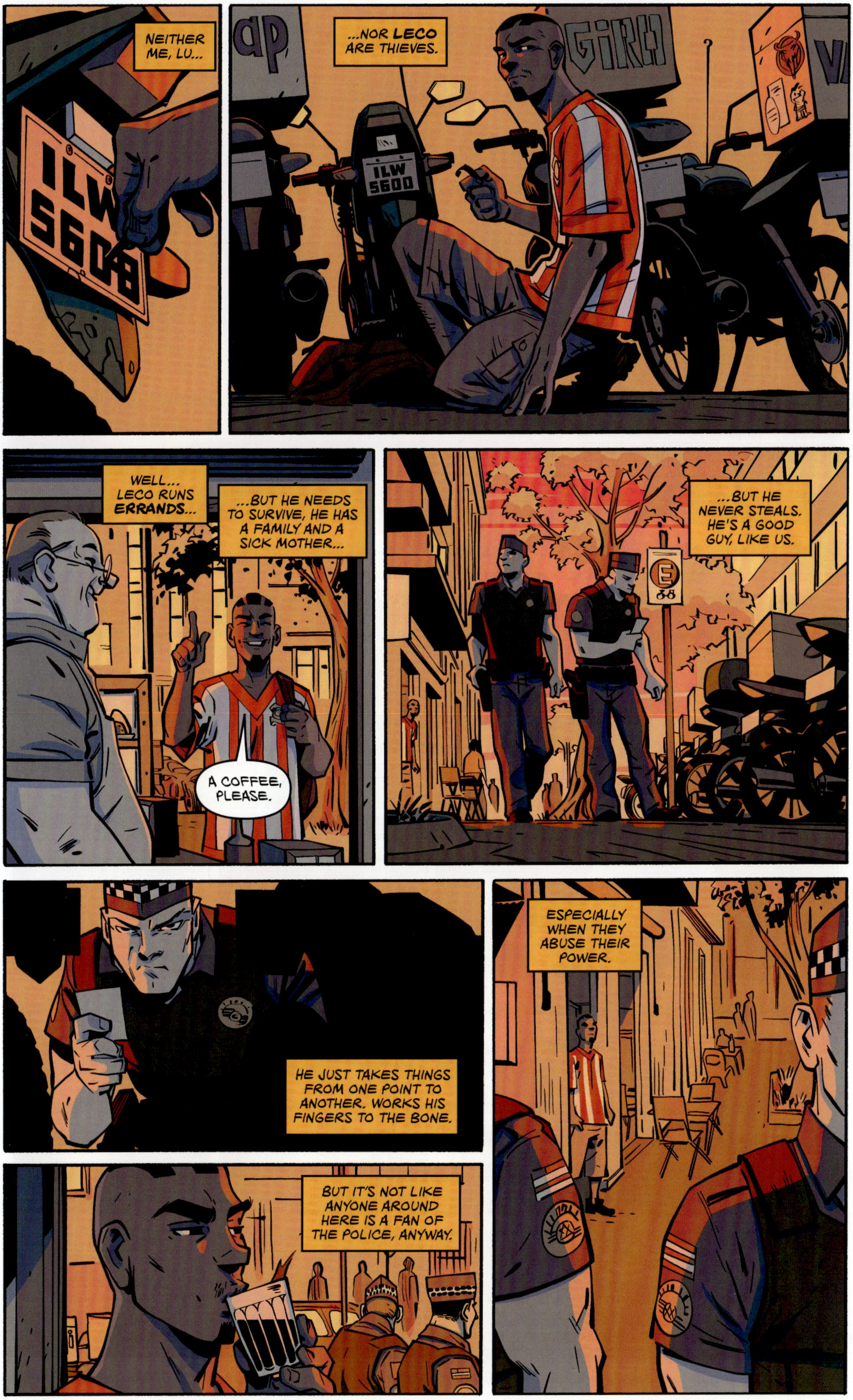
NEITHER ME, LU...
...NOR LECO ARE THIEVES.
ILW 5608
ILW 5600
WELL... LECO RUNS ERRANDS...
...BUT HE NEEDS TO SURVIVE, HE HAS A FAMILY AND A SICK MOTHER...
A COFFEE, PLEASE.
...BUT HE NEVER STEALS. HE'S A GOOD GUY, LIKE US.
HE JUST TAKES THINGS FROM ONE POINT TO ANOTHER. WORKS HIS FINGERS TO THE BONE.
BUT IT'S NOT LIKE ANYONE AROUND HERE IS A FAN OF THE POLICE, ANYWAY.
ESPECIALLY WHEN THEY ABUSE THEIR POWER.

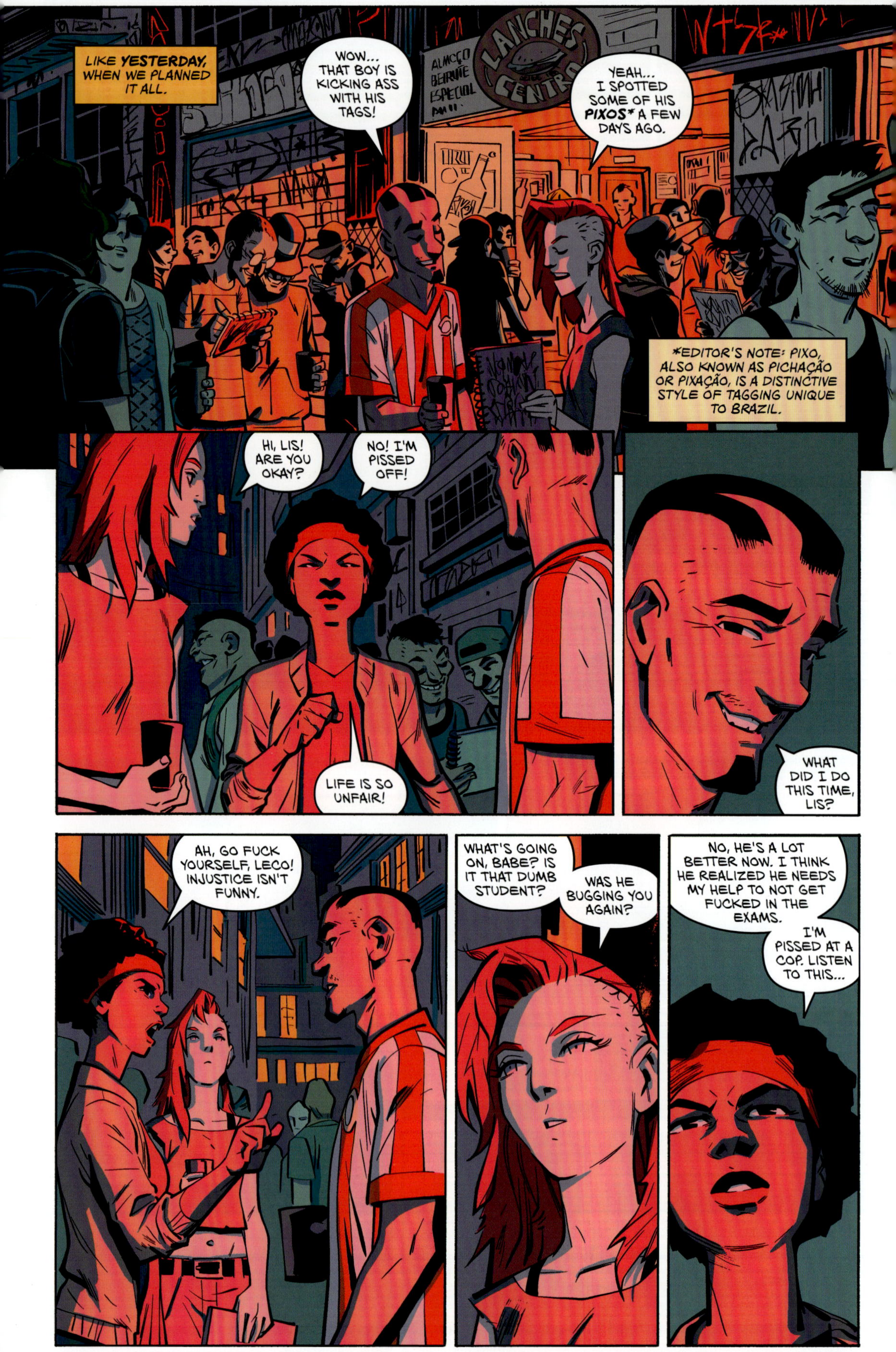
LIKE YESTERDAY, WHEN WE PLANNED IT ALL.
WOW... THAT BOY IS KICKING ASS WITH HIS TAGS!
YEAH... I SPOTTED SOME OF HIS PIXOS* A FEW DAYS AGO.
LANCHES CENTRO
*EDITOR'S NOTE: PIXO, ALSO KNOWN AS PICHAÇÃO OR PIXAÇÃO, IS A DISTINCTIVE STYLE OF TAGGING UNIQUE TO BRAZIL.
HI, LIS! ARE YOU OKAY?
NO! I'M PISSED OFF!
LIFE IS SO UNFAIR!
WHAT DID I DO THIS TIME, LIS?
AH, GO FUCK YOURSELF, LECO! INJUSTICE ISN'T FUNNY.
WHAT'S GOING ON, BABE? IS IT THAT DUMB STUDENT?
WAS HE BUGGING YOU AGAIN?
NO, HE'S A LOT BETTER NOW. I THINK HE REALIZED HE NEEDS MY HELP TO NOT GET FUCKED IN THE EXAMS.
I'M PISSED AT A COP. LISTEN TO THIS...

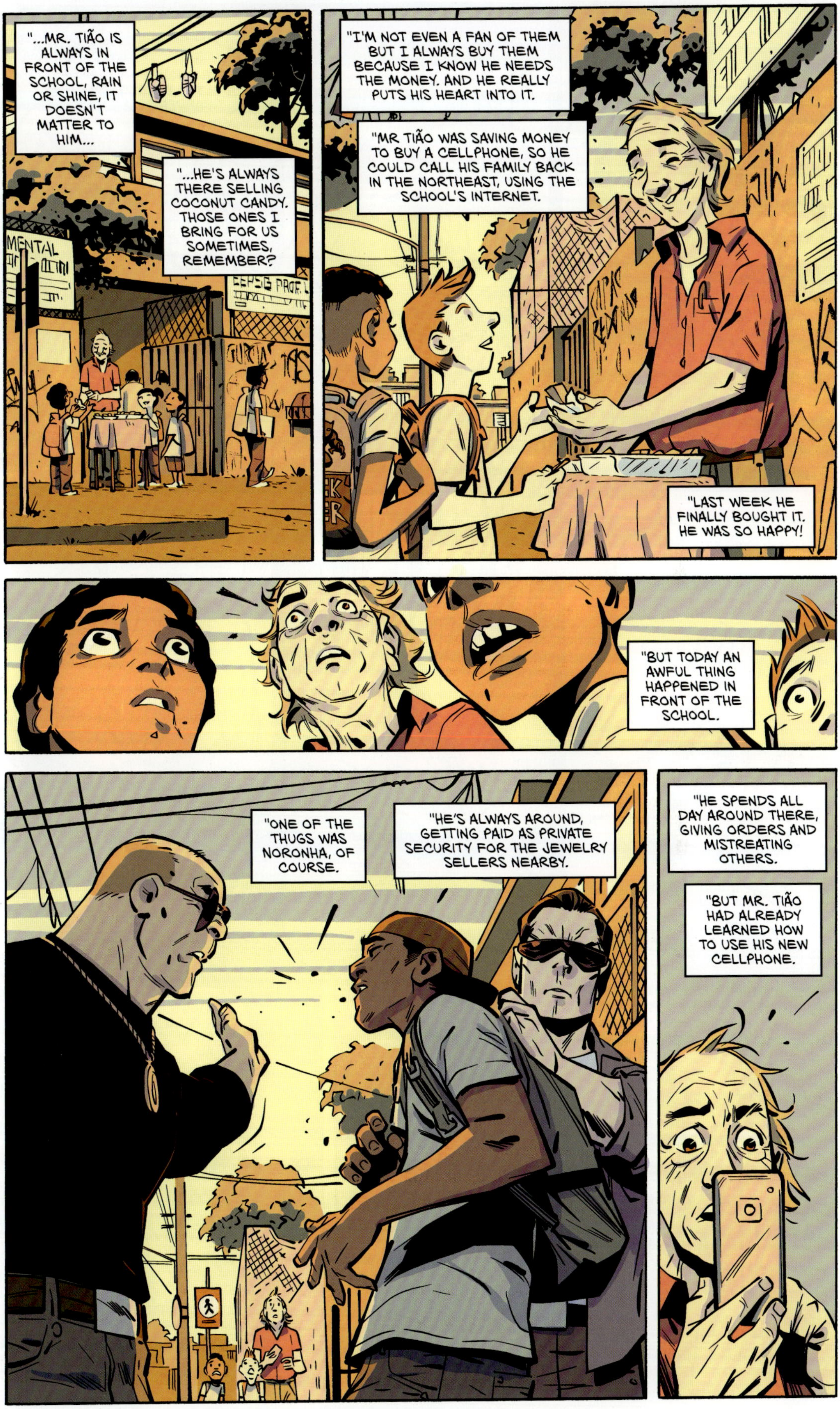
"...MR. TIÃO IS ALWAYS IN FRONT OF THE SCHOOL, RAIN OR SHINE, IT DOESN'T MATTER TO HIM...
"...HE'S ALWAYS THERE SELLING COCONUT CANDY. THOSE ONES I BRING FOR US SOMETIMES, REMEMBER?
"I'M NOT EVEN A FAN OF THEM BUT I ALWAYS BUY THEM BECAUSE I KNOW HE NEEDS THE MONEY. AND HE REALLY PUTS HIS HEART INTO IT.
"MR TIÃO WAS SAVING MONEY TO BUY A CELLPHONE, SO HE COULD CALL HIS FAMILY BACK IN THE NORTHEAST, USING THE SCHOOL'S INTERNET.
"LAST WEEK HE FINALLY BOUGHT IT. HE WAS SO HAPPY!
"BUT TODAY AN AWFUL THING HAPPENED IN FRONT OF THE SCHOOL.
"ONE OF THE THUGS WAS NORONHA, OF COURSE.
"HE'S ALWAYS AROUND, GETTING PAID AS PRIVATE SECURITY FOR THE JEWELRY SELLERS NEARBY.
"HE SPENDS ALL DAY AROUND THERE, GIVING ORDERS AND MISTREATING OTHERS.
"BUT MR. TIÃO HAD ALREADY LEARNED HOW TO USE HIS NEW CELLPHONE.

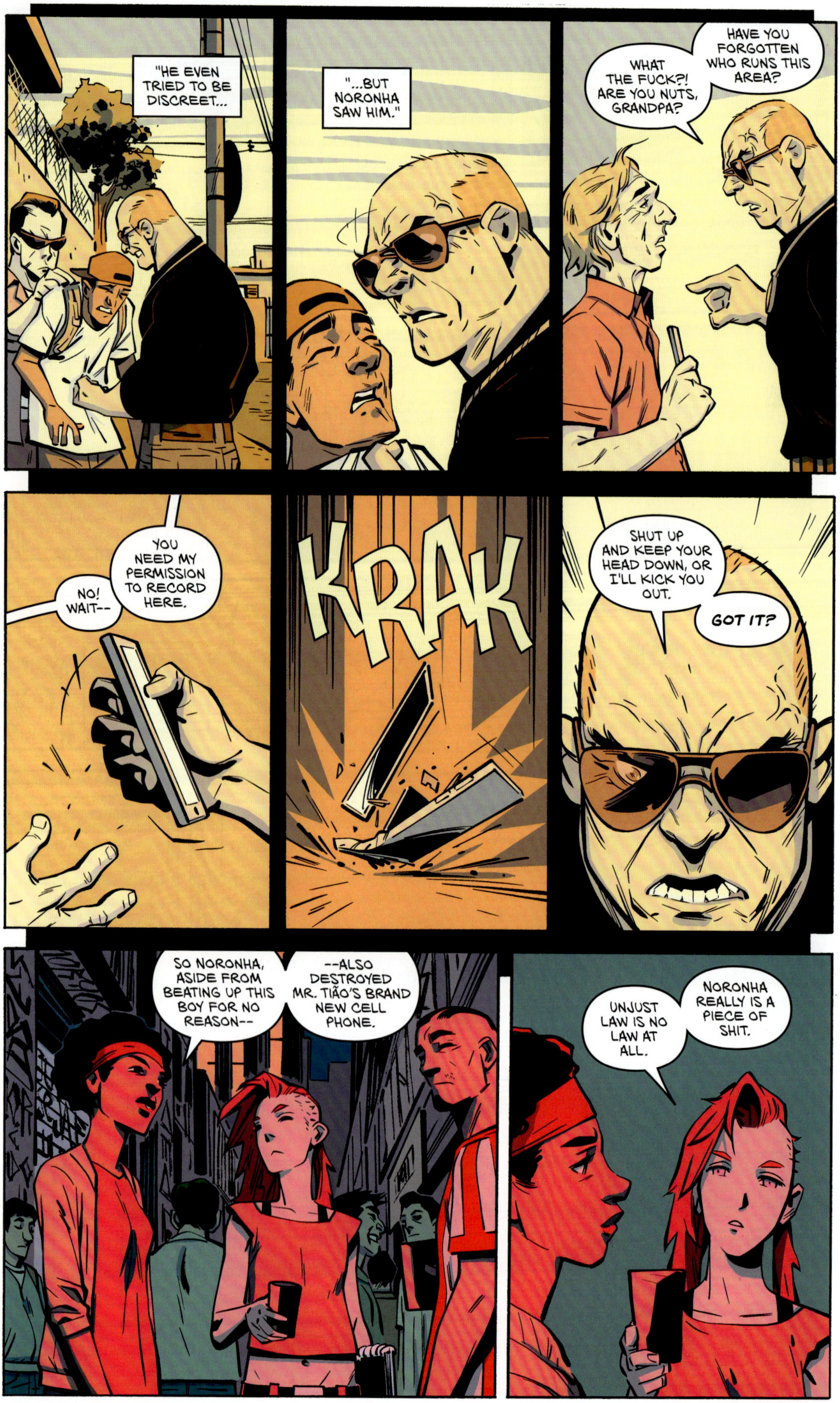
"HE EVEN TRIED TO BE DISCREET...
"...BUT NORONHA SAW HIM."
WHAT THE FUCK?! ARE YOU NUTS, GRANDPA?
HAVE YOU FORGOTTEN WHO RUNS THIS AREA?
YOU NEED MY PERMISSION TO RECORD HERE.
NO! WAIT--
KRAK
SHUT UP AND KEEP YOUR HEAD DOWN, OR I'LL KICK YOU OUT.
GOT IT?
SO NORONHA, ASIDE FROM BEATING UP THIS BOY FOR NO REASON--
--ALSO DESTROYED MR. TIÃO'S BRAND NEW CELL PHONE.
NORONHA REALLY IS A PIECE OF SHIT.
UNJUST LAW IS NO LAW AT ALL.

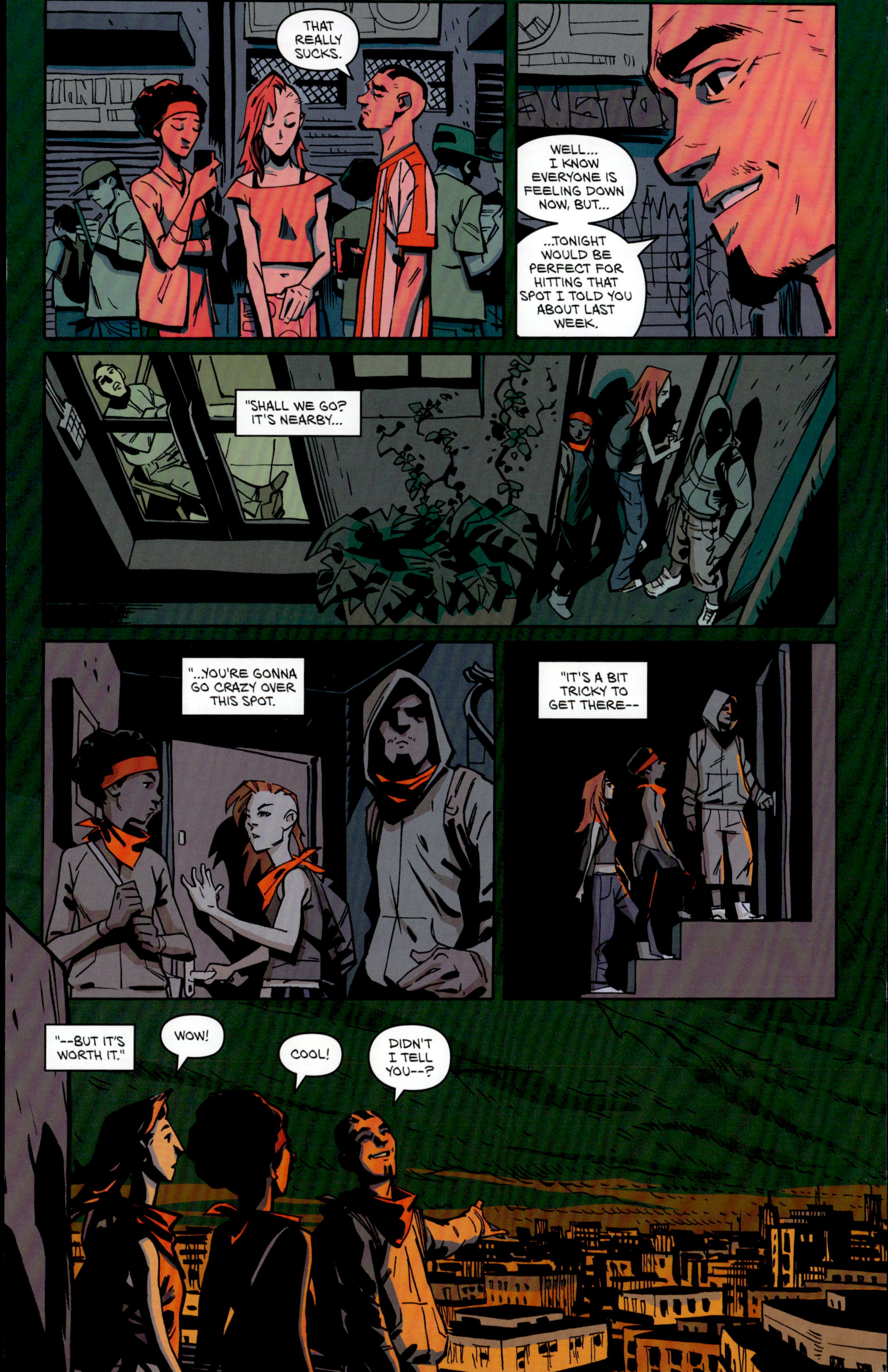
THAT REALLY SUCKS.
WELL... I KNOW EVERYONE IS FEELING DOWN NOW, BUT...
...TONIGHT WOULD BE PERFECT FOR HITTING THAT SPOT I TOLD YOU ABOUT LAST WEEK.
"SHALL WE GO? IT'S NEARBY...
"...YOU'RE GONNA GO CRAZY OVER THIS SPOT.
"IT'S A BIT TRICKY TO GET THERE--
"--BUT IT'S WORTH IT."
WOW!
COOL!
DIDN'T I TELL YOU--?

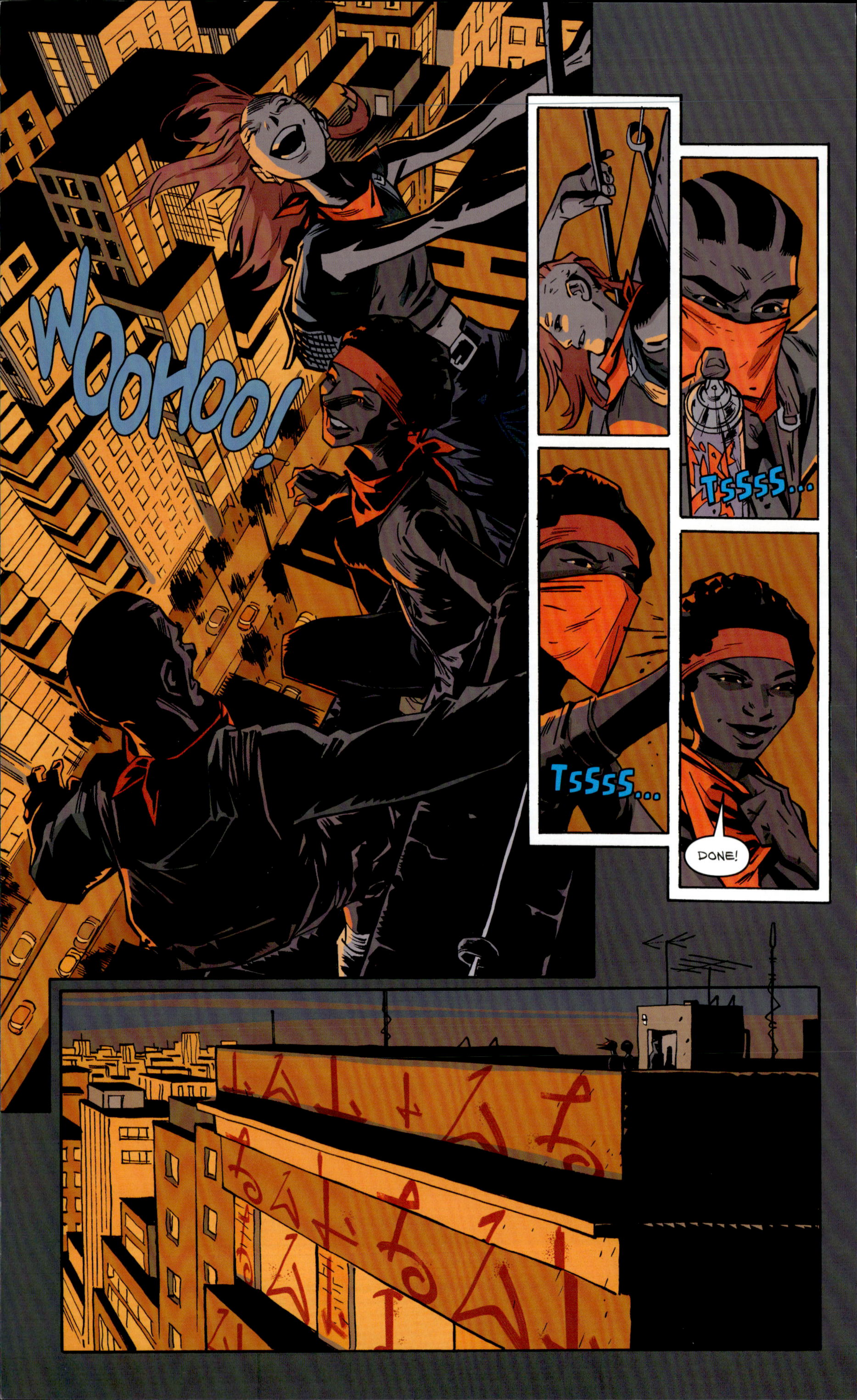
WOOHOO!
TSSSS...
TSSSS...
DONE!

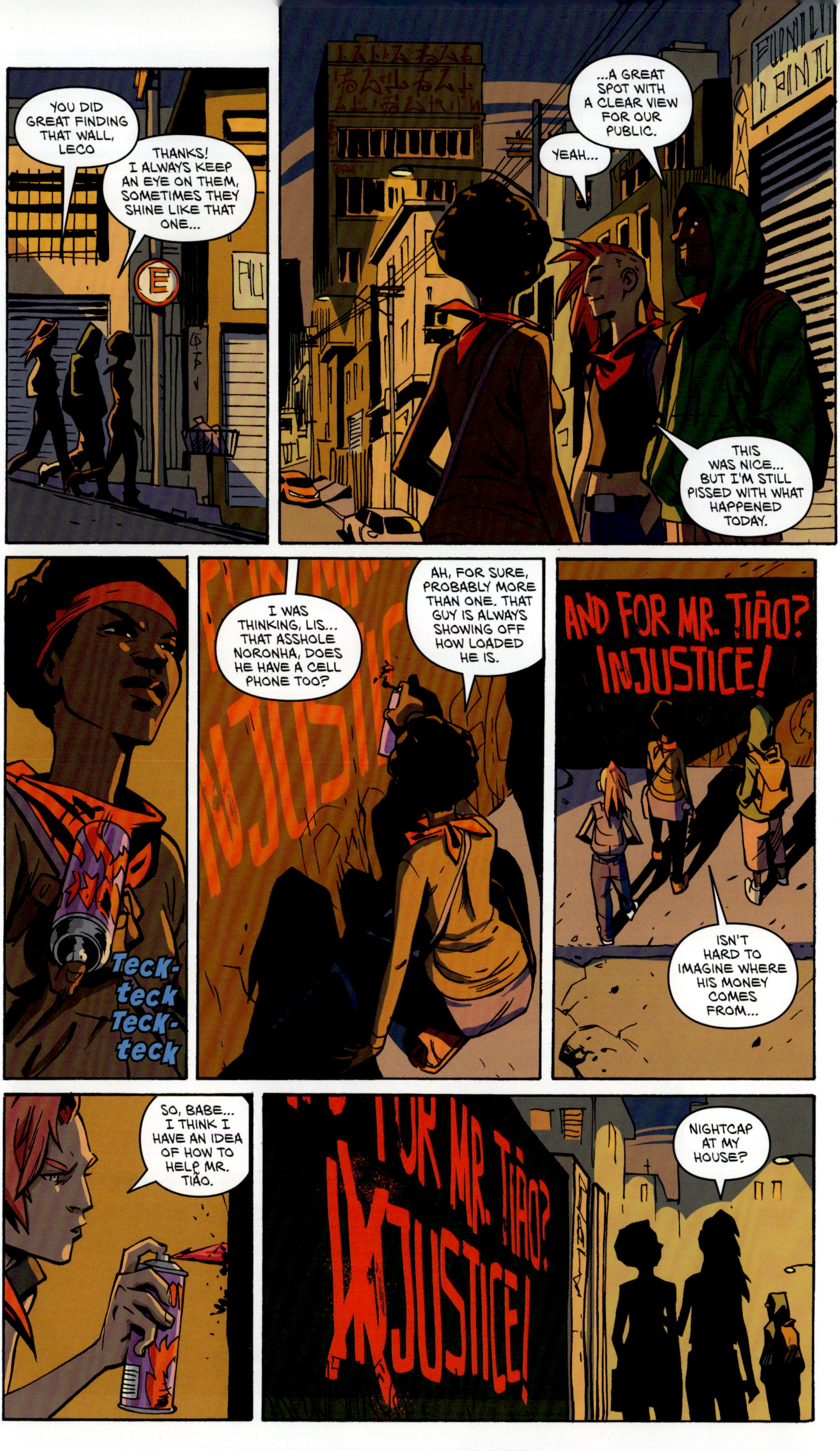
YOU DID GREAT FINDING THAT WALL, LECO
THANKS! I ALWAYS KEEP AN EYE ON THEM, SOMETIMES THEY SHINE LIKE THAT ONE...
...A GREAT SPOT WITH A CLEAR VIEW FOR OUR PUBLIC.
YEAH...
THIS WAS NICE... BUT I'M STILL PISSED WITH WHAT HAPPENED TODAY.
Teck-teck Teck-teck
I WAS THINKING, LIS... THAT ASSHOLE NORONHA, DOES HE HAVE A CELL PHONE TOO?
AH, FOR SURE, PROBABLY MORE THAN ONE. THAT GUY IS ALWAYS SHOWING OFF HOW LOADED HE IS.
AND FOR MR. TIÃO? INJUSTICE!
ISN'T HARD TO IMAGINE WHERE HIS MONEY COMES FROM...
SO, BABE... I THINK I HAVE AN IDEA OF HOW TO HELP MR. TIÃO.
NIGHTCAP AT MY HOUSE?

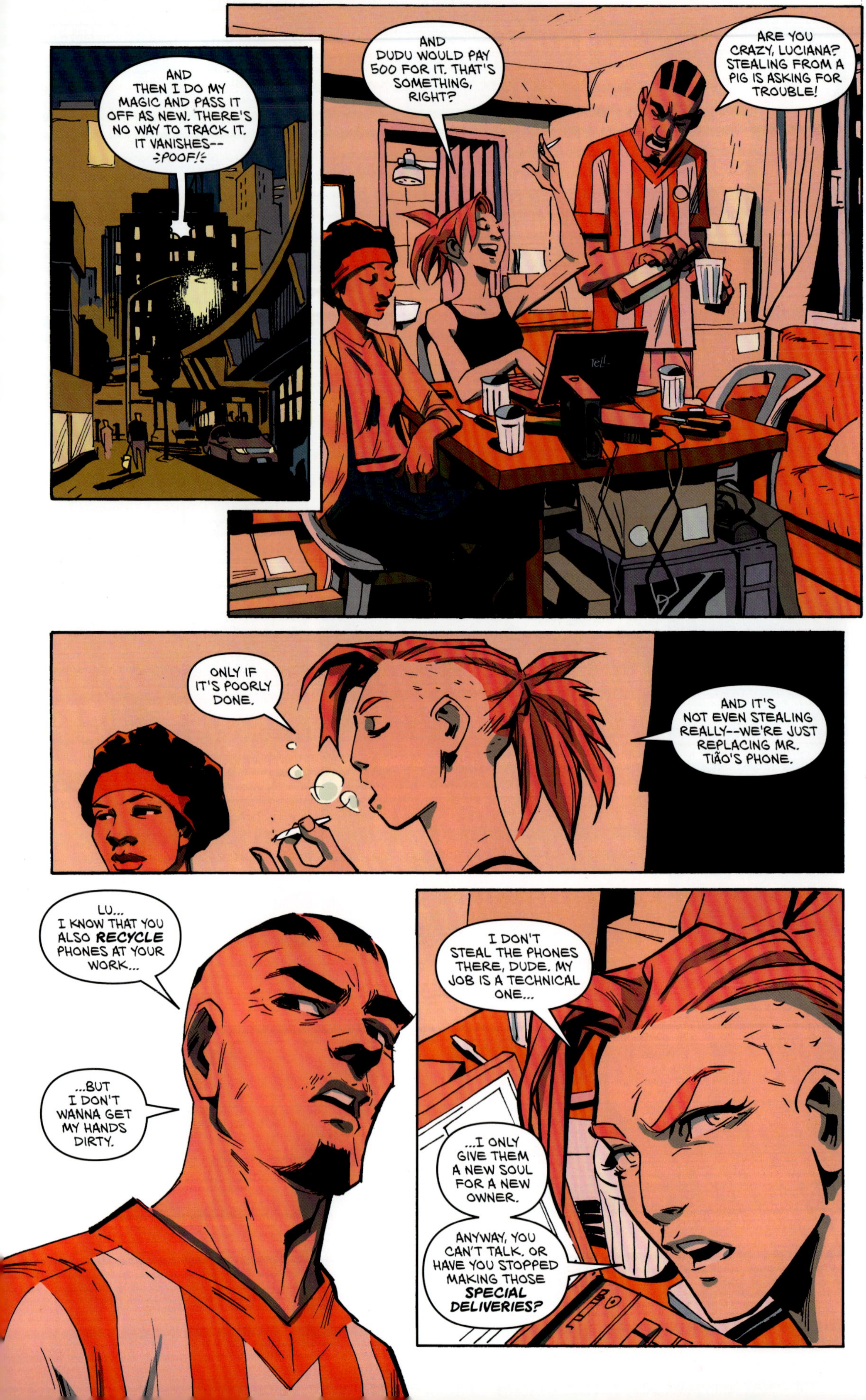
AND THEN I DO MY MAGIC AND PASS IT OFF AS NEW. THERE'S NO WAY TO TRACK IT. IT VANISHES-- POOF!
AND DUDU WOULD PAY 500 FOR IT. THAT'S SOMETHING, RIGHT?
ARE YOU CRAZY, LUCIANA? STEALING FROM A PIG IS ASKING FOR TROUBLE!
ONLY IF IT'S POORLY DONE.
AND IT'S NOT EVEN STEALING REALLY--WE'RE JUST REPLACING MR. TIÃO'S PHONE.
LU... I KNOW THAT YOU ALSO RECYCLE PHONES AT YOUR WORK...
...BUT I DON'T WANNA GET MY HANDS DIRTY.
I DON'T STEAL THE PHONES THERE, DUDE. MY JOB IS A TECHNICAL ONE...
...I ONLY GIVE THEM A NEW SOUL FOR A NEW OWNER.
ANYWAY, YOU CAN'T TALK, OR HAVE YOU STOPPED MAKING THOSE SPECIAL DELIVERIES?

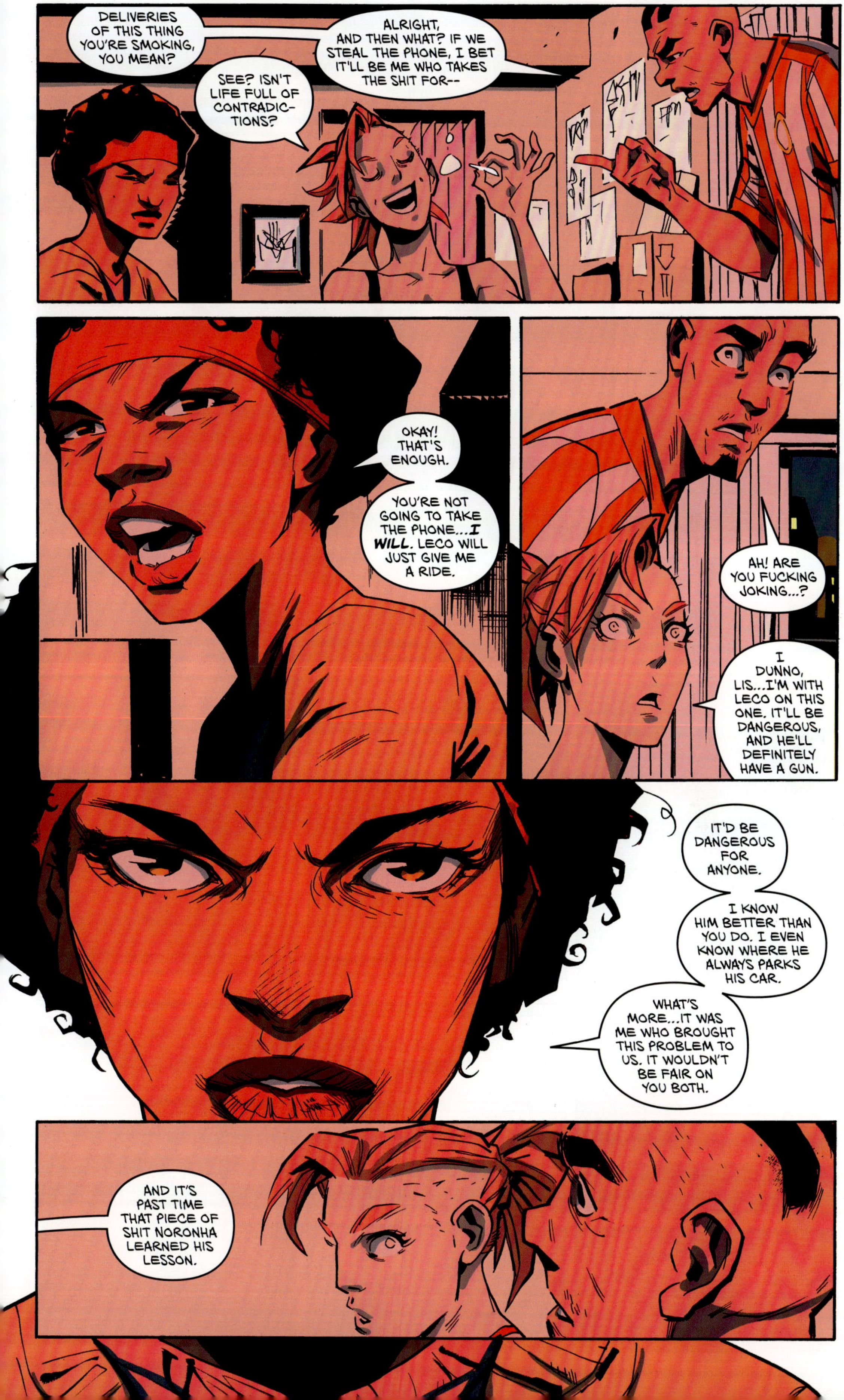
DELIVERIES OF THIS THING YOU'RE SMOKING, YOU MEAN?
ALRIGHT, AND THEN WHAT? IF WE STEAL THE PHONE, I BET IT'LL BE ME WHO TAKES THE SHIT FOR--
SEE? ISN'T LIFE FULL OF CONTRADIC-TIONS?
OKAY! THAT'S ENOUGH.
YOU'RE NOT GOING TO TAKE THE PHONE... I WILL. LECO WILL JUST GIVE ME A RIDE.
AH! ARE YOU FUCKING JOKING...?
I DUNNO, LIS... I'M WITH LECO ON THIS ONE. IT'LL BE DANGEROUS, AND HE'LL DEFINITELY HAVE A GUN.
IT'D BE DANGEROUS FOR ANYONE.
I KNOW HIM BETTER THAN YOU DO. I EVEN KNOW WHERE HE ALWAYS PARKS HIS CAR.
WHAT'S MORE... IT WAS ME WHO BROUGHT THIS PROBLEM TO US. IT WOULDN'T BE FAIR ON YOU BOTH.
AND IT'S PAST TIME THAT PIECE OF SHIT NORONHA LEARNED HIS LESSON.

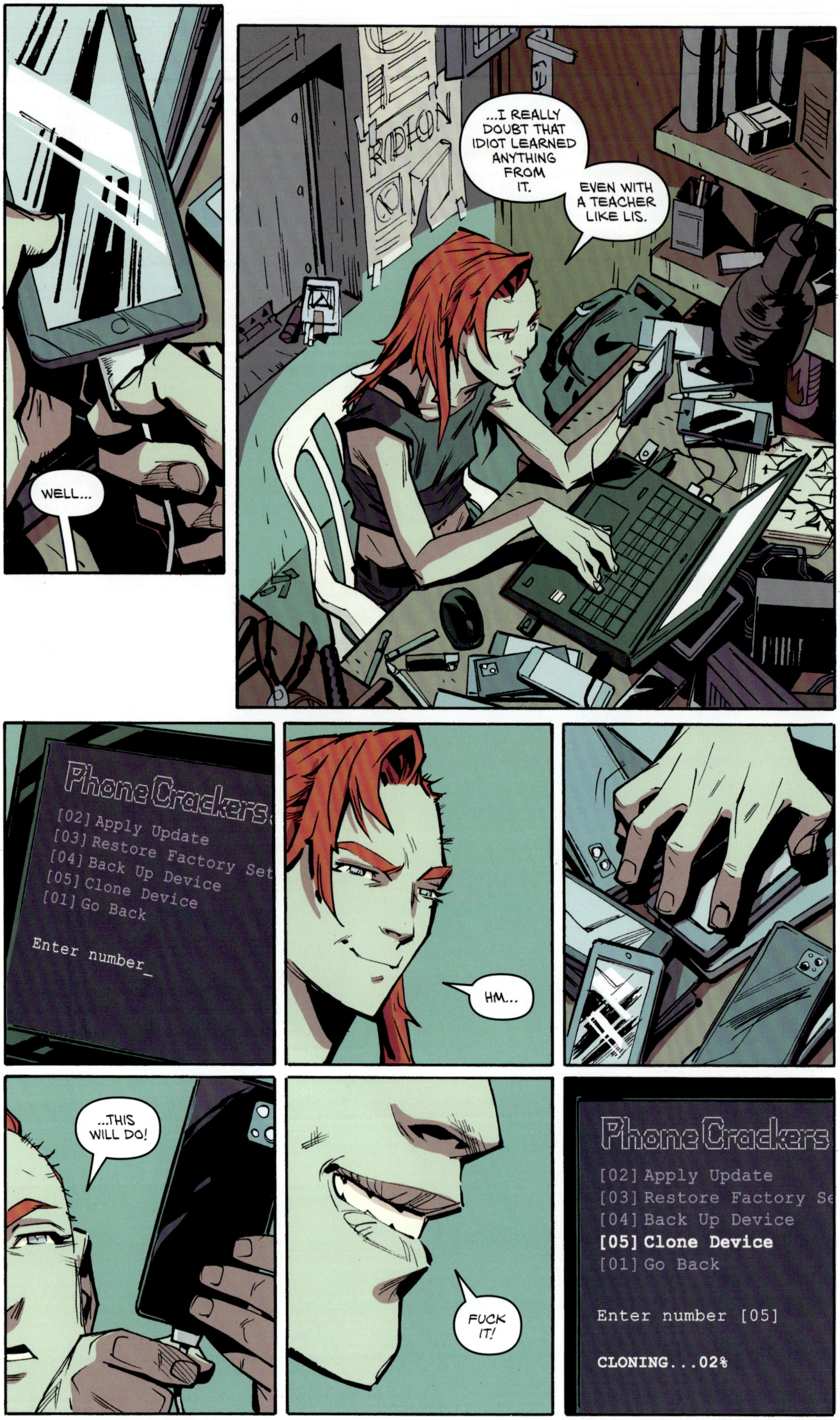
WELL...
...I REALLY DOUBT THAT IDIOT LEARNED ANYTHING FROM IT.
EVEN WITH A TEACHER LIKE LIS.
Phone Crackers
[02] Apply Update
[03] Restore Factory Set
[04] Back Up Device
[05] Clone Device
[01] Go Back
Enter number_
HM...
...THIS WILL DO!
FUCK IT!
Phone Crackers
[02] Apply Update
[03] Restore Factory Se
[04] Back Up Device
[05] Clone Device
[01] Go Back
Enter number [05]
CLONING...02%

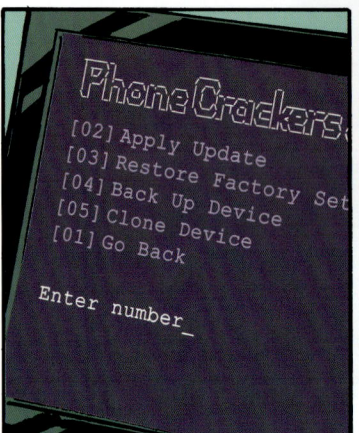

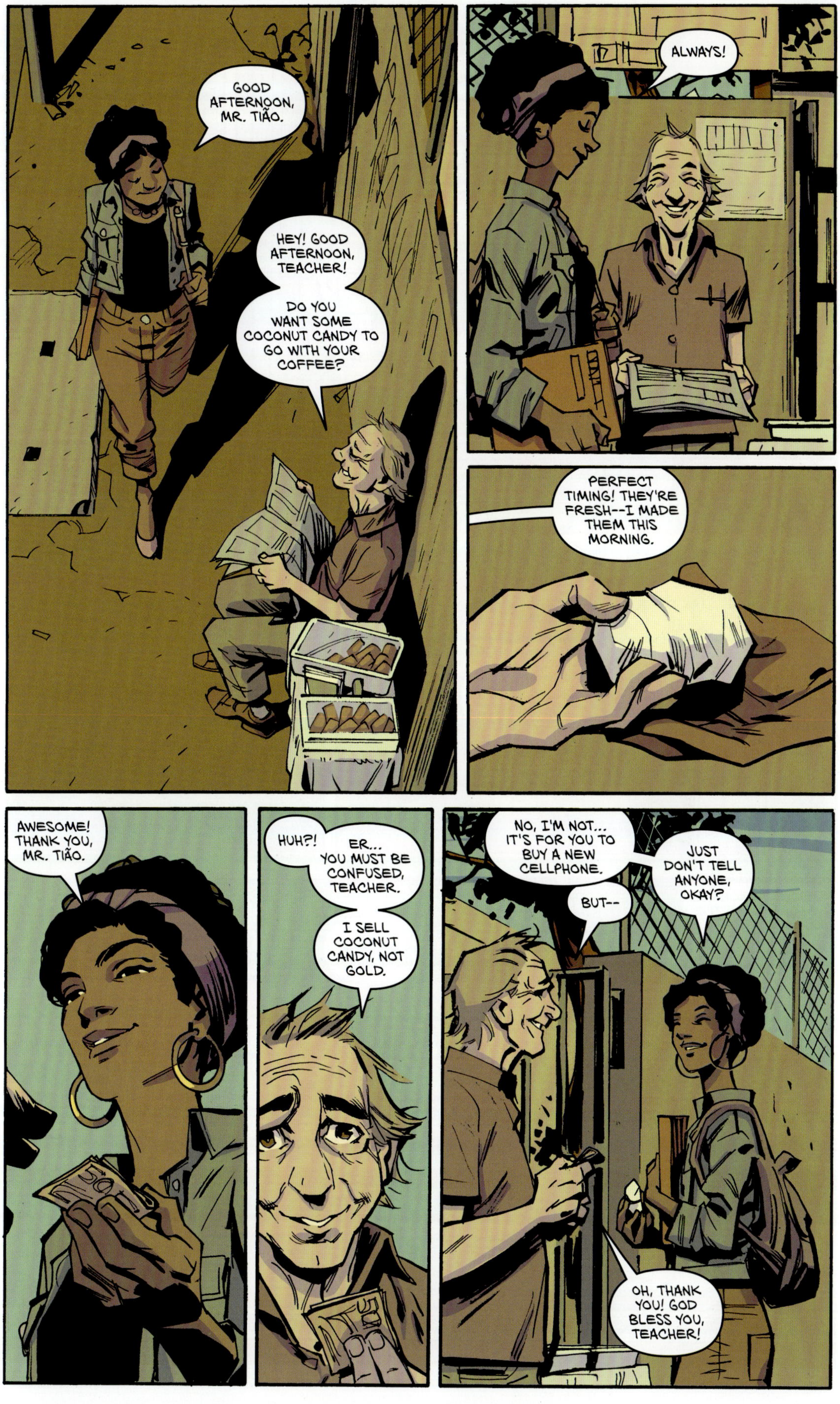
GOOD AFTERNOON, MR. TIÃO.
HEY! GOOD AFTERNOON, TEACHER!
DO YOU WANT SOME COCONUT CANDY TO GO WITH YOUR COFFEE?
ALWAYS!
PERFECT TIMING! THEY'RE FRESH--I MADE THEM THIS MORNING.
AWESOME! THANK YOU, MR. TIÃO.
HUH?!
ER... YOU MUST BE CONFUSED, TEACHER.
I SELL COCONUT CANDY, NOT GOLD.
NO, I'M NOT... IT'S FOR YOU TO BUY A NEW CELLPHONE.
BUT--
JUST DON'T TELL ANYONE, OKAY?
OH, THANK YOU! GOD BLESS YOU, TEACHER!

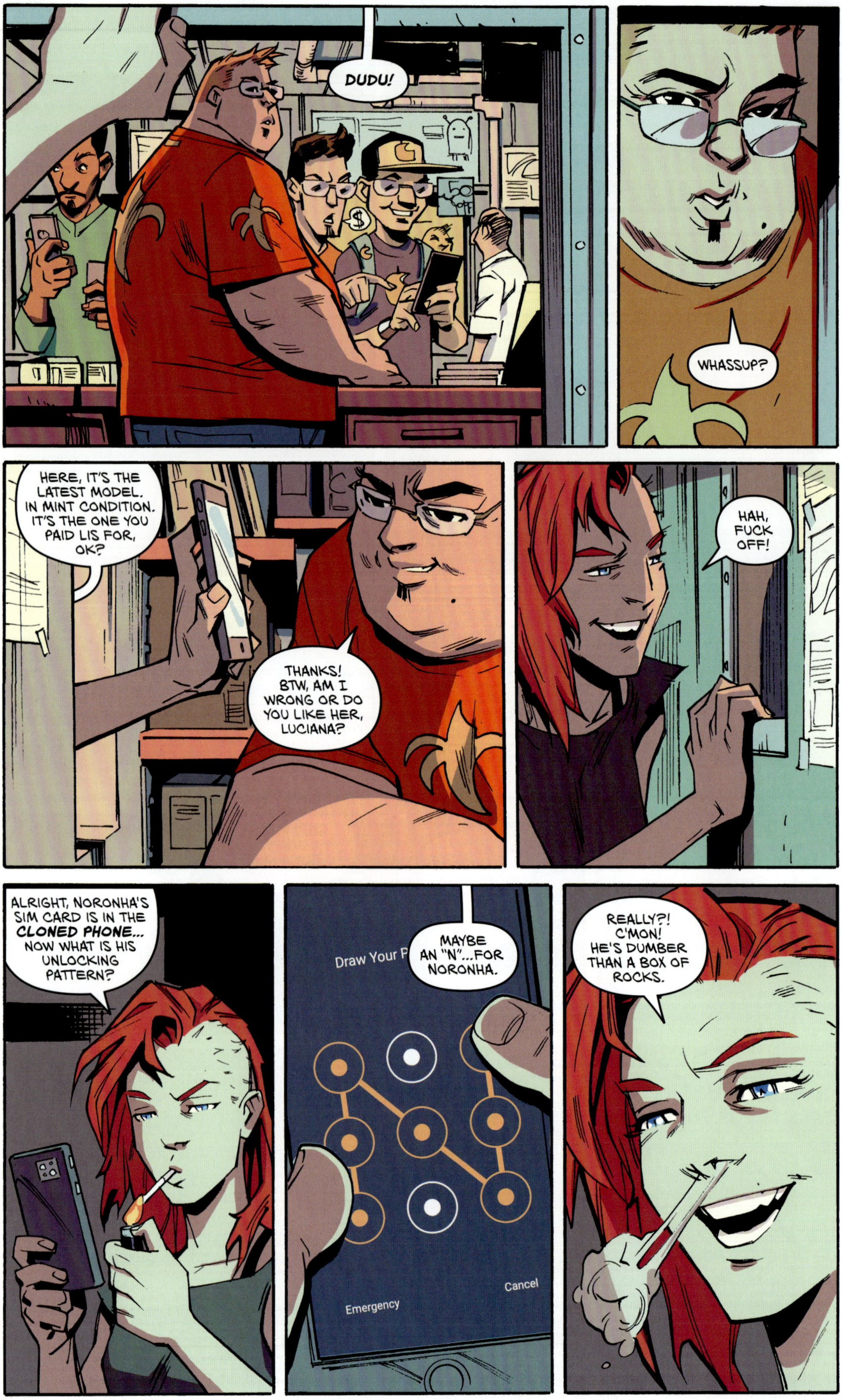
DUDU!
WHASSUP?
HERE, IT'S THE LATEST MODEL. IN MINT CONDITION. IT'S THE ONE YOU PAID US FOR, OK?
THANKS! BTW, AM I WRONG OR DO YOU LIKE HER, LUCIANA?
HAH, FUCK OFF!
ALRIGHT, NORONHA'S SIM CARD IS IN THE CLONED PHONE... NOW WHAT IS HIS UNLOCKING PATTERN?
Draw Your P
MAYBE AN "N"...FOR NORONHA.
Emergency
Cancel
REALLY?! C'MON! HE'S DUMBER THAN A BOX OF ROCKS.

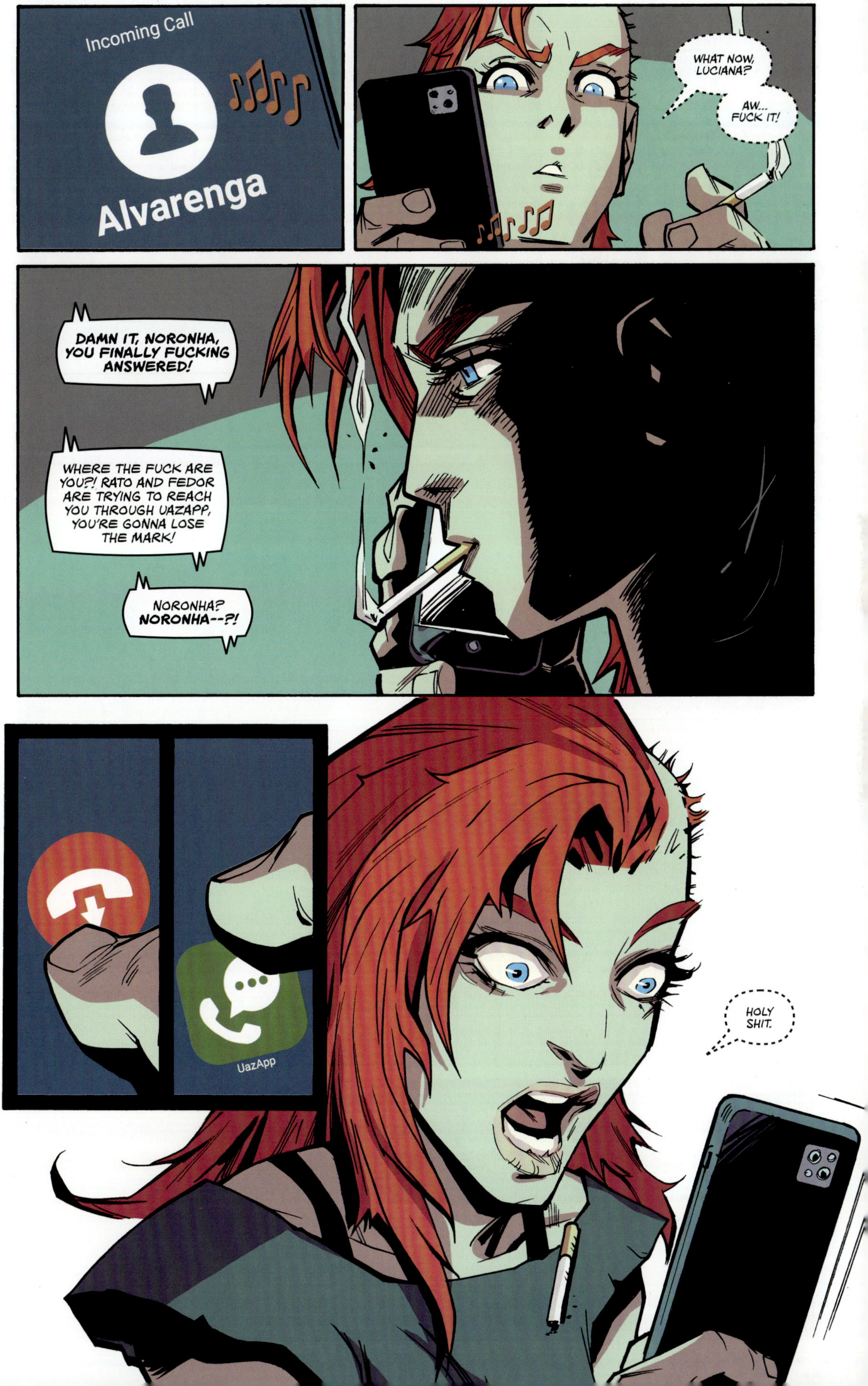
Incoming Call
Alvarenga
WHAT NOW, LUCIANA?
AW... FUCK IT!
DAMN IT, NORONHA, YOU FINALLY FUCKING ANSWERED!
WHERE THE FUCK ARE YOU?! RATO AND FEDOR ARE TRYING TO REACH YOU THROUGH UAZAPP, YOU'RE GONNA LOSE THE MARK!
NORONHA? NORONHA--?!
UazApp
HOLY SHIT.

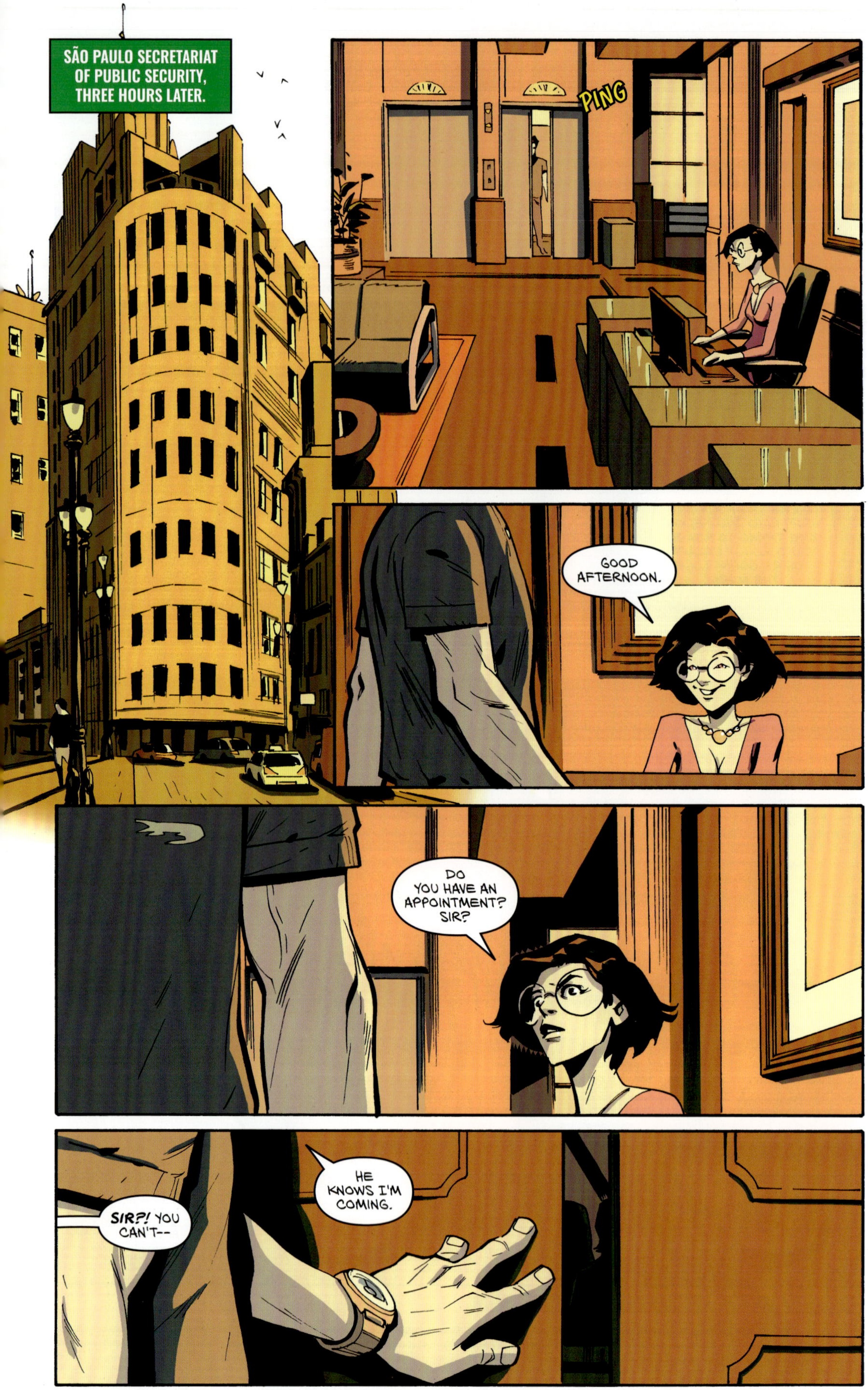
SÃO PAULO SECRETARIAT OF PUBLIC SECURITY, THREE HOURS LATER.
PING
GOOD AFTERNOON.
DO YOU HAVE AN APPOINTMENT? SIR?
HE KNOWS I'M COMING.
SIR?! YOU CAN'T--

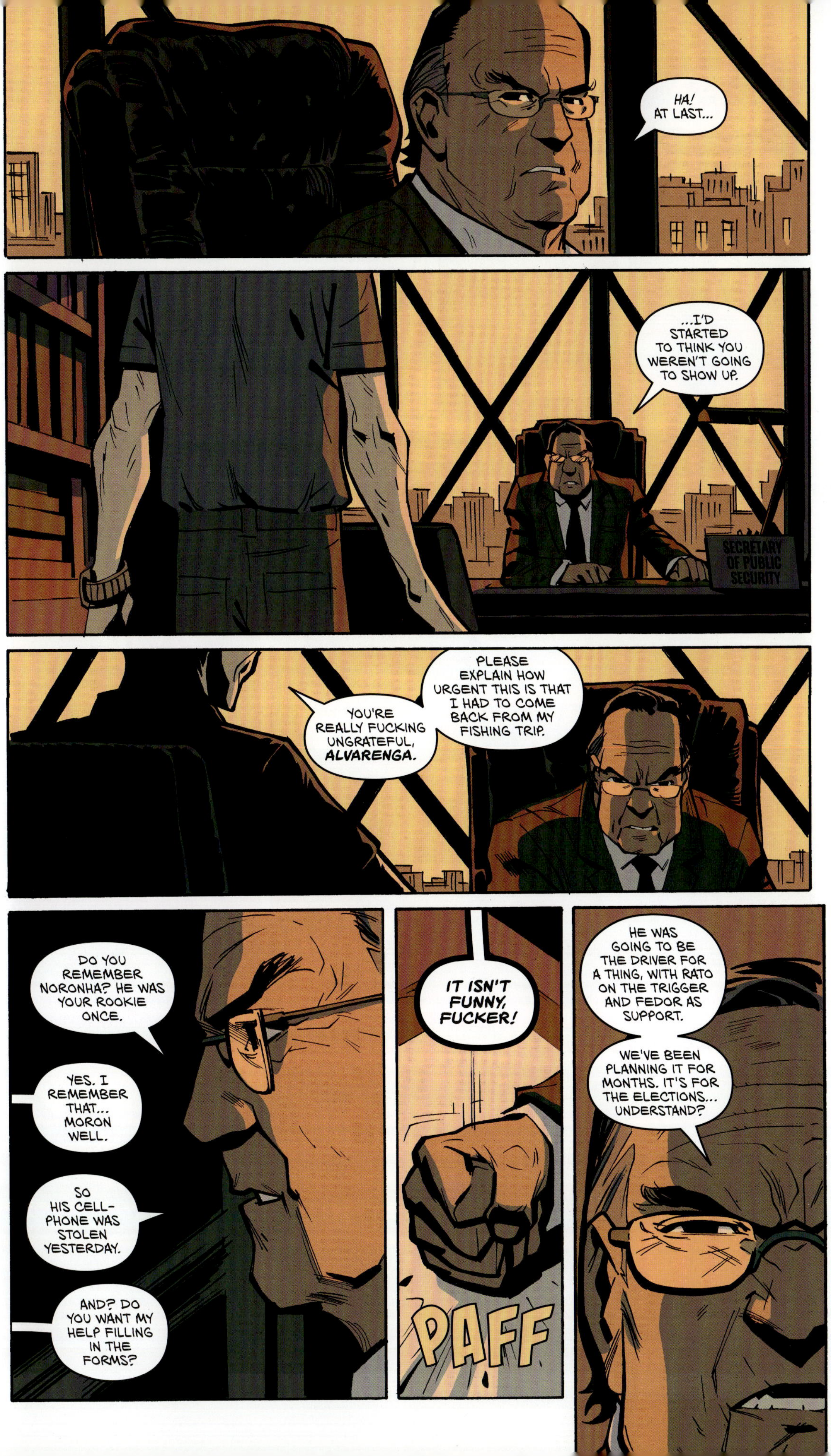
HA! AT LAST...
...I'D STARTED TO THINK YOU WEREN'T GOING TO SHOW UP.
PLEASE EXPLAIN HOW URGENT THIS IS THAT I HAD TO COME BACK FROM MY FISHING TRIP.
YOU'RE REALLY FUCKING UNGRATEFUL, ALVARENGA.
SECRETARY OF PUBLIC SECURITY
DO YOU REMEMBER NORONHA? HE WAS YOUR ROOKIE ONCE.
YES. I REMEMBER THAT... MORON WELL.
SO HIS CELL-PHONE WAS STOLEN YESTERDAY.
AND? DO YOU WANT MY HELP FILLING IN THE FORMS?
IT ISN'T FUNNY, FUCKER!
PAFF
HE WAS GOING TO BE THE DRIVER FOR A THING, WITH RATO ON THE TRIGGER AND FEDOR AS SUPPORT.
WE'VE BEEN PLANNING IT FOR MONTHS. IT'S FOR THE ELECTIONS... UNDERSTAND?

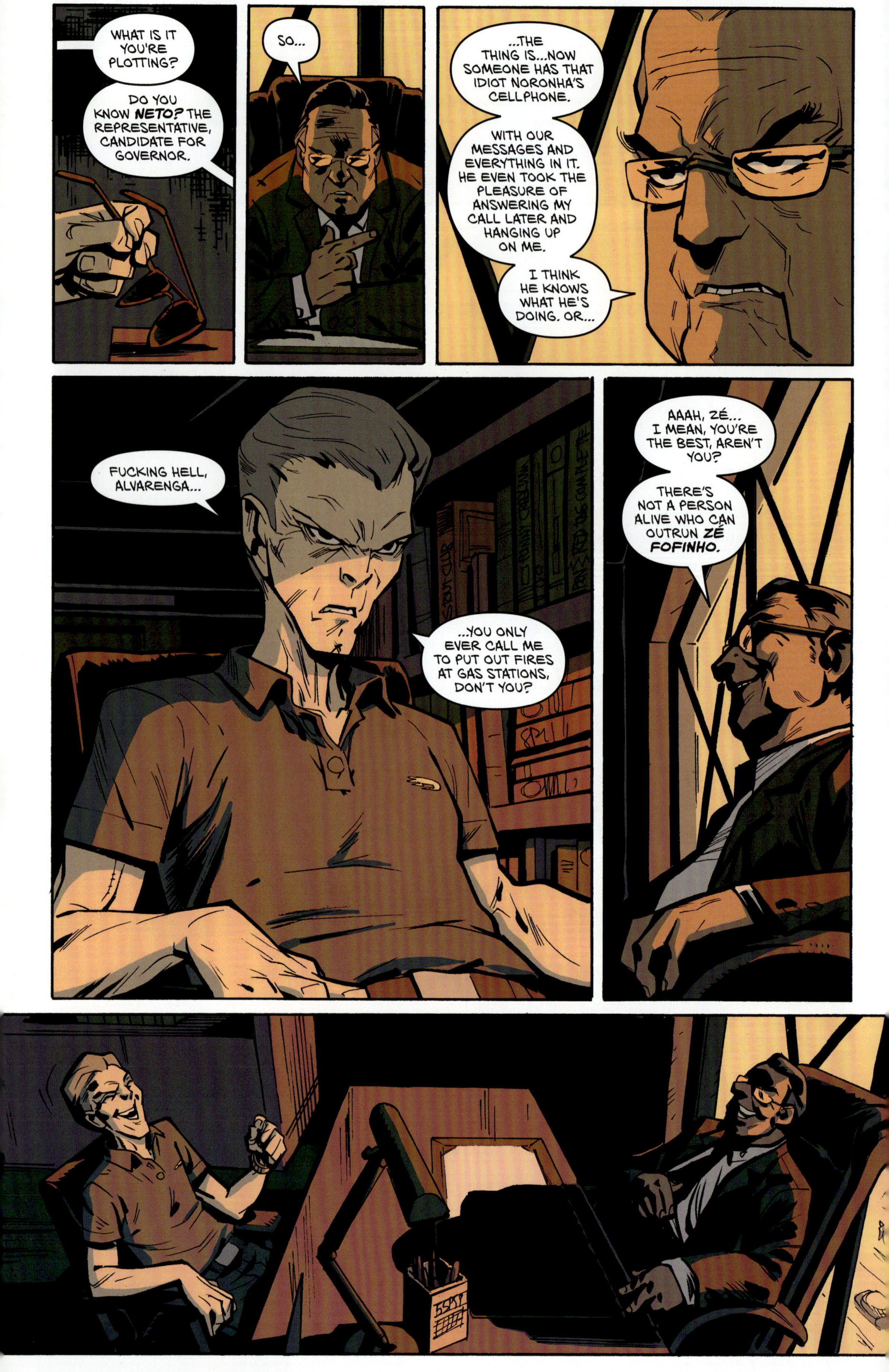

WHAT IS IT YOU'RE PLOTTING?
DO YOU KNOW **NETO?** THE REPRESENTATIVE, CANDIDATE FOR GOVERNOR.
SO...
...THE THING IS...NOW SOMEONE HAS THAT IDIOT NORONHA'S CELLPHONE.
WITH OUR MESSAGES AND EVERYTHING IN IT. HE EVEN TOOK THE PLEASURE OF ANSWERING MY CALL LATER AND HANGING UP ON ME.
I THINK HE KNOWS WHAT HE'S DOING. OR...
FUCKING HELL, ALVARENGA...
...YOU ONLY EVER CALL ME TO PUT OUT FIRES AT GAS STATIONS, DON'T YOU?
AAAH, ZÉ... I MEAN, YOU'RE THE BEST, AREN'T YOU?
THERE'S NOT A PERSON ALIVE WHO CAN OUTRUN **ZÉ FOFINHO.**

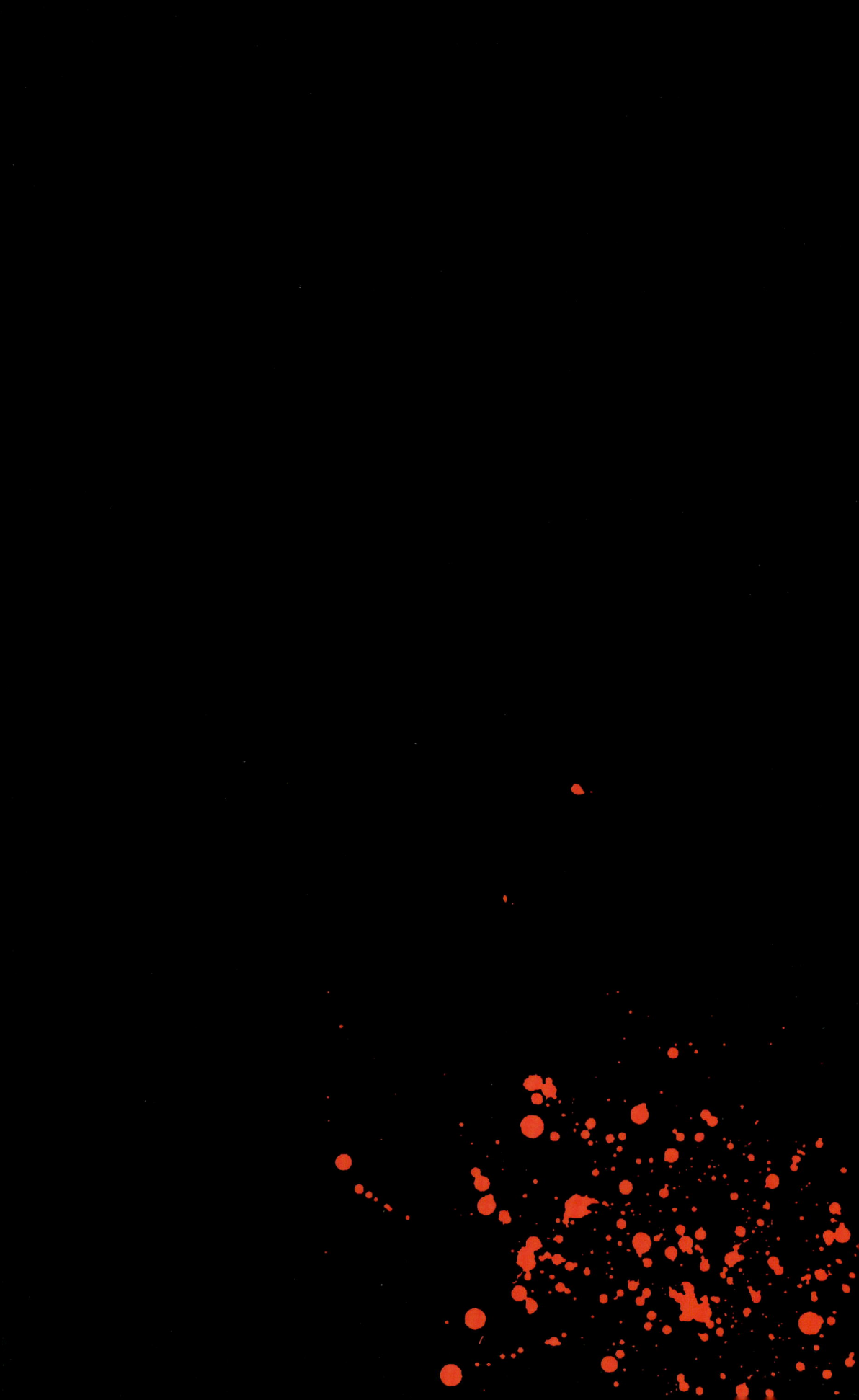

CHAPTER TWO
FOOD CHAIN

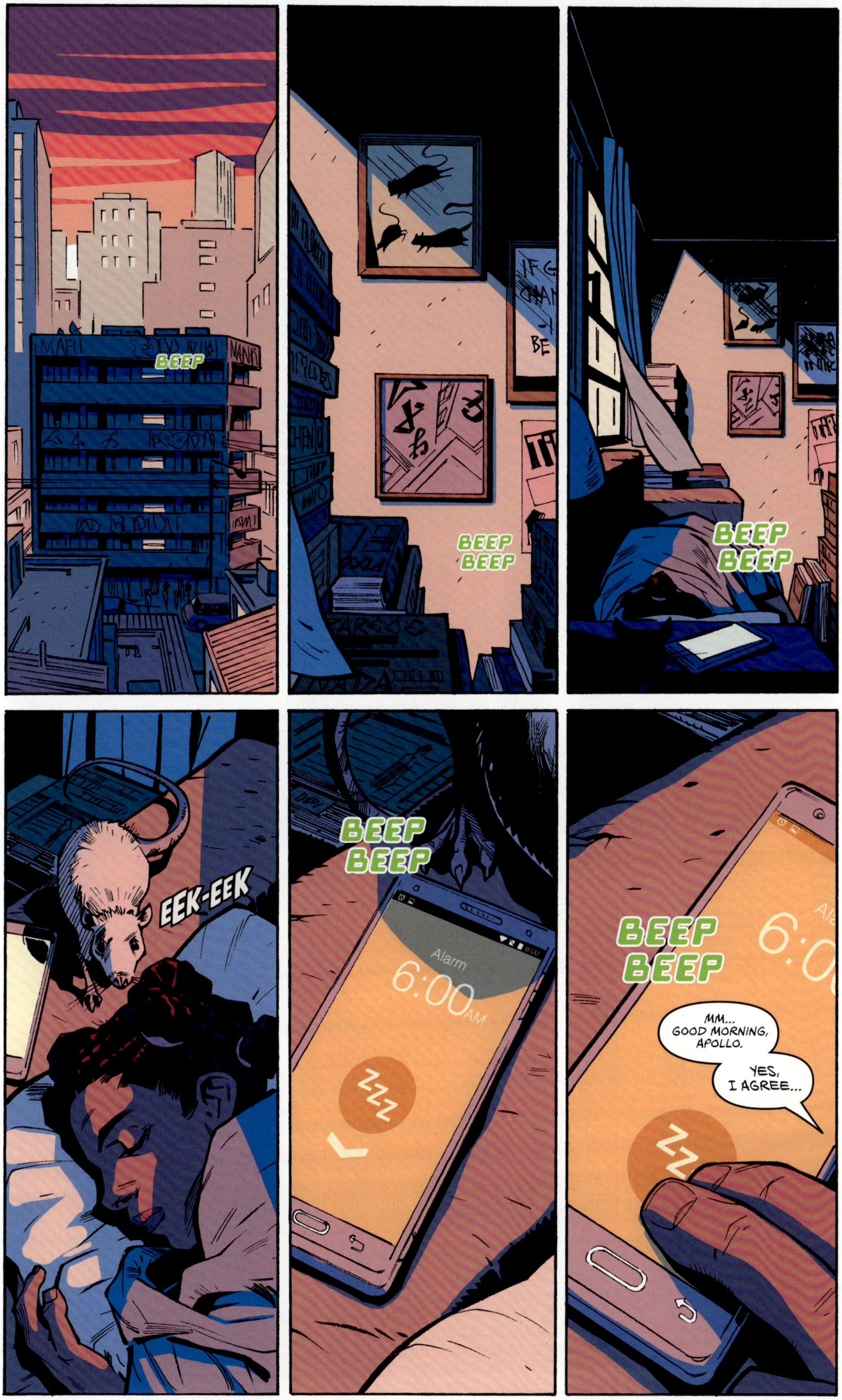
BEEP
BEEP
BEEP
BEEP
BEEP
EEK-EEK
BEEP
BEEP
Alarm
6:00AM
BEEP
BEEP
MM... GOOD MORNING, APOLLO.
YES, I AGREE...

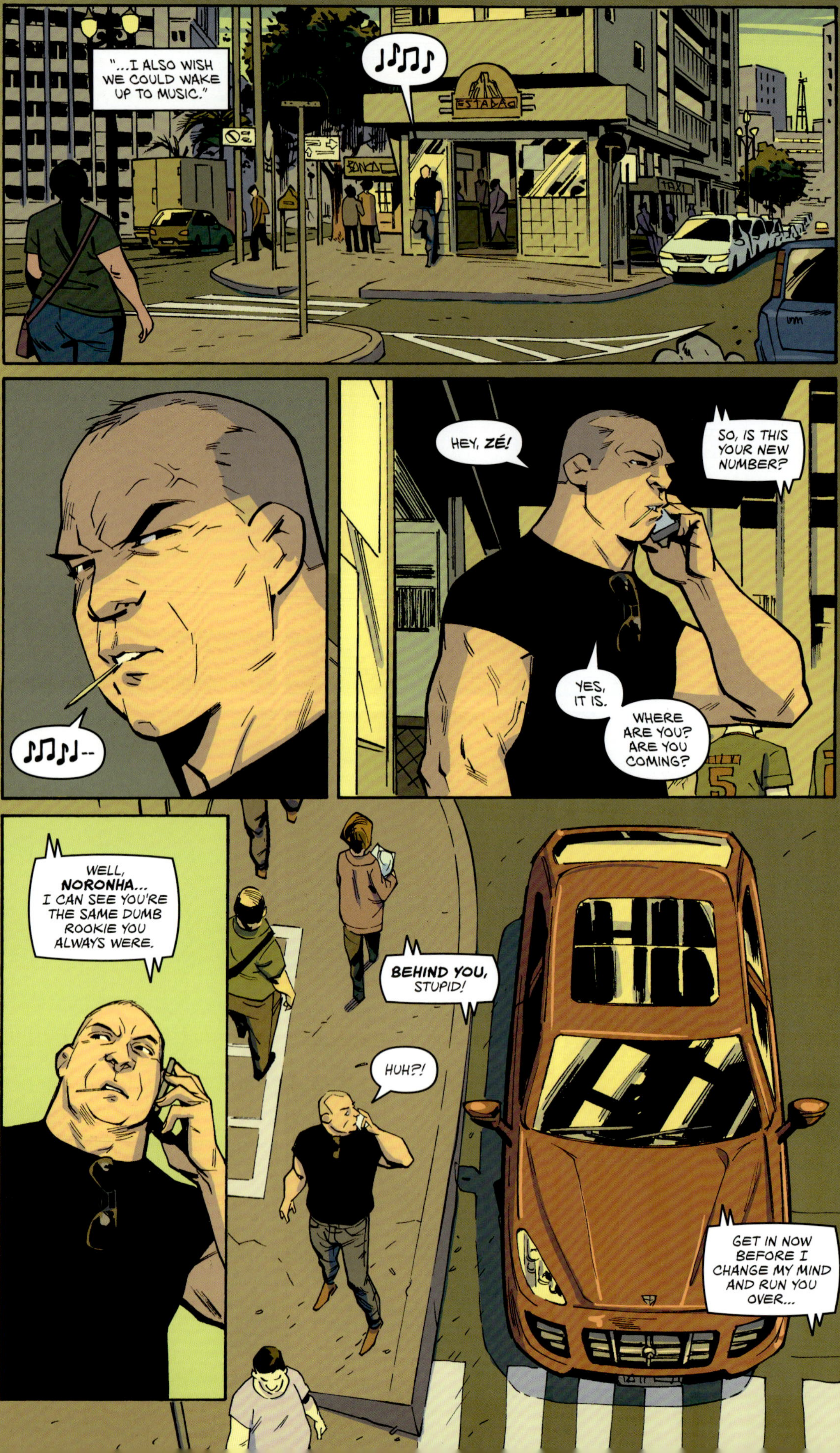

"...I ALSO WISH WE COULD WAKE UP TO MUSIC."
♪♫♪
ESTADÃO
TAXI
♫♪♪--
HEY, ZÉ!
SO, IS THIS YOUR NEW NUMBER?
YES, IT IS.
WHERE ARE YOU? ARE YOU COMING?
WELL, NORONHA... I CAN SEE YOU'RE THE SAME DUMB ROOKIE YOU ALWAYS WERE.
BEHIND YOU, STUPID!
HUH?!
GET IN NOW BEFORE I CHANGE MY MIND AND RUN YOU OVER...

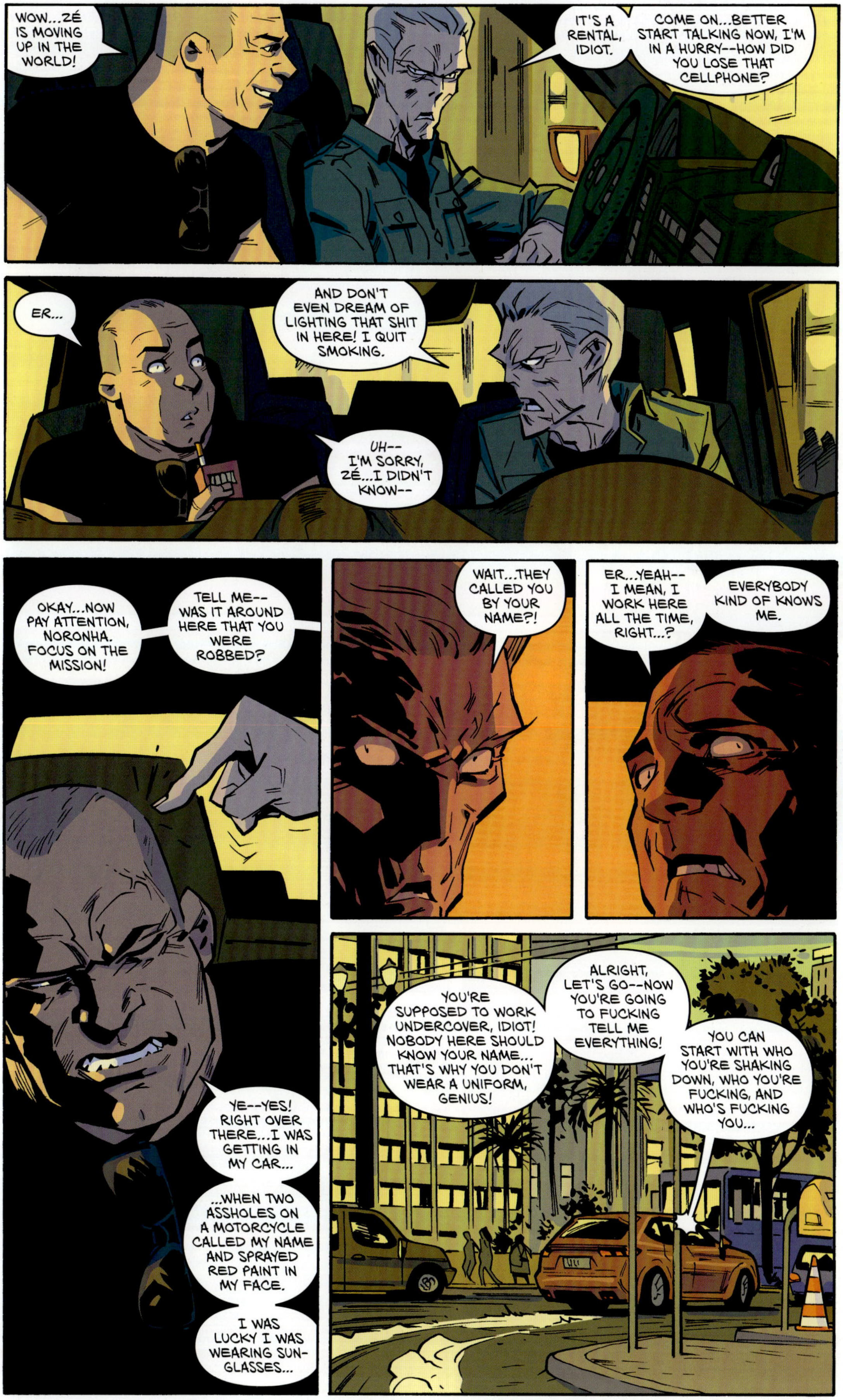
WOW...ZÉ IS MOVING UP IN THE WORLD!
IT'S A RENTAL, IDIOT.
COME ON...BETTER START TALKING NOW, I'M IN A HURRY--HOW DID YOU LOSE THAT CELLPHONE?
ER...
AND DON'T EVEN DREAM OF LIGHTING THAT SHIT IN HERE! I QUIT SMOKING.
UH-- I'M SORRY, ZÉ...I DIDN'T KNOW--
OKAY...NOW PAY ATTENTION, NORONHA. FOCUS ON THE MISSION!
TELL ME-- WAS IT AROUND HERE THAT YOU WERE ROBBED?
YE--YES! RIGHT OVER THERE...I WAS GETTING IN MY CAR...
...WHEN TWO ASSHOLES ON A MOTORCYCLE CALLED MY NAME AND SPRAYED RED PAINT IN MY FACE.
I WAS LUCKY I WAS WEARING SUN-GLASSES...
WAIT...THEY CALLED YOU BY YOUR NAME?!
ER...YEAH-- I MEAN, I WORK HERE ALL THE TIME, RIGHT...?
EVERYBODY KIND OF KNOWS ME.
YOU'RE SUPPOSED TO WORK UNDERCOVER, IDIOT! NOBODY HERE SHOULD KNOW YOUR NAME... THAT'S WHY YOU DON'T WEAR A UNIFORM, GENIUS!
ALRIGHT, LET'S GO--NOW YOU'RE GOING TO FUCKING TELL ME EVERYTHING!
YOU CAN START WITH WHO YOU'RE SHAKING DOWN, WHO YOU'RE FUCKING, AND WHO'S FUCKING YOU...

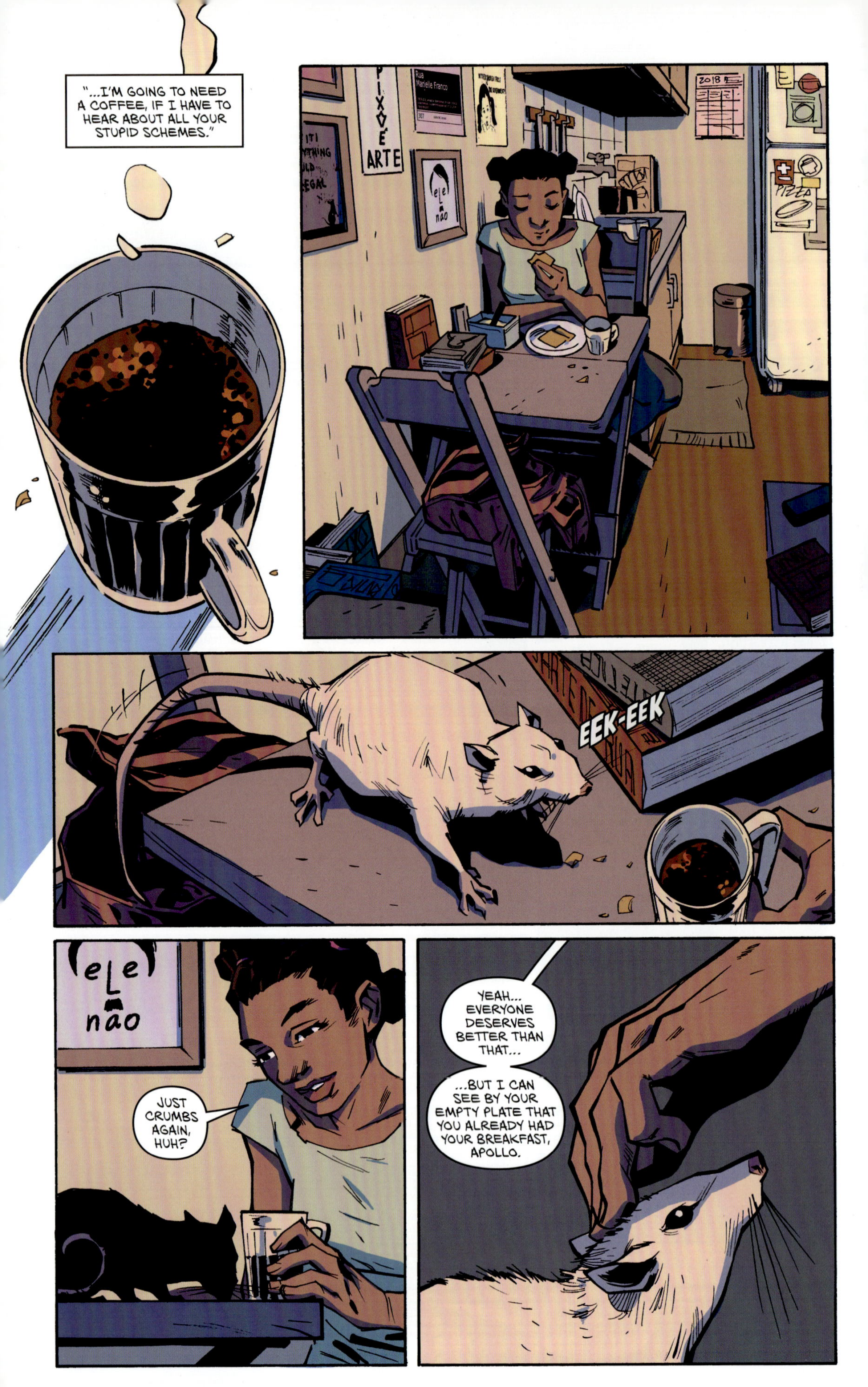
"...I'M GOING TO NEED A COFFEE, IF I HAVE TO HEAR ABOUT ALL YOUR STUPID SCHEMES."
EEK-EEK
JUST CRUMBS AGAIN, HUH?
YEAH... EVERYONE DESERVES BETTER THAN THAT...
...BUT I CAN SEE BY YOUR EMPTY PLATE THAT YOU ALREADY HAD YOUR BREAKFAST, APOLLO.

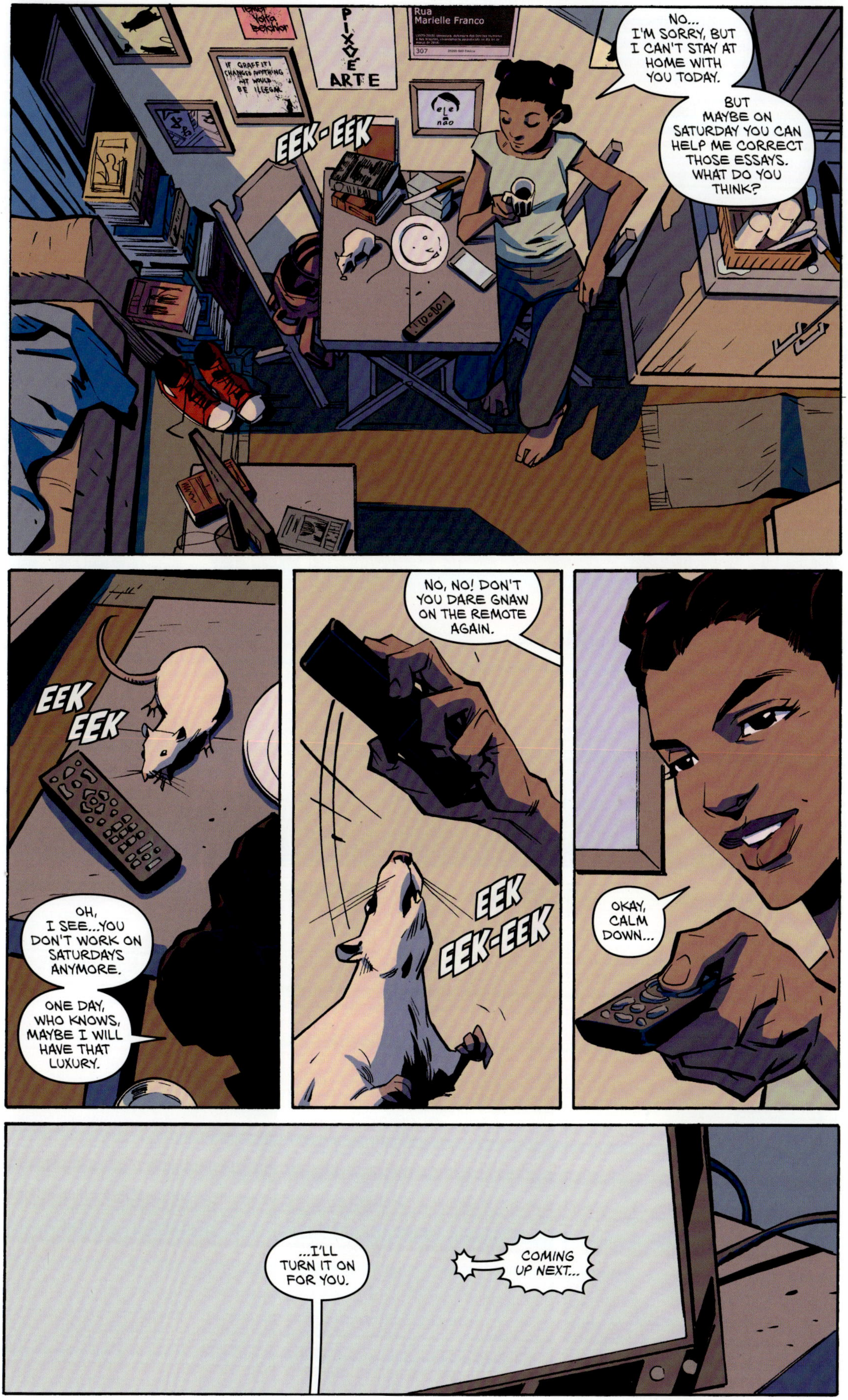
PIXO É ARTE
Rua Marielle Franco
IF GRAFFITI CHANGED ANYTHING IT WOULD BE ILLEGAL
NO... I'M SORRY, BUT I CAN'T STAY AT HOME WITH YOU TODAY.
BUT MAYBE ON SATURDAY YOU CAN HELP ME CORRECT THOSE ESSAYS. WHAT DO YOU THINK?
EEK-EEK
EEK EEK
OH, I SEE...YOU DON'T WORK ON SATURDAYS ANYMORE.
ONE DAY, WHO KNOWS, MAYBE I WILL HAVE THAT LUXURY.
NO, NO! DON'T YOU DARE GNAW ON THE REMOTE AGAIN.
EEK EEK-EEK
OKAY, CALM DOWN...
...I'LL TURN IT ON FOR YOU.
COMING UP NEXT...

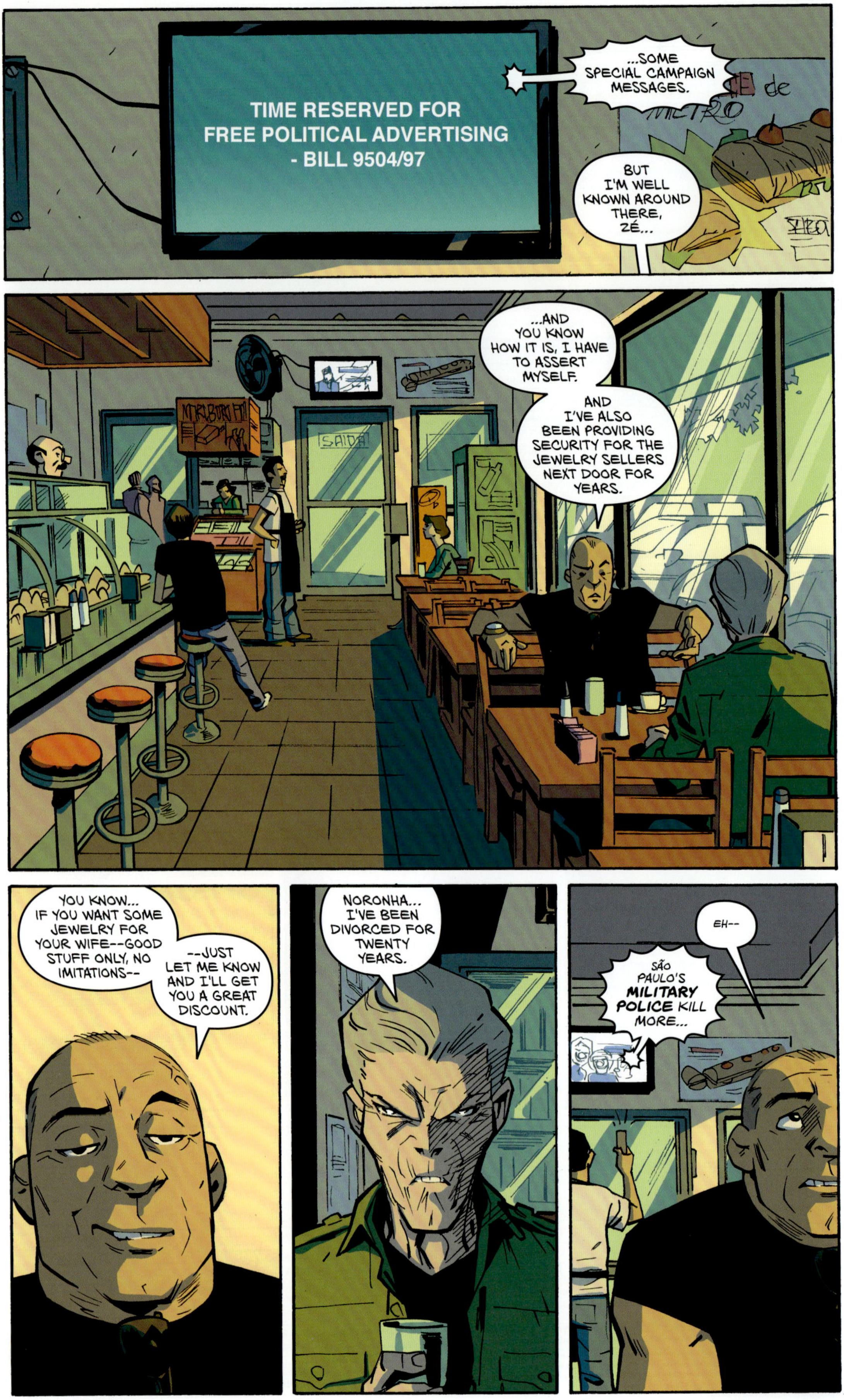
TIME RESERVED FOR FREE POLITICAL ADVERTISING - BILL 9504/97
...SOME SPECIAL CAMPAIGN MESSAGES.
BUT I'M WELL KNOWN AROUND THERE, ZÉ...
...AND YOU KNOW HOW IT IS, I HAVE TO ASSERT MYSELF.
AND I'VE ALSO BEEN PROVIDING SECURITY FOR THE JEWELRY SELLERS NEXT DOOR FOR YEARS.
SAIDA
YOU KNOW... IF YOU WANT SOME JEWELRY FOR YOUR WIFE--GOOD STUFF ONLY, NO IMITATIONS--
--JUST LET ME KNOW AND I'LL GET YOU A GREAT DISCOUNT.
NORONHA... I'VE BEEN DIVORCED FOR TWENTY YEARS.
EH--
SÃO PAULO'S **MILITARY POLICE** KILL MORE...

...AND DIE MORE THAN NEARLY ANYWHERE ELSE IN THE WORLD.
IT'S UNACCEPTABLE THAT A STATE AS RICH AND DIVERSE AS OURS HAS THIS KIND OF POLICE FORCE.
THEREFORE, WHEN ELECTED, I WILL MOVE MOUNTAINS TO MAKE SÃO PAULO THE FIRST STATE IN THE FEDERATION TO ABOLISH THE MILITARY POLICE...
...AND THEN TRANSFER ITS PERSONNEL TO A MORE HUMANE POLICE FORCE, ONE THAT CAN BE HELD ACCOUNTABLE FOR ITS ACTIONS BY CIVIL LAW. WE MUST SET AN EXAMPLE FOR OUR CHILDREN AND OUR FUTURE...
WHOA! WHO'S THIS GUY!?
HE'S NETO! HE'S RUNNING FOR GOVERNOR.
HE'S GOOD! HE'S FACING THAT POLICE MAFIA OUT THERE...HE'S CLIMBING UP THE POLLS FAST.
IF HE GETS TO THE SECOND ROUND, HE'LL WIN FOR SURE.
GULP
GO AND PAY FOR MY COFFEE, NORONHA.
LET'S GO FOR A RIDE...

"...YOU STILL HAVE A LOT TO TELL ME."
YES, SHE'S FINE, TOO...HER SURGERY WENT WELL.
SURE, YOU TAKE CARE OF YOURSELF TOO, COUSIN.
AND SEND A KISS TO THE KIDS, TOO! BYE BYE!
GOOD MORNING, MR. TIÃO!
GOOD MORNING, TEACHER! LOOK, HERE IT IS... I ALREADY CALLED MY FAMILY TODAY...
THAT'S WONDERFUL, MR. TIÃO! I'M LOOKING FORWARD TO HEARING ALL ABOUT IT LATER ON. I'M RUNNING LATE FOR CLASS RIGHT NOW...
PING
07:59
LU just now
Morning, babe... Can we talk tonight at the Point? It's very important. Xoxo!
GOOD MORNING, CLASS!
GOOD MORNING, TEACHER!

COME ON, ZÉ, WE'VE BEEN GOING OVER THIS ALL DAY...
...GUARAPIRANGA? THE RESERVOIR?!
WHY DID WE HAVE TO COME THIS FAR OUT?
HA-- WHERE WOULD YOU PREFER? THE MALL?
RATO AND FEDOR GOT SUSPICIOUS AFTER YOUR BLUNDER...
...YOU MIGHT HAVE FUCKING EXPOSED EVERYONE!
NOW HOLD ON AND ENJOY THE RIDE. WE'RE ALMOST THERE.
HUMPH OKAY.
ZÉ...DO YOU REMEMBER THAT TIME WHEN YOU, ME, RATO, AND FEDOR WENT FISHING AT THE RESERVOIR?
YES, I DO.
HA-HA! I THINK I EVEN HAVE PICTURES OF THAT DAY. I'LL SEND THEM TO YOU...

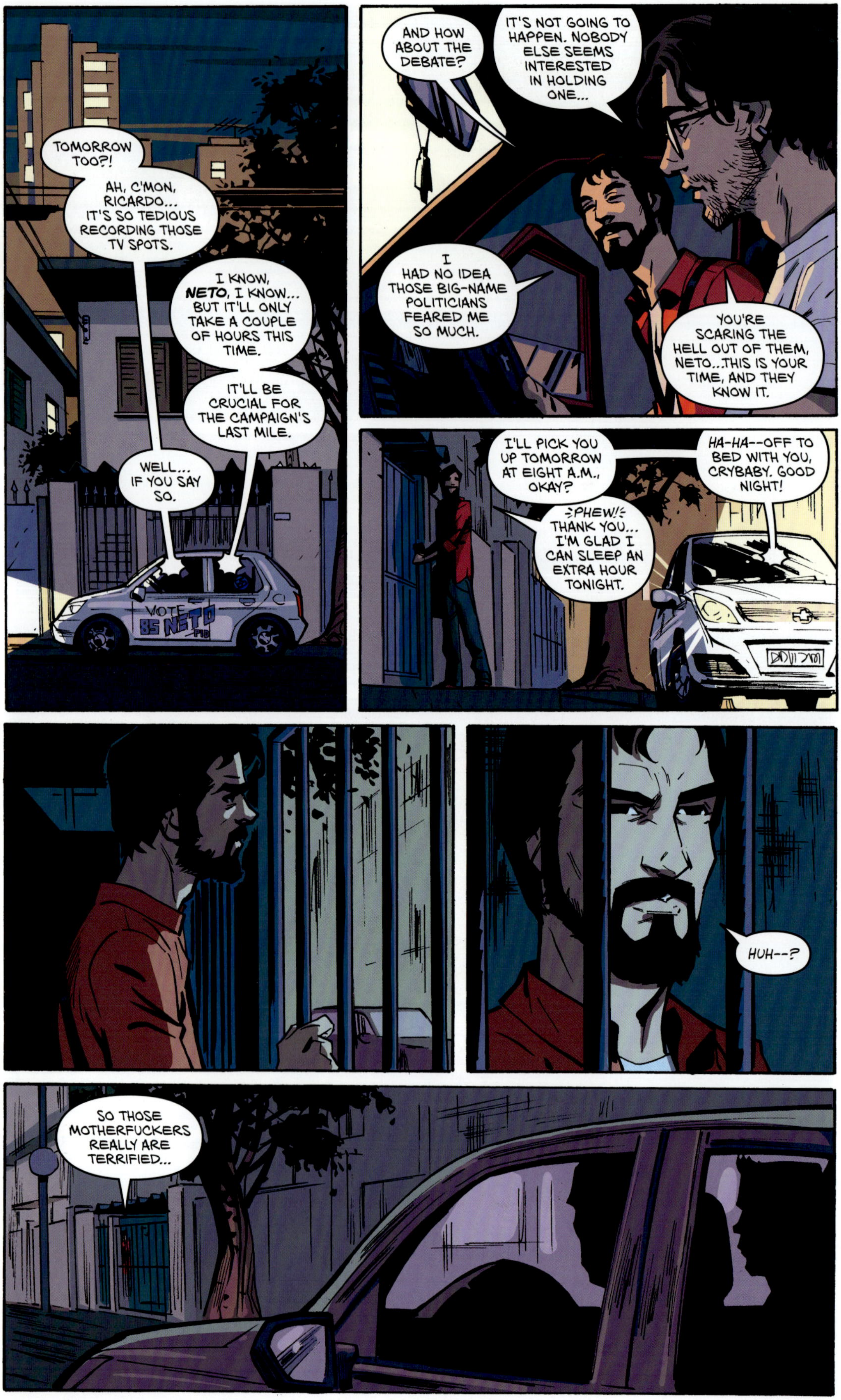
TOMORROW TOO?!
AH, C'MON, RICARDO... IT'S SO TEDIOUS RECORDING THOSE TV SPOTS.
I KNOW, NETO, I KNOW... BUT IT'LL ONLY TAKE A COUPLE OF HOURS THIS TIME.
IT'LL BE CRUCIAL FOR THE CAMPAIGN'S LAST MILE.
WELL... IF YOU SAY SO.
VOTE 85 NETO
AND HOW ABOUT THE DEBATE?
IT'S NOT GOING TO HAPPEN. NOBODY ELSE SEEMS INTERESTED IN HOLDING ONE...
I HAD NO IDEA THOSE BIG-NAME POLITICIANS FEARED ME SO MUCH.
YOU'RE SCARING THE HELL OUT OF THEM, NETO...THIS IS YOUR TIME, AND THEY KNOW IT.
I'LL PICK YOU UP TOMORROW AT EIGHT A.M., OKAY?
HA-HA--OFF TO BED WITH YOU, CRYBABY. GOOD NIGHT!
PHEW!! THANK YOU... I'M GLAD I CAN SLEEP AN EXTRA HOUR TONIGHT.
HUH--?
SO THOSE MOTHERFUCKERS REALLY ARE TERRIFIED...

AND WHY DIDN'T YOU GUYS LET ME CANCEL THE OLD NUMBER, NOW I'VE GOT A NEW ONE?
THIS ONE ISN'T EVEN IN MY NAME, SO WE WON'T HAVE ANY MORE ISSUES... HA-HA.
TOMORROW I'LL PAY A VISIT TO THOSE ELECTRONICS SHOPPING MALLS IN SANTA IFIGÊNIA--
SOME ASSHOLES OVER THERE OWE ME A FEW FAVORS... I'LL FIND THE MOTHERFUCKERS WHO--
LISTEN HERE-- YOU'RE NOT GOING TO PAY A VISIT TO ANYONE!
UNTIL WE FIX YOUR MESS, YOU'LL DANCE TO MY TUNE.
YE-- YES, SIR...
...SO... CAN I SMOKE NOW?
HOLD ON--
YES, YES--GOOD. OKAY! WE'RE ALREADY HERE.

FINE, YOU CAN SMOKE.
BUT BLOW THE SMOKE OVER THERE!
RATO AND FEDOR ARE ALMOST HERE...
I HAVEN'T SPOKEN TO THEM SINCE YESTERDAY... THEY MUST BE PISSED AT ME.
DO YOU THINK THAT--
POW
POW
POW
SHUT THE FUCK UP.
SPLOOSH

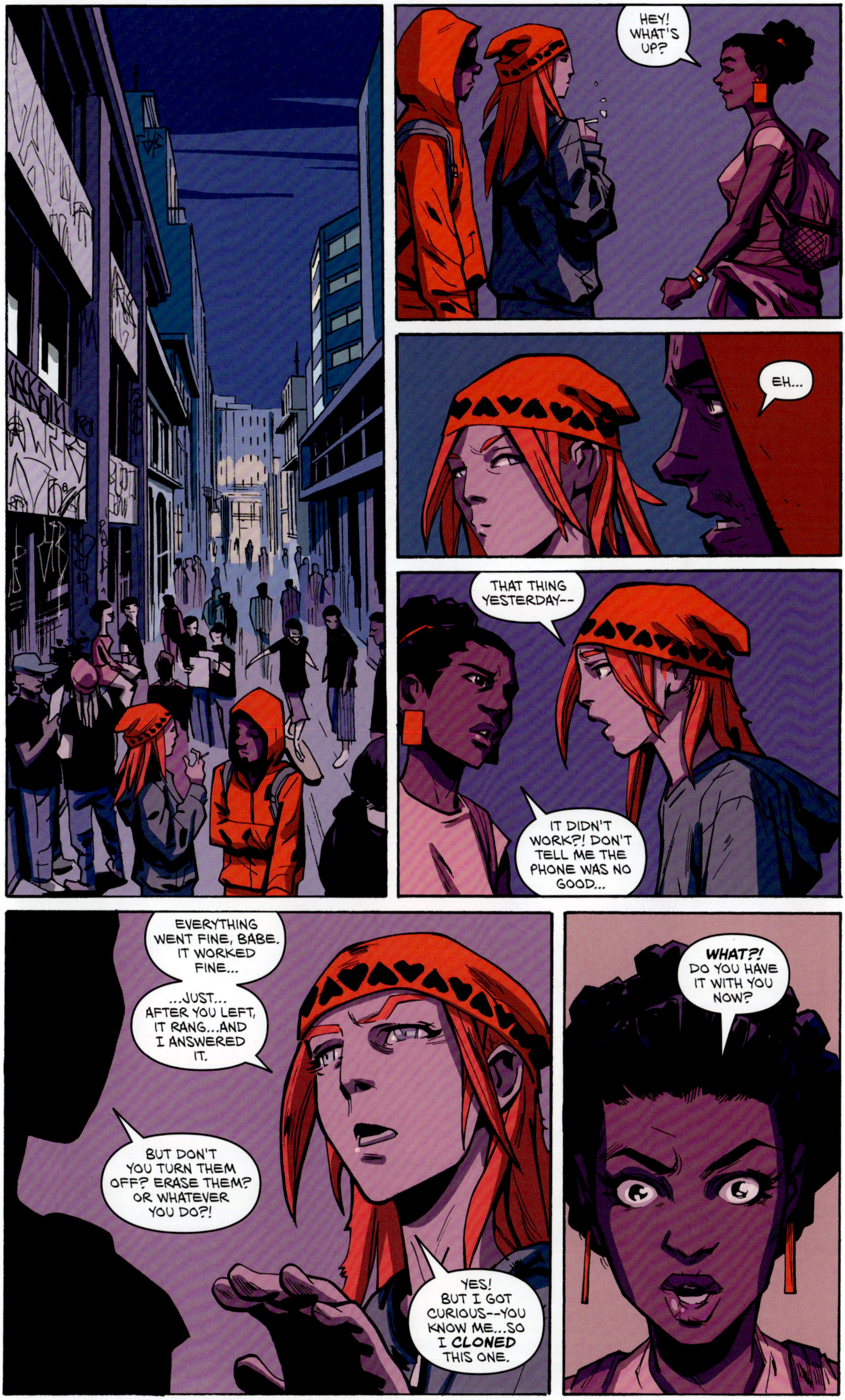
HEY! WHAT'S UP?
EH...
THAT THING YESTERDAY--
IT DIDN'T WORK?! DON'T TELL ME THE PHONE WAS NO GOOD...
EVERYTHING WENT FINE, BABE. IT WORKED FINE...
...JUST... AFTER YOU LEFT, IT RANG...AND I ANSWERED IT.
BUT DON'T YOU TURN THEM OFF? ERASE THEM? OR WHATEVER YOU DO?!
YES! BUT I GOT CURIOUS--YOU KNOW ME...SO I CLONED THIS ONE.
WHAT?! DO YOU HAVE IT WITH YOU NOW?

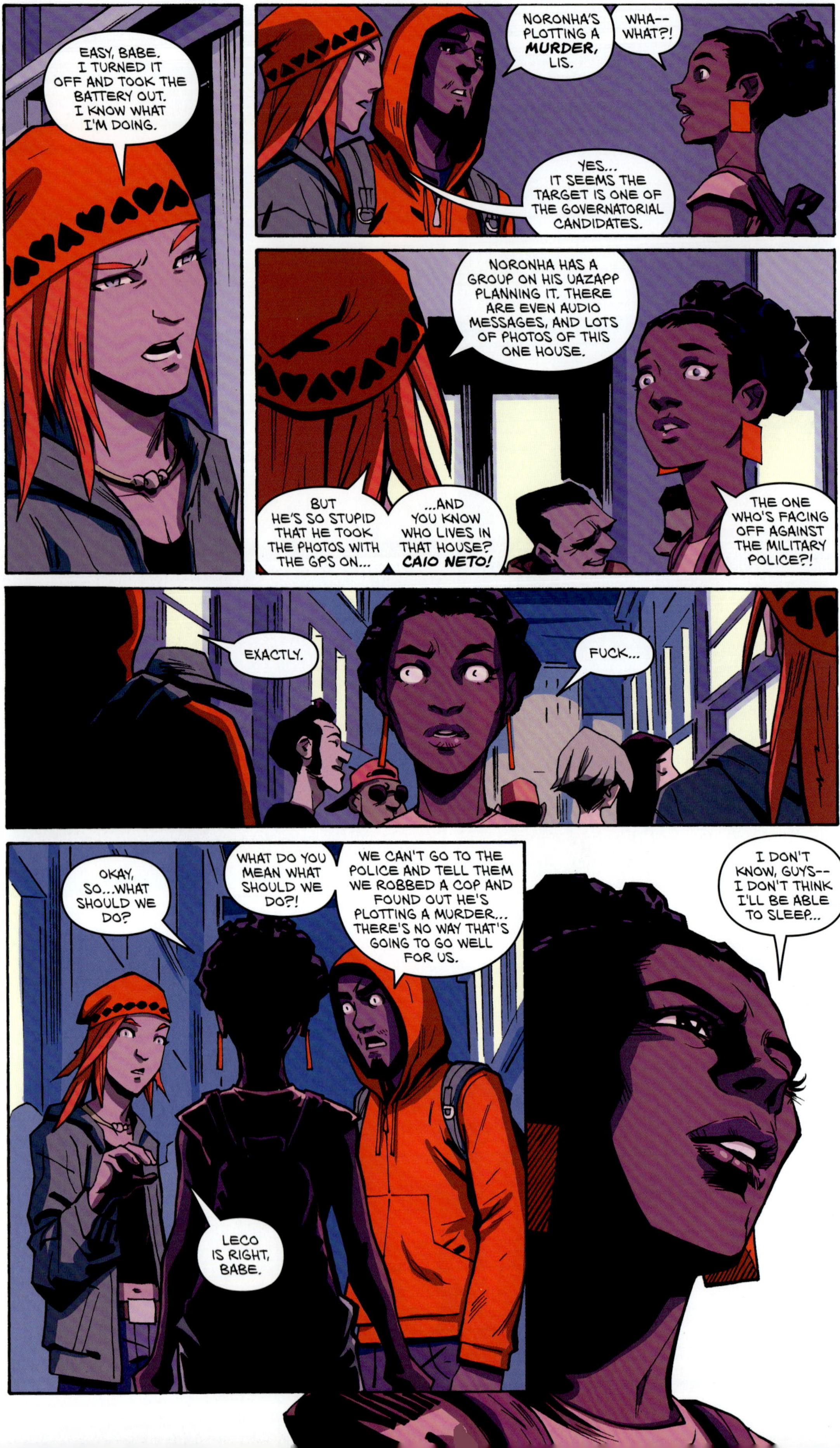
EASY, BABE. I TURNED IT OFF AND TOOK THE BATTERY OUT. I KNOW WHAT I'M DOING.
NORONHA'S PLOTTING A **MURDER,** LIS.
WHA-- WHAT?!
YES... IT SEEMS THE TARGET IS ONE OF THE GOVERNATORIAL CANDIDATES.
NORONHA HAS A GROUP ON HIS UAZAPP PLANNING IT. THERE ARE EVEN AUDIO MESSAGES, AND LOTS OF PHOTOS OF THIS ONE HOUSE.
BUT HE'S SO STUPID THAT HE TOOK THE PHOTOS WITH THE GPS ON...
...AND YOU KNOW WHO LIVES IN THAT HOUSE? **CAIO NETO!**
THE ONE WHO'S FACING OFF AGAINST THE MILITARY POLICE?!
EXACTLY.
FUCK...
OKAY, SO...WHAT SHOULD WE DO?
WHAT DO YOU MEAN WHAT SHOULD WE DO?!
WE CAN'T GO TO THE POLICE AND TELL THEM WE ROBBED A COP AND FOUND OUT HE'S PLOTTING A MURDER... THERE'S NO WAY THAT'S GOING TO GO WELL FOR US.
LECO IS RIGHT, BABE.
I DON'T KNOW, GUYS-- I DON'T THINK I'LL BE ABLE TO SLEEP...

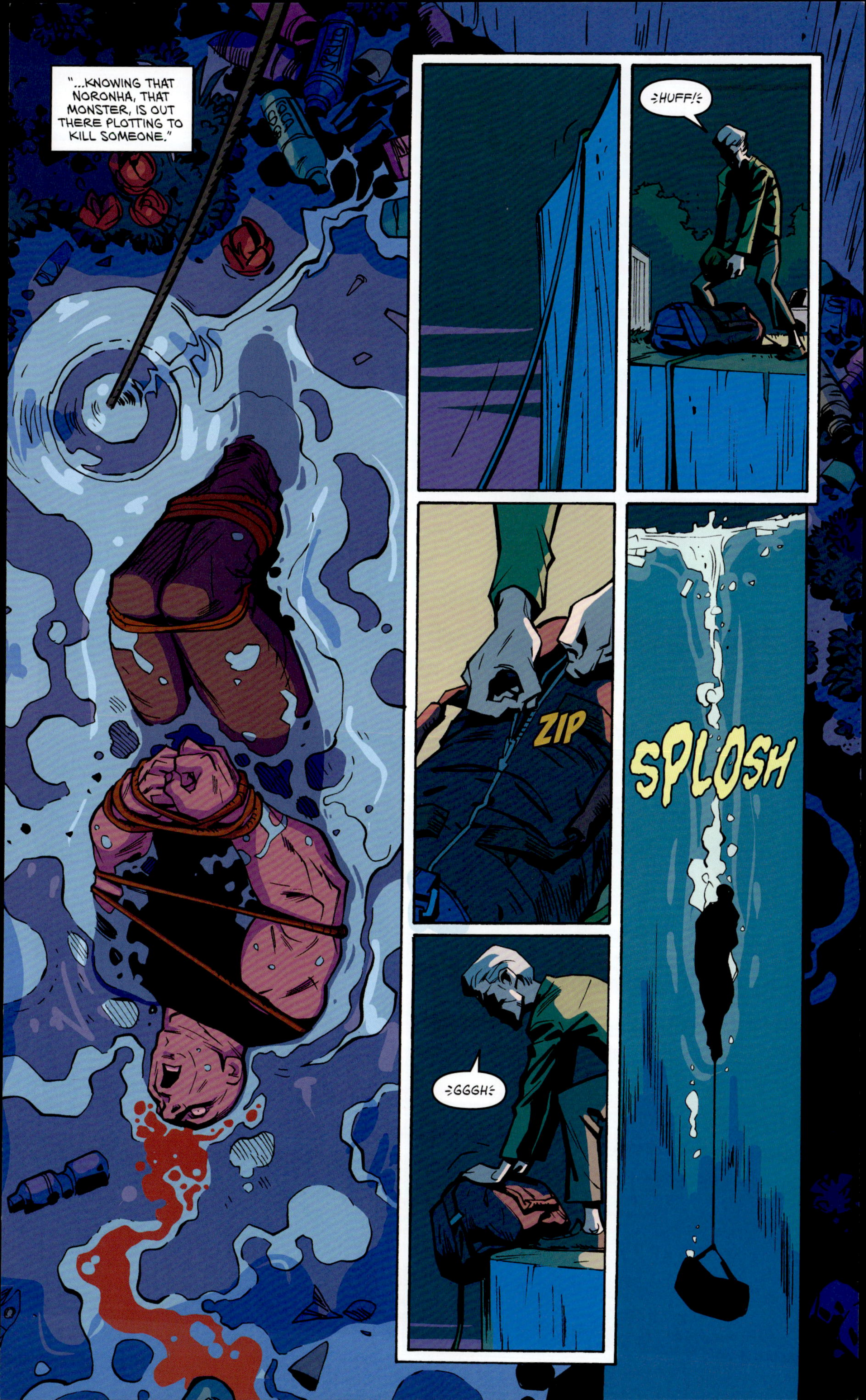
"...KNOWING THAT NORONHA, THAT MONSTER, IS OUT THERE PLOTTING TO KILL SOMEONE."
HUFF!
ZIP
SPLOSH
GGGH

NOW THE FISH CAN DEAL WITH YOUR STUPIDITY.
IT'S ME. NORONHA IS OUT...YEAH, IT WENT FINE. HE'S MET HIS FATE.
YES, I NEED...WHO'S TRUSTWORTHY IN INTELLIGENCE?
YES. SURE, I KNOW HIM. LET HIM KNOW I'M GOING TO NEED HIM TODAY...
...WE'VE GOT SOME BUSY DAYS AHEAD.
Ongoing Call
Alvarenga
KRAKK
São Paulo
30 km

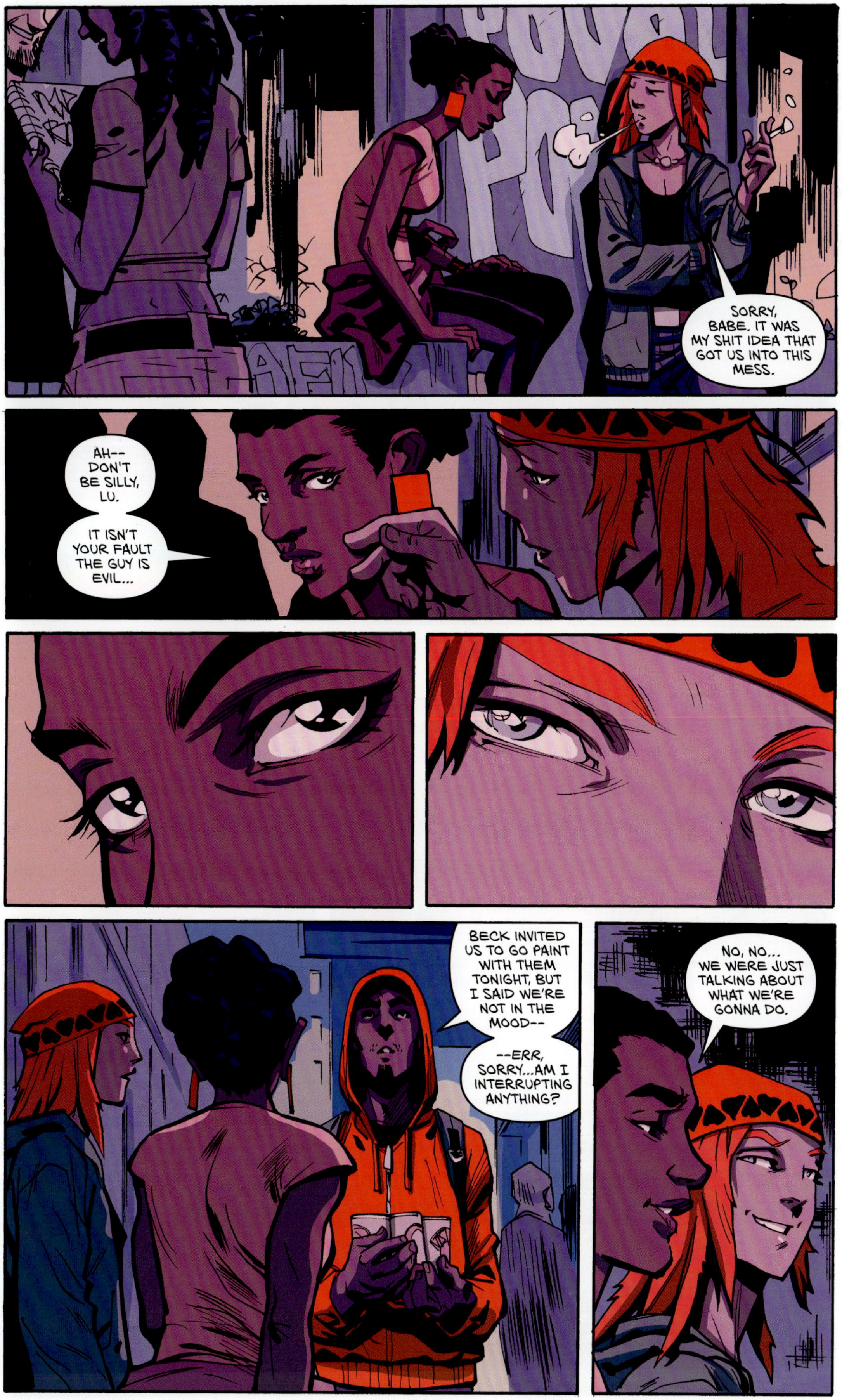
SORRY, BABE. IT WAS MY SHIT IDEA THAT GOT US INTO THIS MESS.
AH-- DON'T BE SILLY, LU.
IT ISN'T YOUR FAULT THE GUY IS EVIL...
BECK INVITED US TO GO PAINT WITH THEM TONIGHT, BUT I SAID WE'RE NOT IN THE MOOD--
--ERR, SORRY...AM I INTERRUPTING ANYTHING?
NO, NO... WE WERE JUST TALKING ABOUT WHAT WE'RE GONNA DO.

WHAT IF WE GO TO A NEWSPAPER AND TELL THEM ABOUT THIS CONSPIRACY?
AND HOW WOULD YOU EXPLAIN THAT WE FOUND OUT ABOUT IT FROM A STOLEN **AND** CLONED CELL-PHONE?
THAT'S ILLEGAL, TOO...
TSSS
HMM...
YES-- BUT DON'T FORGET THAT THE **ART** WE DO...
...OUR **VOICES** HERE, ARE ALSO ILLEGAL.

YOU BET...
TRUE...
ARE YOU THINKING WHAT I'M THINKING?
HEY, BEEECK!
COME HERE...

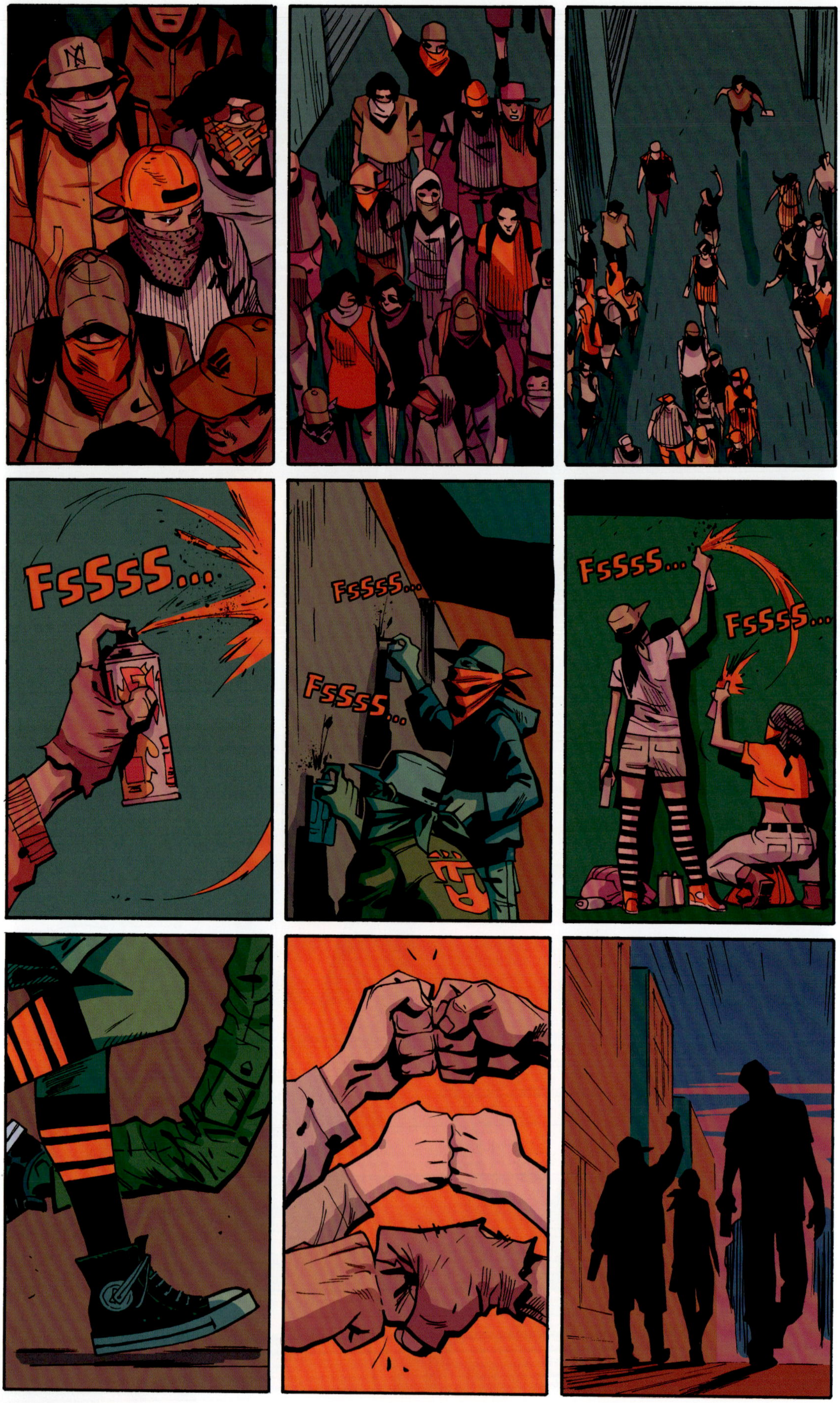
FsSSS...
FsSSS...
FsSSS...
FsSSS...
FsSSS...

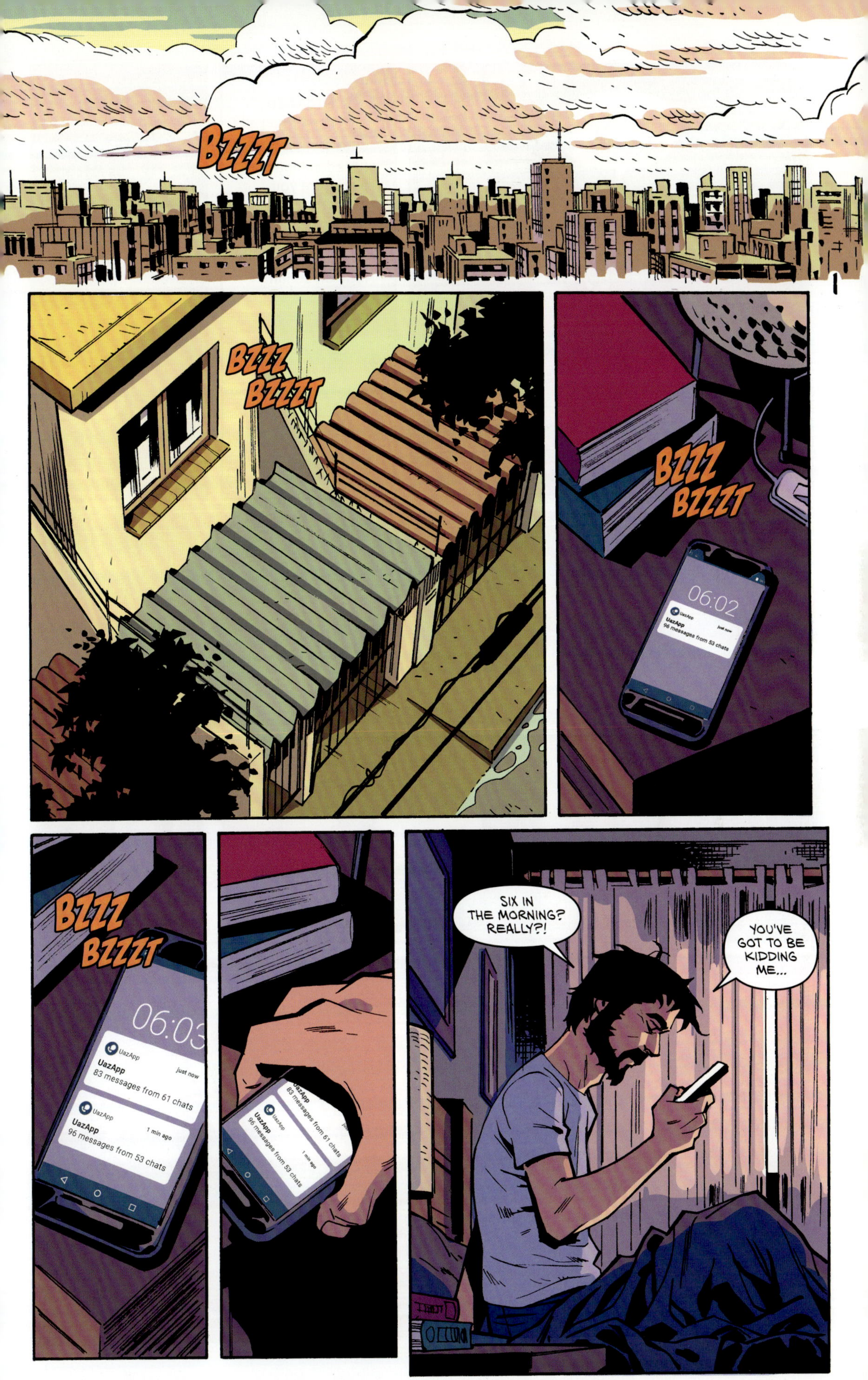
BZZZT
BZZZ
BZZZT
BZZZ
BZZZT
06:02
UazApp
UazApp
96 messages from 53 chats
just now
BZZZ
BZZZT
06:03
UazApp
UazApp
83 messages from 61 chats
just now
UazApp
UazApp
96 messages from 53 chats
1 min ago
SIX IN THE MORNING? REALLY?!
YOU'VE GOT TO BE KIDDING ME...

WHAT THE HELL-- HOW MANY MESSAGES?!
Ricardo
seen today at 06
I tried calling you, Neto! Are you alright?!
Call me back, please...and take a look on social media.
QWERT
ASDFG
HUMPH
THANKS, EVERYONE...SO MUCH FOR THAT LIE IN--
--HUH?!
WHAT THE FUCK?
NETO, YOUR LIFE IS IN DANGER

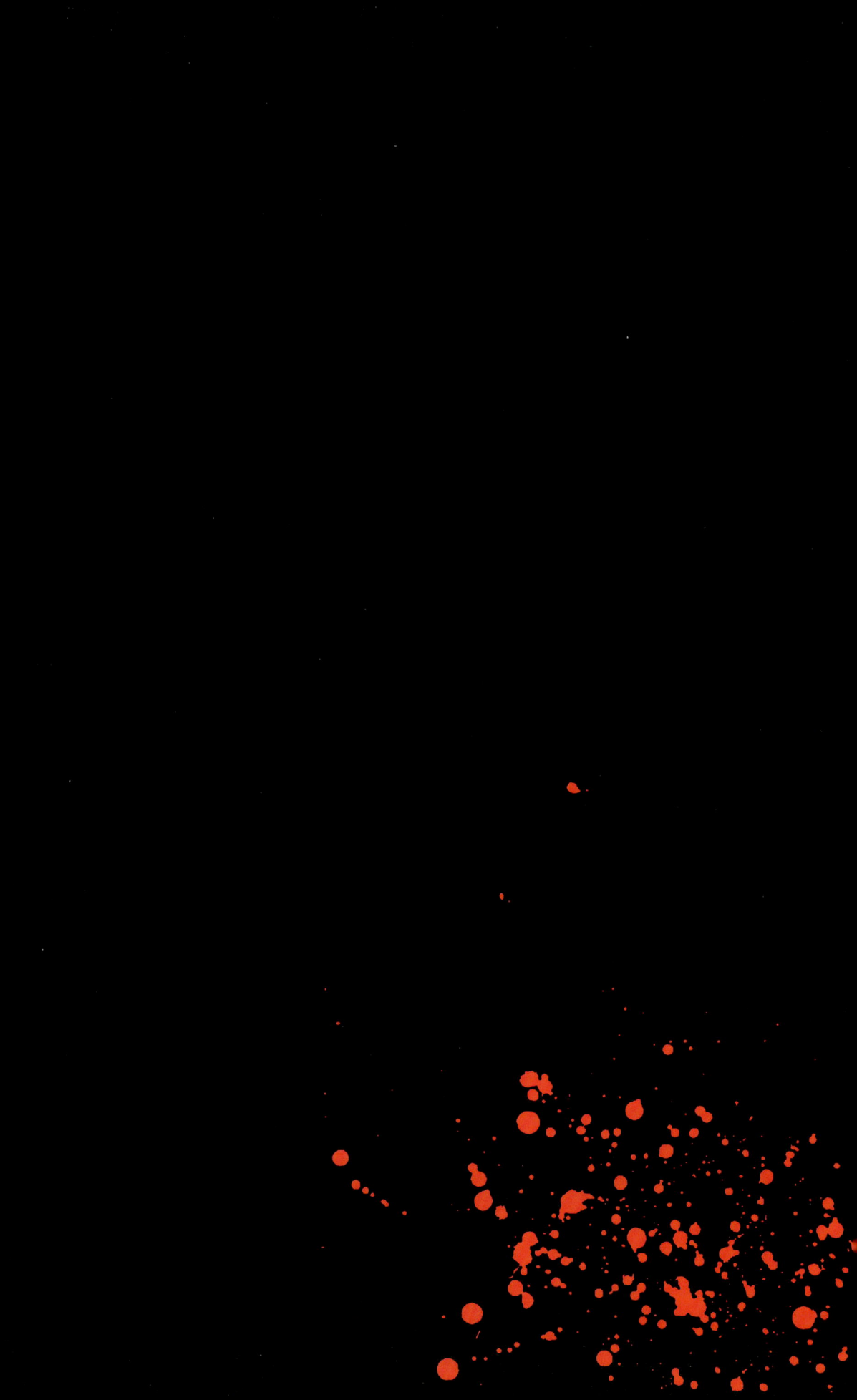

CHAPTER THREE

THE FICKLE FINGER OF FATE

I SAW IT ALL ROUND DOWNTOWN.
YES! I SAW IT TOO, ON PAULISTA AVENUE AND MARGINAL PINHEIROS.
HEY, BRUNA! GOOD MORNING!
CRIS! DO YOU REMEMBER ROGER?
OF COURSE!
THANKS FOR SAVING THIS SEAT, GUYS.
I JUST CAME FROM JARDINS AND IT'S ALL OVER THERE TOO.
REALLY? FUCK!
SSH! IT'S STARTING...
GOOD MORNING, EVERYONE.
FIRST OF ALL, I WANT TO THANK YOU ALL...

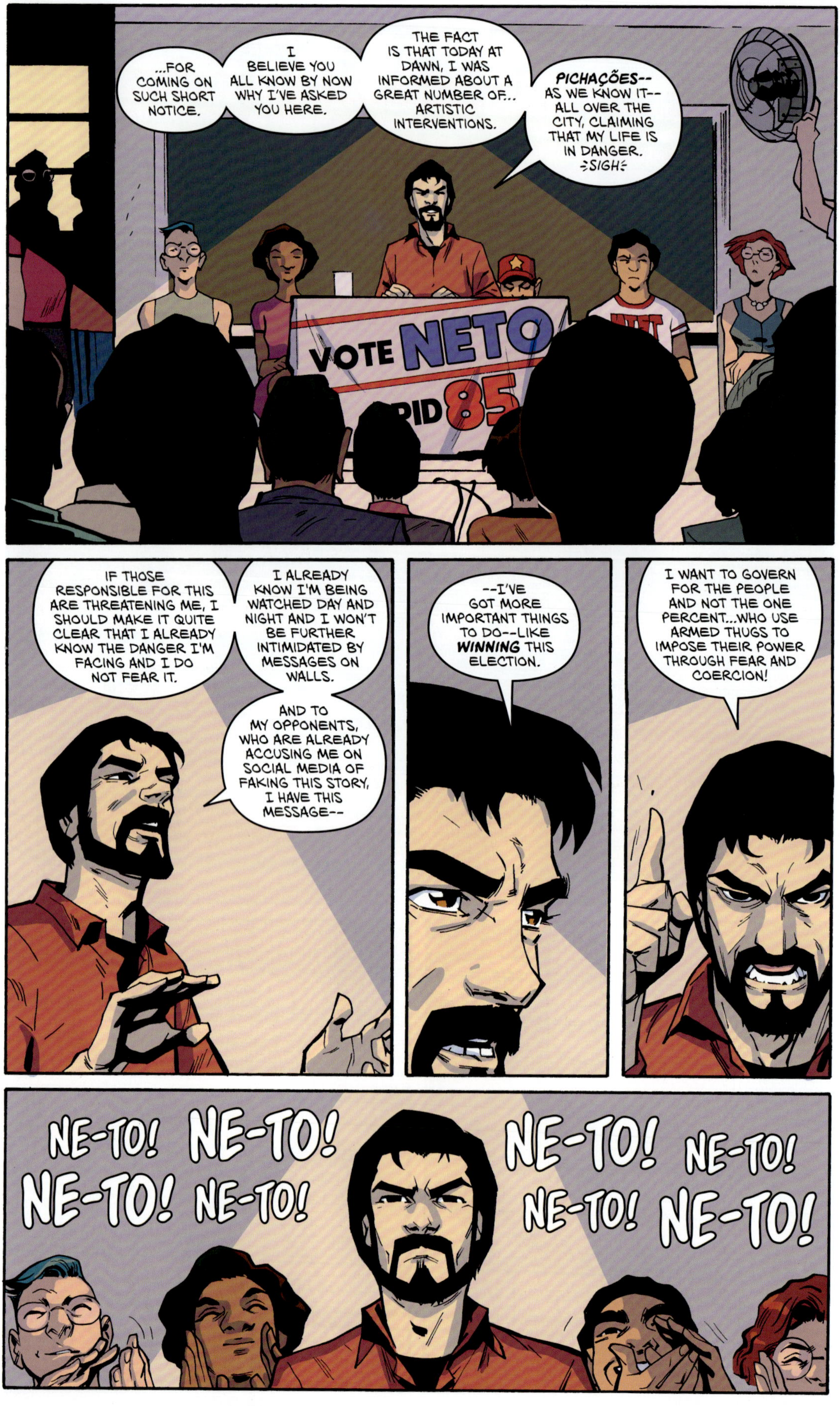

...FOR COMING ON SUCH SHORT NOTICE.
I BELIEVE YOU ALL KNOW BY NOW WHY I'VE ASKED YOU HERE.
THE FACT IS THAT TODAY AT DAWN, I WAS INFORMED ABOUT A GREAT NUMBER OF... ARTISTIC INTERVENTIONS.
PICHAÇÕES-- AS WE KNOW IT-- ALL OVER THE CITY, CLAIMING THAT MY LIFE IS IN DANGER. SIGH
VOTE NETO
PID 85
IF THOSE RESPONSIBLE FOR THIS ARE THREATENING ME, I SHOULD MAKE IT QUITE CLEAR THAT I ALREADY KNOW THE DANGER I'M FACING AND I DO NOT FEAR IT.
I ALREADY KNOW I'M BEING WATCHED DAY AND NIGHT AND I WON'T BE FURTHER INTIMIDATED BY MESSAGES ON WALLS.
AND TO MY OPPONENTS, WHO ARE ALREADY ACCUSING ME ON SOCIAL MEDIA OF FAKING THIS STORY, I HAVE THIS MESSAGE--
--I'VE GOT MORE IMPORTANT THINGS TO DO--LIKE WINNING THIS ELECTION.
I WANT TO GOVERN FOR THE PEOPLE AND NOT THE ONE PERCENT...WHO USE ARMED THUGS TO IMPOSE THEIR POWER THROUGH FEAR AND COERCION!
NE-TO! NE-TO! NE-TO! NE-TO! NE-TO! NE-TO! NE-TO! NE-TO!

SHHH-- PLEASE, GUYS...

TO FINISH, I WANT TO ADDRESS THE PEOPLE BEHIND THESE MESSAGES...

"...IF YOUR OBJECTIVE WASN'T TO THREATEN, BUT TO WARN ME-- IF YOU HAVE MORE INFORMATION, OR EVEN PROOF..."

"...BRING IT FORWARD."

THANK YOU, SON.

YOU'RE WELCOME, MA'AM.

NETO, YOUR LIFE IS IN DANG!

WELL... LOOK WHO'S HERE.
GOOD MORNING TO YOU TOO, MR. RAMIRO.
SO I'M ALL YOURS TODAY... AND I'M UP FOR DOING SOME EXPRESS DELIVERIES.
I'M NOT SURE, LEANDRO... LAST WEEK YOU LEFT THAT CLIENT WAITING ALL DAY. I HAD TO GIVE HIM A FULL REFUND!
ARE YOU DELIVERING FOR MY COMPETITORS NOW TOO, ON THE DAYS YOU WORK FOR ME?!
OF COURSE NOT, MR. RAMIRO. I'M JUST WITH YOU ON FRIDAYS.
I SENT YOU A MESSAGE ABOUT LAST WEEK-- MY BIKE BROKE IN THE MIDDLE OF MARGINAL PINHEIROS. IT TOOK ME ALL DAY TO FIX IT.
I THINK IT'S RUNNING OUT OF STEAM ALREADY... SO I'M IN A HURRY TO MAKE ENOUGH MONEY TO REPLACE IT...

Panel 1
"...SO I'M NOT CAUGHT ON THE WRONG FOOT AGAIN WHEN DELIVERING FOR YOU."

♪♪ ♪♪♪

Panel 2
PING

Panel 3
< Lis
Check this out! 10:13

Candidate Neto is threatened
Posted by BRBC News
The candidate for governor held a last-minute press conference this morning after a great number of pichações were seen in town claiming his life is in

Panel 4
GOOD!

Panel 5
THEIR UAZAPP GROUP SHOULD BE ON FIRE.

Panel 6
BATTERY... BATTERY...?

Panel 8
=SIGH=

Panel 9
NO--!

"--I BET THEY'RE ALREADY TRACING THIS NUMBER."
HMM...
NORONHA'S PHONE PINGED FROM HERE, TWO DAYS AGO.
AH--
DuduPhone
--LOOK AT THAT...
HEY, GOOD MORNING! FEEL FREE TO HAVE A LOOK AT THE PHONES...
SO THIS IS WHY I THINK YOU SHOULD GET A DUAL SIM, GUYS.
...I'LL BE WITH YOU IN A MINUTE.

IT'S AN URGENT MATTER-- I'M DETECTIVE SALDANHA, FROM THE CIVIL POLICE.
I HAVE INTEL THAT THIS STORE IS SELLING **STOLEN** PHONES.
I'LL NEED A LIST OF ALL YOUR EMPLOYEES AND SUPPLIERS.
I'LL ALSO NEED TO INSPECT THE STORE--
HEY-- MY MAN...
...WHAT YOU REALLY NEED, FIRST OF ALL, IS A **WARRANT.**
AS LONG AS YOU DON'T HAVE ONE, YOU TALK ONLY TO MY **LAWYER...** AND I SHOULD WARN YOU THAT HE'S NOT AS FRIENDLY AS I AM.
AH... AND HE ALSO HAS ACCESS TO ALL THE CAMERAS IN THE STORE, TO AVOID SHAKEDOWNS... GET IT?
SO, GUYS--HAVE YOU DECIDED ON THE DUAL-CHIP?
I'VE BEEN USING IT FOR ABOUT TWO YEARS AND NEVER HAD ANY PROBLEMS. I HIGHLY RECOMMEND IT.
HUMPH
IF YOU GET TWO OF THE SAME MODEL, I CAN GIVE YOU A BIG DISCOUNT.

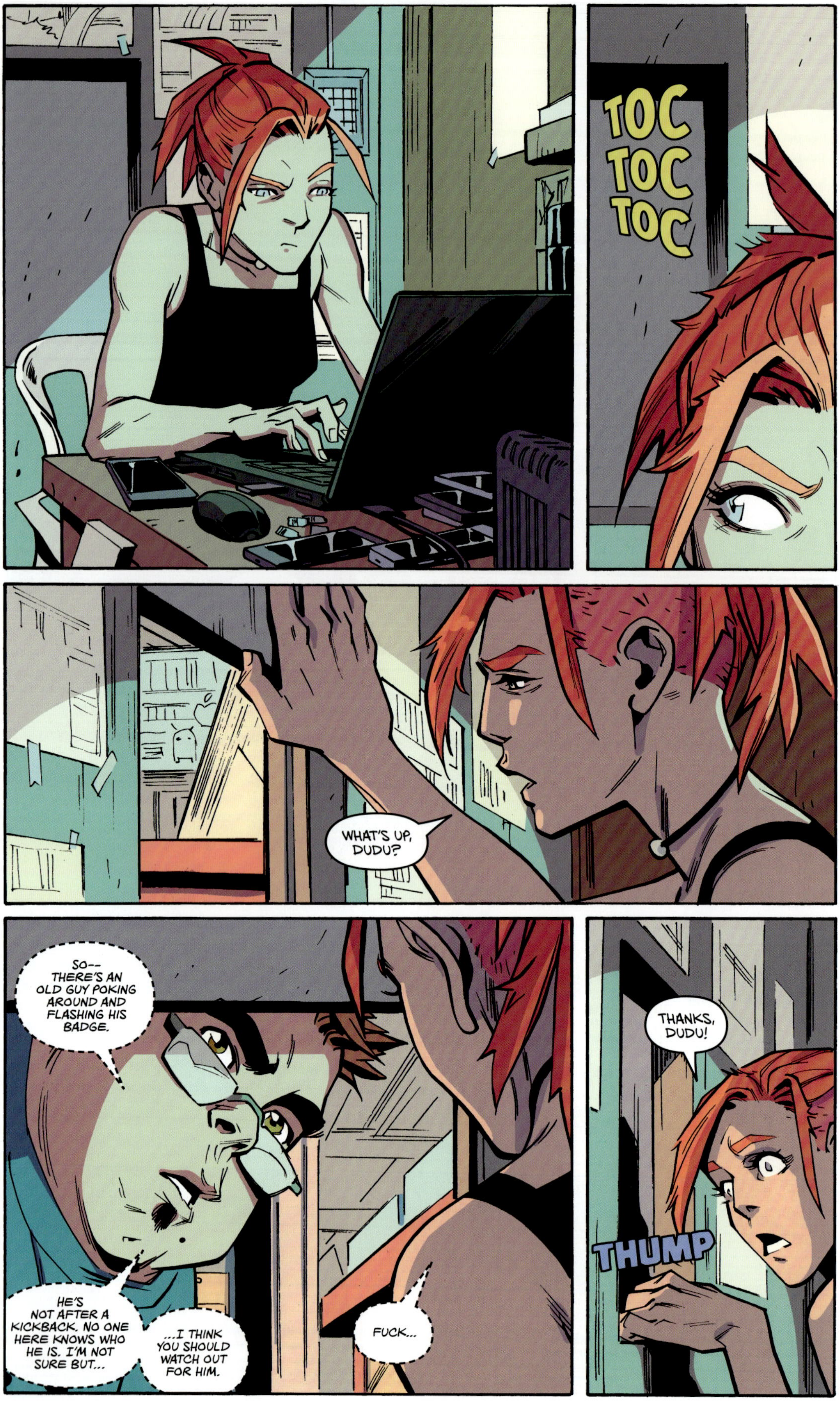
TOC TOC TOC
WHAT'S UP, DUDU?
SO-- THERE'S AN OLD GUY POKING AROUND AND FLASHING HIS BADGE.
HE'S NOT AFTER A KICKBACK. NO ONE HERE KNOWS WHO HE IS. I'M NOT SURE BUT...
...I THINK YOU SHOULD WATCH OUT FOR HIM.
FUCK...
THANKS, DUDU!
THUMP

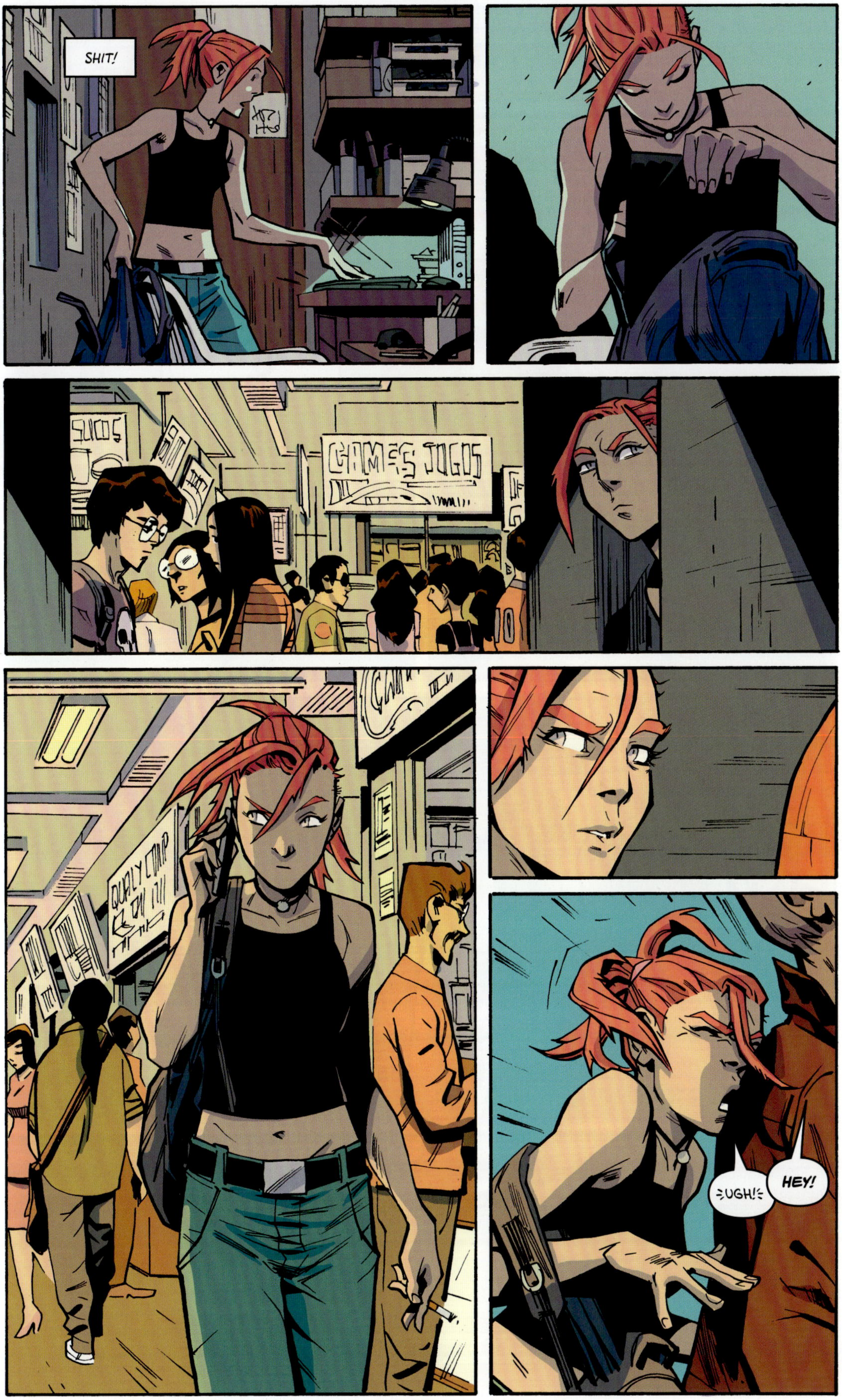
SHIT!
GAMES JOGOS
SUCOS
QUALY COMP
UGH!
HEY!

WATCH OUT, LADY!
OH...
ER... I'M SORRY, MISTER.
NO SWEAT... JUST WATCH WHERE YOU'RE GOING.
YES, SIR!
HMM...
GOT YOU.

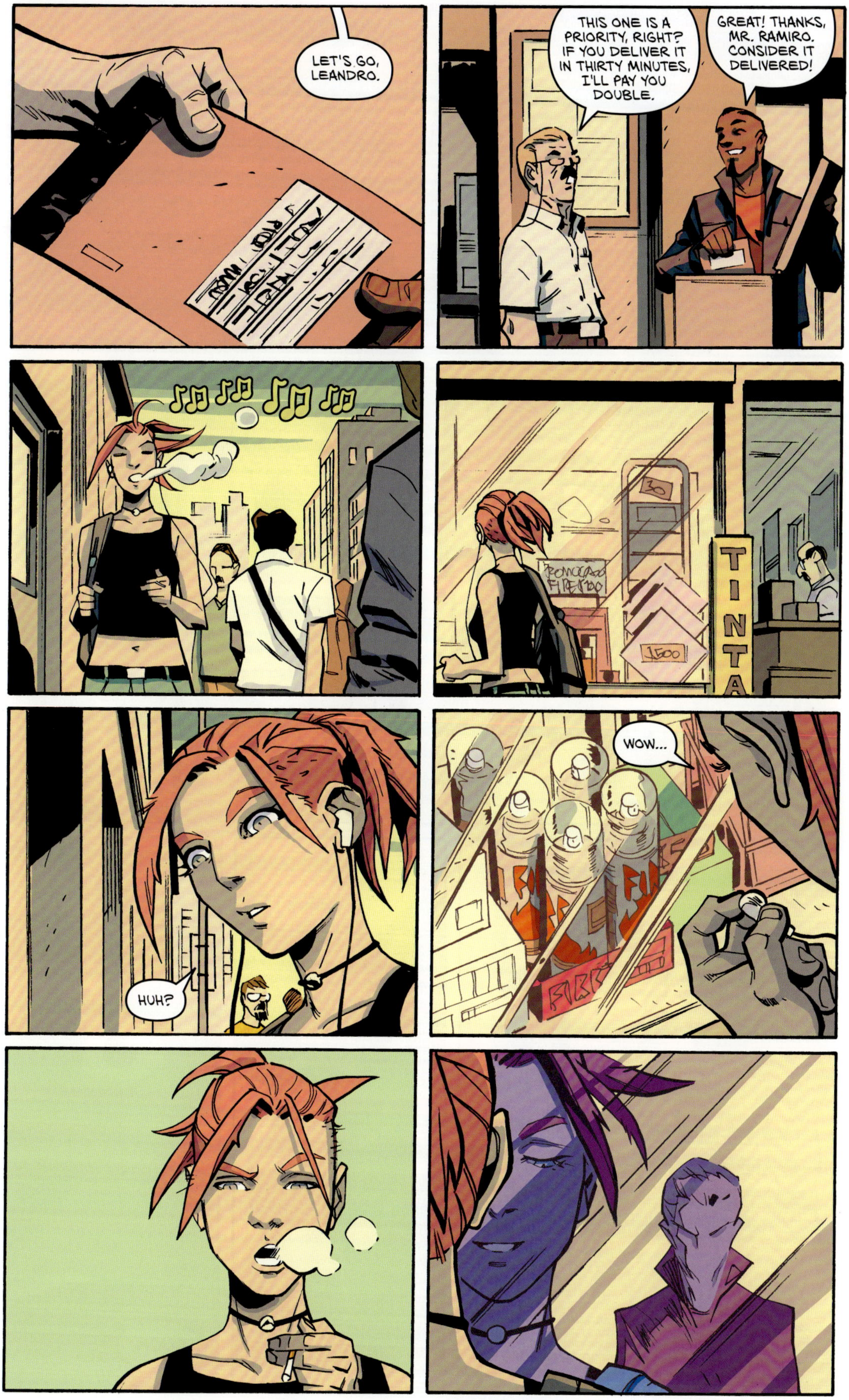
LET'S GO, LEANDRO.
THIS ONE IS A PRIORITY, RIGHT? IF YOU DELIVER IT IN THIRTY MINUTES, I'LL PAY YOU DOUBLE.
GREAT! THANKS, MR. RAMIRO. CONSIDER IT DELIVERED!
TINTA
HUH?
WOW...

YOU...
HUH?!
...COME WITH ME--!
SHIT!
TINTA
HI, YES... WHAT?!
NO, NO! NOT NOW!
WHAT--?!
AH, FUCK, LUCIANA!
LUCIANA?
FUCK!

HUMPH!
AH... DUDE--!
LISTEN HERE--
UGH!
GO-- GOOO!
SKREEECHH
PUFF! PUFF! SHIT...
...WHO WAS THAT?

AND ANOTHER FIGURE OF SPEECH, THAT YOU ALL PROBABLY KNOW WELL...
...IS ONOMATOPOEIA.
IT IS THE REPRODUCTION OF A SOUND IN WRITING AND IS WIDELY USED IN COMIC BOOKS, FOR EXAMPLE.
WHO KNOWS WHAT THIS ONE HERE REPRESENTS?
RIIIING
AN OLD TELEPHONE! LIKE MY GRANNY'S!
VERY GOOD! AND WHAT ELSE?
THINK ABOUT SCHOOL. IT'S SOMETHING YOU ALL LIKE A LOT...
RIIIING
BREAK TIME!
HA-HA-- SEE YOU AFTER THE BREAK. AND DON'T BE LATE!
BZZZ BZZZ
LU? AT THIS TIME?
HI, LU.
WHAT?!

...YES, BABE. BUT WE'RE GOOD NOW. YEAH--WE WILL. BYE-BYE.
PUFFF
OKAY. LIS IS UP TO SPEED NOW...
WHO WAS THAT GUY, LUCIANA? HOW DID HE FIND YOU?!
I DON'T KNOW, LECO. I'VE NEVER SEEN HIM BEFORE...
IS IT ABOUT THE PHONE? DO YOU HAVE IT ON YOU?
YES...BUT I TOOK THE BATTERY OUT. IT'S IMPOSSIBLE TO TRACE WITHOUT IT.
UNLESS... WAIT, LET'S SEE.
ARE YOU CRAZY?!
DONE! IT'S ON...
WHAT?!
EASY, LECO... I KNOW WHAT I'M DOING.
I CAN SEE YOUR TAG ON THAT BUILDING. DO YOU STILL REMEMBER HOW TO GET UP THERE?
ER... YES-- WHY?
HURRY, PARK YOUR BIKE IN THE NEXT STREET AND FIND ME ON THAT BUILDING.
YOU'RE FUCKING CRAZY, LUCIANA.
THANKS--

ARE YOU SURE YOU TURNED IT OFF AGAIN?
YES... I ALREADY TOLD YOU, I TOOK THE BATTERY OUT.
AH-- SHIT!
SKREEEECH
HUMPH
SON OF A BITCH!
KRAKK
VROOOM
HA! SEE? THEY CAN'T TRACK US WITHOUT THE BATTERY.
OKAY... AND NOW WHAT?

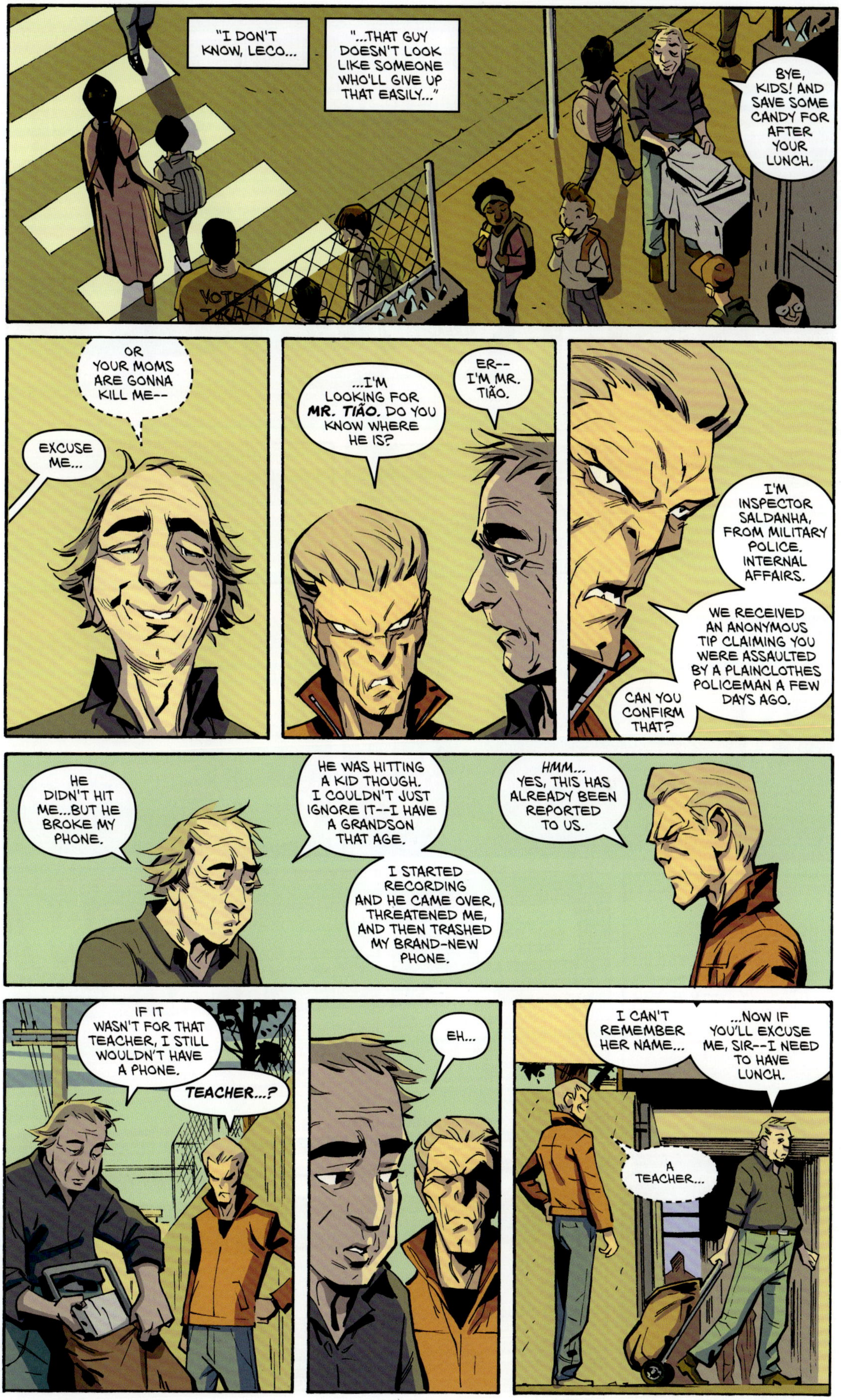
"I DON'T KNOW, LECO...
"...THAT GUY DOESN'T LOOK LIKE SOMEONE WHO'LL GIVE UP THAT EASILY..."
BYE, KIDS! AND SAVE SOME CANDY FOR AFTER YOUR LUNCH.
OR YOUR MOMS ARE GONNA KILL ME--
EXCUSE ME...
...I'M LOOKING FOR **MR. TIÃO.** DO YOU KNOW WHERE HE IS?
ER-- I'M MR. TIÃO.
I'M INSPECTOR SALDANHA, FROM MILITARY POLICE. INTERNAL AFFAIRS.
WE RECEIVED AN ANONYMOUS TIP CLAIMING YOU WERE ASSAULTED BY A PLAINCLOTHES POLICEMAN A FEW DAYS AGO.
CAN YOU CONFIRM THAT?
HE DIDN'T HIT ME...BUT HE BROKE MY PHONE.
HE WAS HITTING A KID THOUGH. I COULDN'T JUST IGNORE IT--I HAVE A GRANDSON THAT AGE.
I STARTED RECORDING AND HE CAME OVER, THREATENED ME, AND THEN TRASHED MY BRAND-NEW PHONE.
HMM... YES, THIS HAS ALREADY BEEN REPORTED TO US.
IF IT WASN'T FOR THAT TEACHER, I STILL WOULDN'T HAVE A PHONE.
TEACHER...?
EH...
I CAN'T REMEMBER HER NAME...
...NOW IF YOU'LL EXCUSE ME, SIR--I NEED TO HAVE LUNCH.
A TEACHER...

BRIZA
AH, FUCK, BRO... MR. RAMIRO'S GIVEN ME UP ALREADY?!
I'LL NEVER BE ABLE TO WORK NOW.
I BET THEY ALREADY HAVE MY BIKE'S LICENSE PLATE, MY NAME, ADDRESS--
MOM! AND PAULINHA--!
C'MON... PICK UP, PICK UP!
MOM!? *PHEW*
IS EVERYTHING ALL RIGHT?
KLIK BEEP BEEP BEEP--
HELLO-- HELLO?!
VROOOOOM
AH-- FUCK! FUCK!

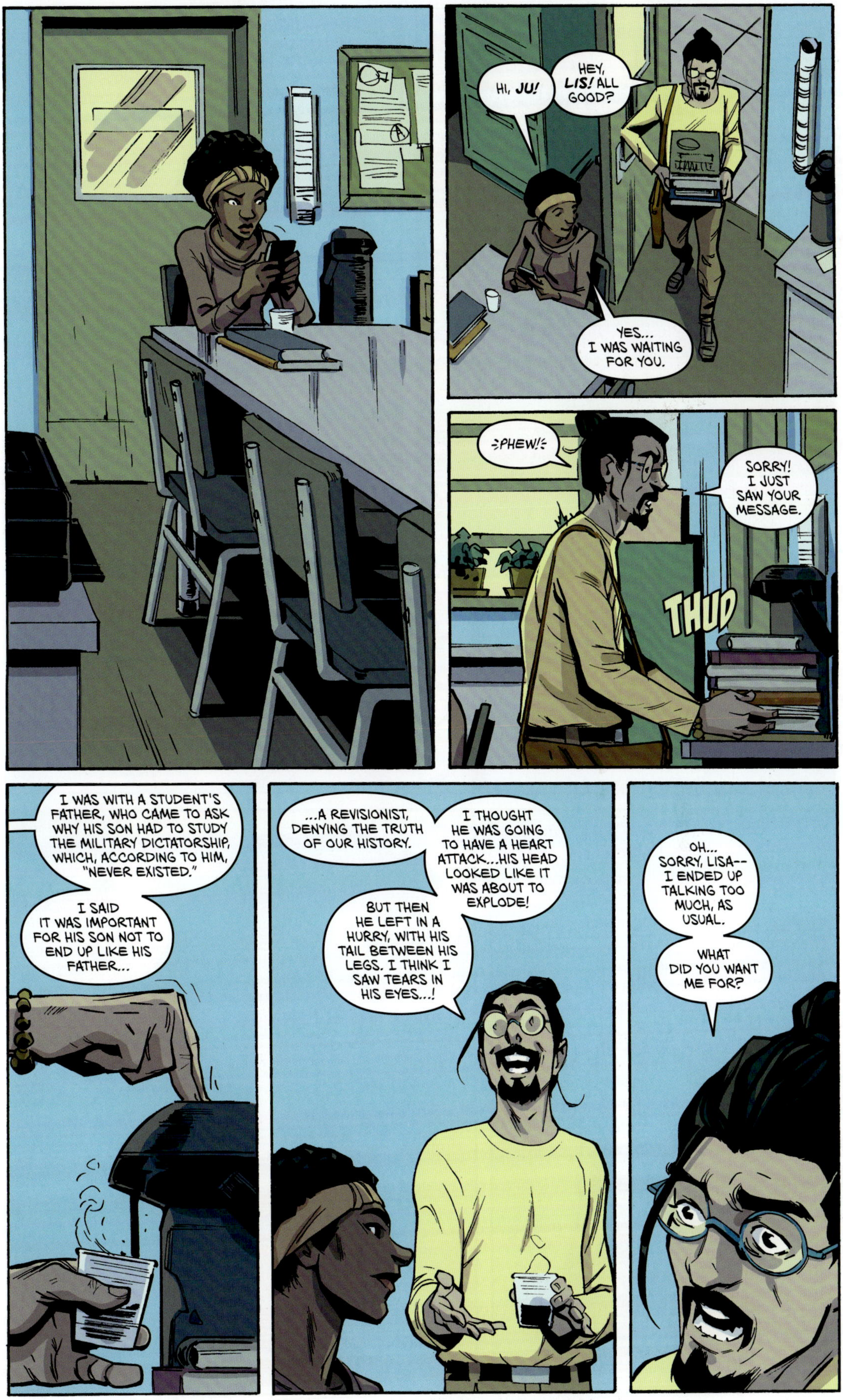
HI, JU!
HEY, LIS! ALL GOOD?
YES... I WAS WAITING FOR YOU.
PHEW!
SORRY! I JUST SAW YOUR MESSAGE.
THUD
I WAS WITH A STUDENT'S FATHER, WHO CAME TO ASK WHY HIS SON HAD TO STUDY THE MILITARY DICTATORSHIP, WHICH, ACCORDING TO HIM, "NEVER EXISTED."
I SAID IT WAS IMPORTANT FOR HIS SON NOT TO END UP LIKE HIS FATHER...
...A REVISIONIST, DENYING THE TRUTH OF OUR HISTORY.
I THOUGHT HE WAS GOING TO HAVE A HEART ATTACK...HIS HEAD LOOKED LIKE IT WAS ABOUT TO EXPLODE!
BUT THEN HE LEFT IN A HURRY, WITH HIS TAIL BETWEEN HIS LEGS. I THINK I SAW TEARS IN HIS EYES...!
OH... SORRY, LISA-- I ENDED UP TALKING TOO MUCH, AS USUAL.
WHAT DID YOU WANT ME FOR?

SO, SORRY FOR ASKING, JU, BUT-- YOU'RE CLOSE WITH ROQUE ALVES, AREN'T YOU?
THE JOURNALIST...
HE'S MY EX, BUT WE'RE STILL GOOD FRIENDS.
WHY THE INTEREST IN ROQUE?
DO YOU THINK HE'S TRUSTWORTHY? AS A JOURNALIST, I MEAN.
IT'S ABOUT SOMETHING SERIOUS, IMPORTANT PEOPLE... A MATTER OF LIFE AND DEATH, I SUPPOSE.
HMM... IF IT'S THAT SERIOUS...
...YOU CAN BE SURE THAT ROQUE IS THE RIGHT PERSON TO TALK TO.
DO YOU WANT HIS NUMBER?
OR SHALL I GET HIM TO CONTACT YOU?
SEND ME HIS NUMBER, PLEASE. I'LL CALL HIM AT NOON.

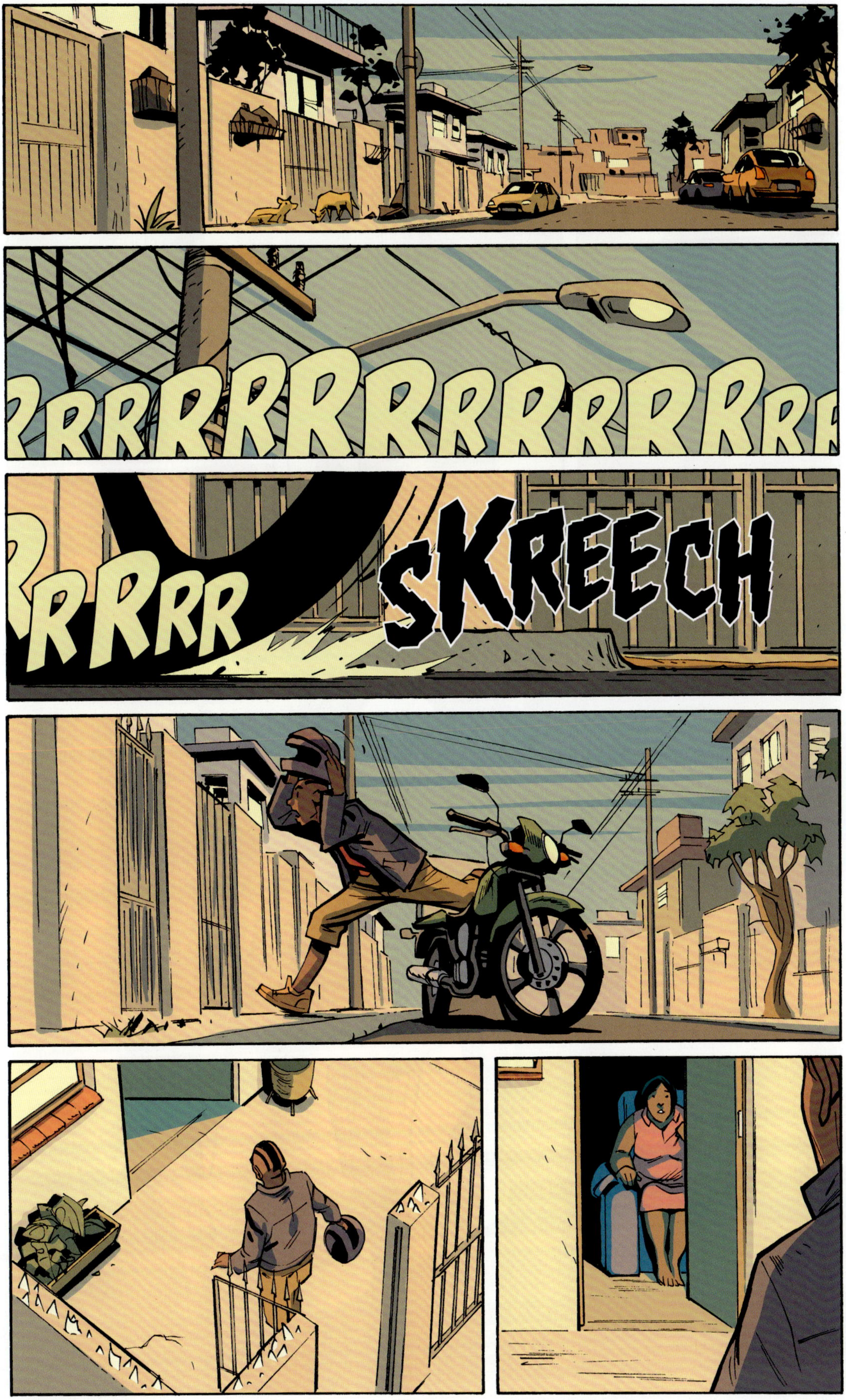
RRRRRRRRRRRRR
RRRR
SKREECH

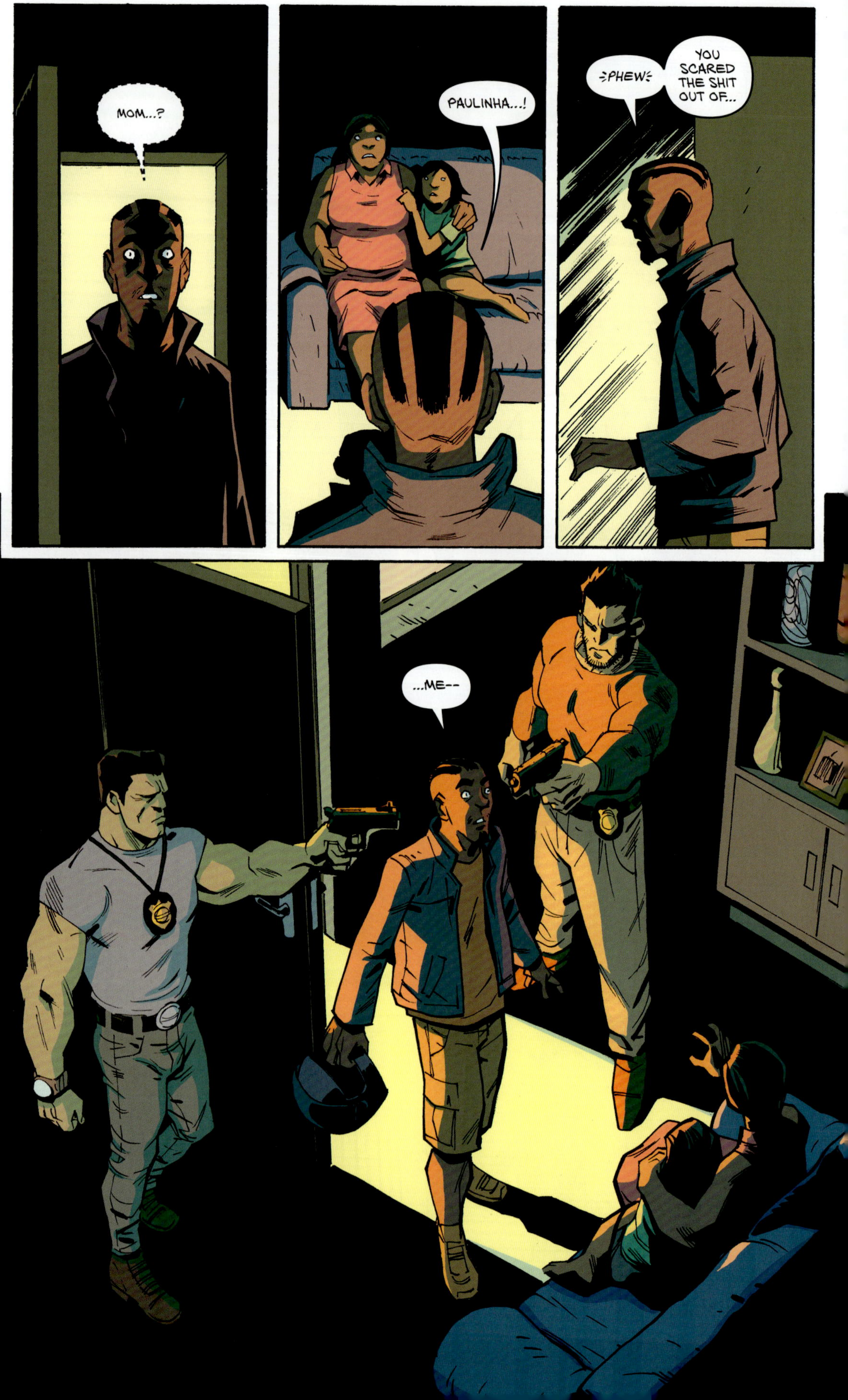
MOM...?
PAULINHA...!
PHEW
YOU SCARED THE SHIT OUT OF...
...ME--

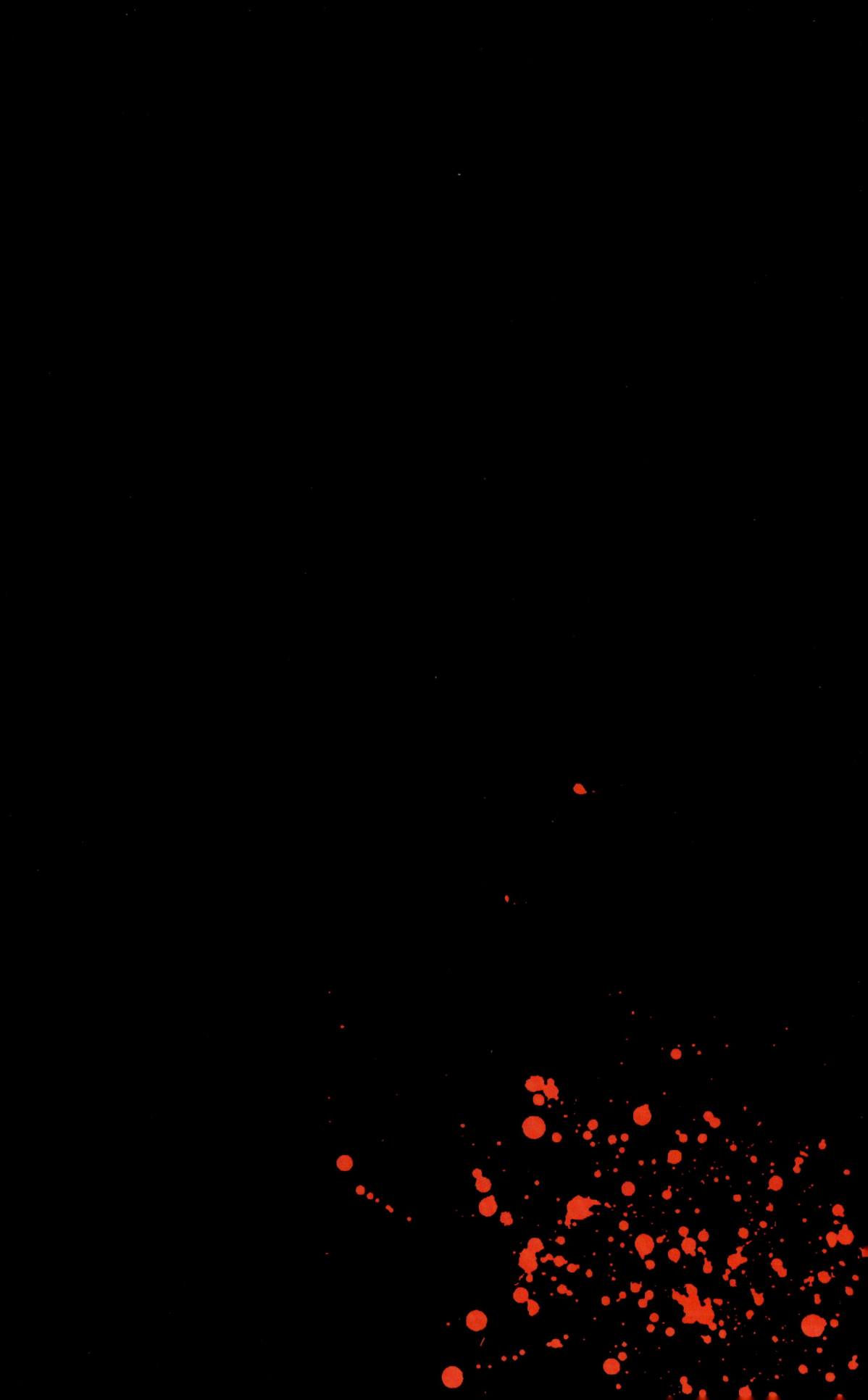

CHAPTER FOUR
DROPPING THE BOMB

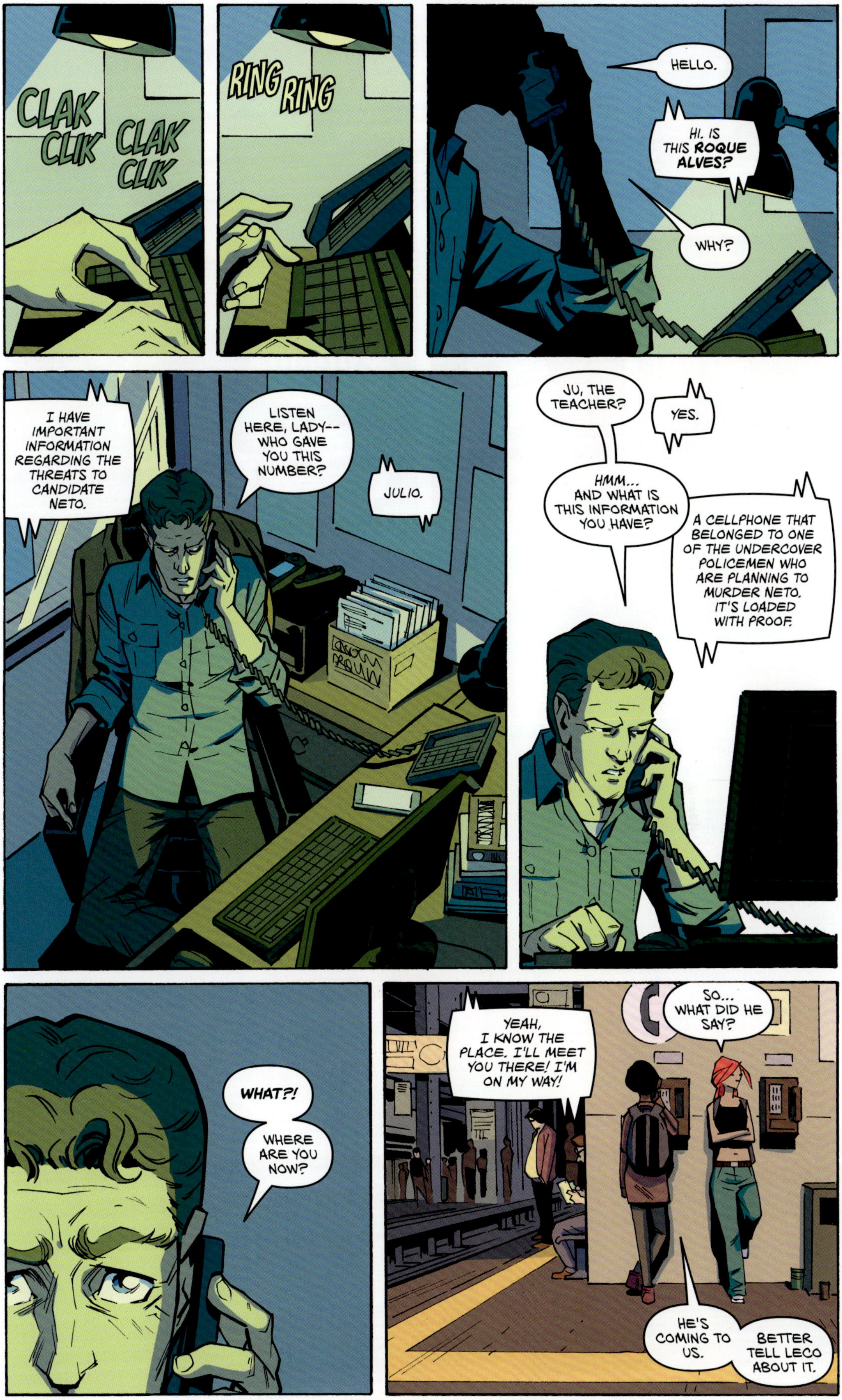
CLAK CLIK CLAK CLIK
RING RING
HELLO.
HI. IS THIS ROQUE ALVES?
WHY?
I HAVE IMPORTANT INFORMATION REGARDING THE THREATS TO CANDIDATE NETO.
LISTEN HERE, LADY-- WHO GAVE YOU THIS NUMBER?
JULIO.
JU, THE TEACHER?
YES.
HMM... AND WHAT IS THIS INFORMATION YOU HAVE?
A CELLPHONE THAT BELONGED TO ONE OF THE UNDERCOVER POLICEMEN WHO ARE PLANNING TO MURDER NETO. IT'S LOADED WITH PROOF.
WHAT?!
WHERE ARE YOU NOW?
YEAH, I KNOW THE PLACE. I'LL MEET YOU THERE! I'M ON MY WAY!
SO... WHAT DID HE SAY?
HE'S COMING TO US.
BETTER TELL LECO ABOUT IT.

"MAYBE HE CAN RELAX A BIT."
NO! NO, NO, NO... PLEASE...
16:51
UazApp
Lis
12 messages
BZZZZ
BZZZZ
AAARGH--!
BZZZZ
BZZZZ
16:52
UazApp
Lu
4 messages
UazApp
Lis
12 messages
AHHHH!
MY GOD-- P-P-PLEASE, STOP... *COUGH*
...STOOOOP... *COUGH*
THIS IS ONLY A SAMPLE OF COURSE...

STOP! I'LL TALK... I'LL TALK-- =COUGH=
I NAMED THIS COLLECTION THE BEST OF SCREAMS, VOLUME 3.
THE TWO FIRST VOLUMES ARE OLDER...STILL ON CASSETTE TAPES.
AAHHH--!
HAVE YOU LEARNED THE MELODY? OR DO YOU NEED TO LISTEN TO IT AGAIN?
YOU'D BETTER KNOW IT, BECAUSE YOU'LL HAVE THE HONOR OF DOING THE CHORUS.
IT WORKS LIKE A MUSICAL INSTRUMENT-- I PLAY. YOU SCREAM.
BUT SINCE WE'RE IN A HURRY, AND I DON'T HAVE THE PROPER TOOLS HERE...
...I'LL HAVE TO IMPROVISE WITH THIS.
=GHH=

I PROBABLY WON'T REACH THE HIGH PITCHES I'M LOOKING FOR...
...BUT BELIEVE ME, I CAN GET CLOSE.
I CAN PLAY WITH YOUR NAILS.
OR EVEN WITH YOUR VOICE.
BUT AS WITH ALL FORMS OF ART...IT'S MAINLY ABOUT FEELING.
AND ONE THING I CAN GUARANTEE YOU, IT'LL FUCKING HURT!
GGHN NO...
OR WE DON'T EVEN NEED TO GET DIRTY IF YOU JUST TELL ME...
...WHO HAS THAT FUCKING PHONE?
AAAHHHH!

VIADUTO DO CHÁ, DOWNTOWN SÃO PAULO.
ROQUE?
HI! SO, WHAT DO YOU HAVE FOR ME?
FIRST I WANT TO KNOW THAT YOU WON'T OUT ME--
--YOU KNOW... AS YOUR SOURCE.
LISTEN-- I WON'T REVEAL MY SOURCE EVEN AT GUNPOINT.
I ALSO DON'T CARE HOW YOU GOT THIS THING.
OKAY...THE PHONE IS NEARBY, WITH A FRIEND, FOR SAFETY.
IT IS STILL FUNCTIONAL BUT IT CAN ONLY BE TRACKED WHEN TURNED ON.
IT HAS CONTACTS, CHAT HISTORY, PHOTOS, VIDEOS... EVERYTHING.

AND HOW DO YOU KNOW IT'S LEGIT?
ONE OF THE CONSPIRATORS-- A BIG NAME-- CALLED BACK...
BEEP BEEP
...THEY ARE HOT ON OUR HEELS...
FUCK...
HEY, LECO! DID YOU GET MY--?
LUCIANA?
WHO IS THIS?
IT DOESN'T MATTER... LISTEN CAREFULLY-- MY PISTOL IS NOW AIMED AT LEANDRO'S GUTS.
IF I DON'T HAVE THAT PHONE IN ONE HOUR, I'LL PULL THE TRIGGER AND WATCH YOUR FRIEND BLEED TO DEATH.
BECAUSE PAIN, WELL... HE'S ALREADY HAD ENOUGH OF THAT FOR ONE DAY.
PUT HIM ON THE LINE, NOW!
I--I'M GOOD, LU, I'M GOOD! SOCK! UGH
SORRY, HE WON'T BE ABLE TO TALK FOR A WHILE...
...ONE LAST THING-- IF YOU TELL ANYONE ELSE ABOUT THIS, YOU'LL NEVER SEE LEANDRO AGAIN.
I'LL BE WAITING FOR YOUR CALL. THE CLOCK IS TICKING--
LIS! LIS! THEY HAVE LECO.
AH... SHIT--
WE'VE GOT TO GO...
...I'LL REACH OUT AGAIN AS SOON AS I CAN.
TAKE CARE.

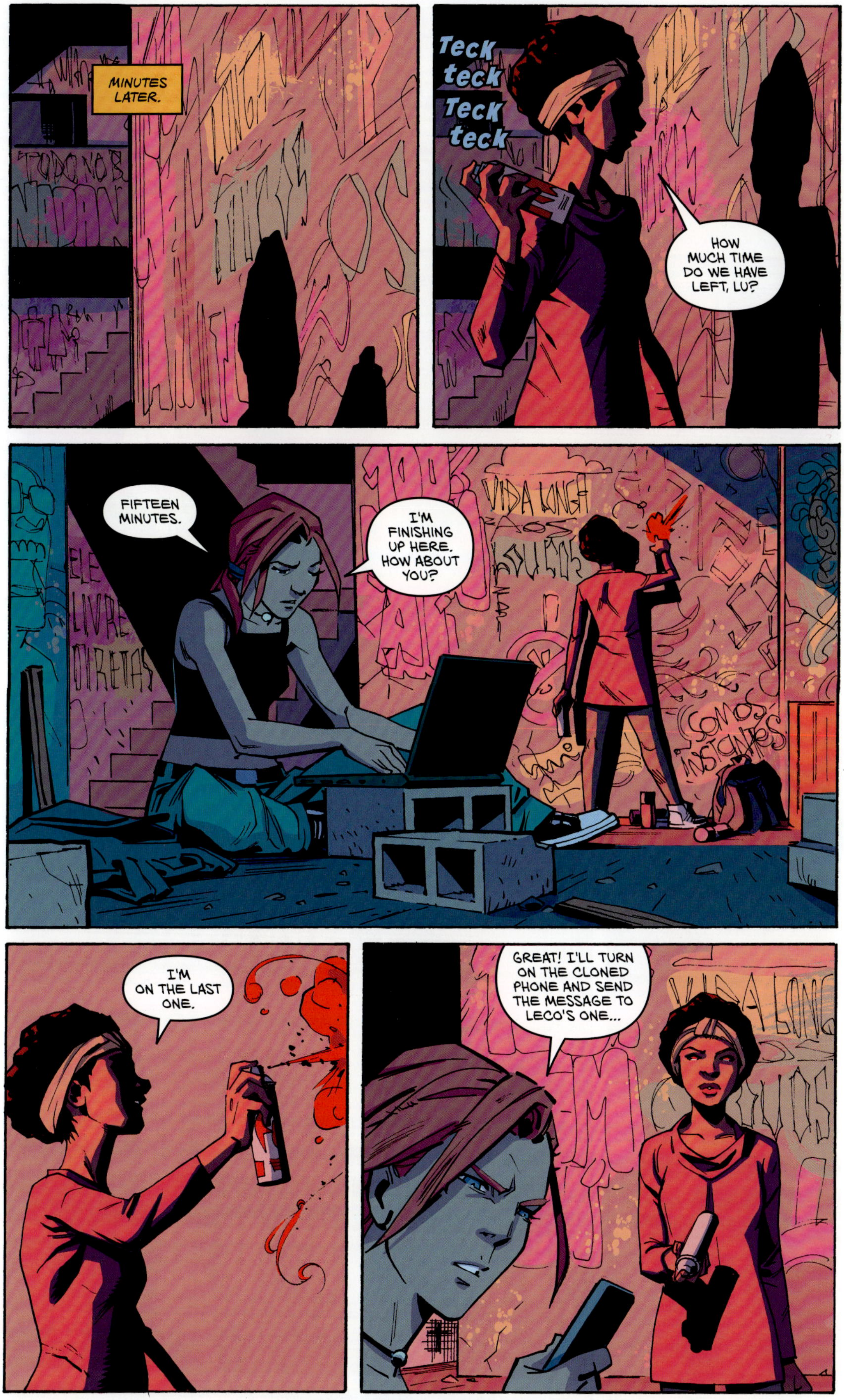
MINUTES LATER.
Teck teck Teck teck
HOW MUCH TIME DO WE HAVE LEFT, LU?
FIFTEEN MINUTES.
I'M FINISHING UP HERE. HOW ABOUT YOU?
I'M ON THE LAST ONE.
GREAT! I'LL TURN ON THE CLONED PHONE AND SEND THE MESSAGE TO LECO'S ONE...

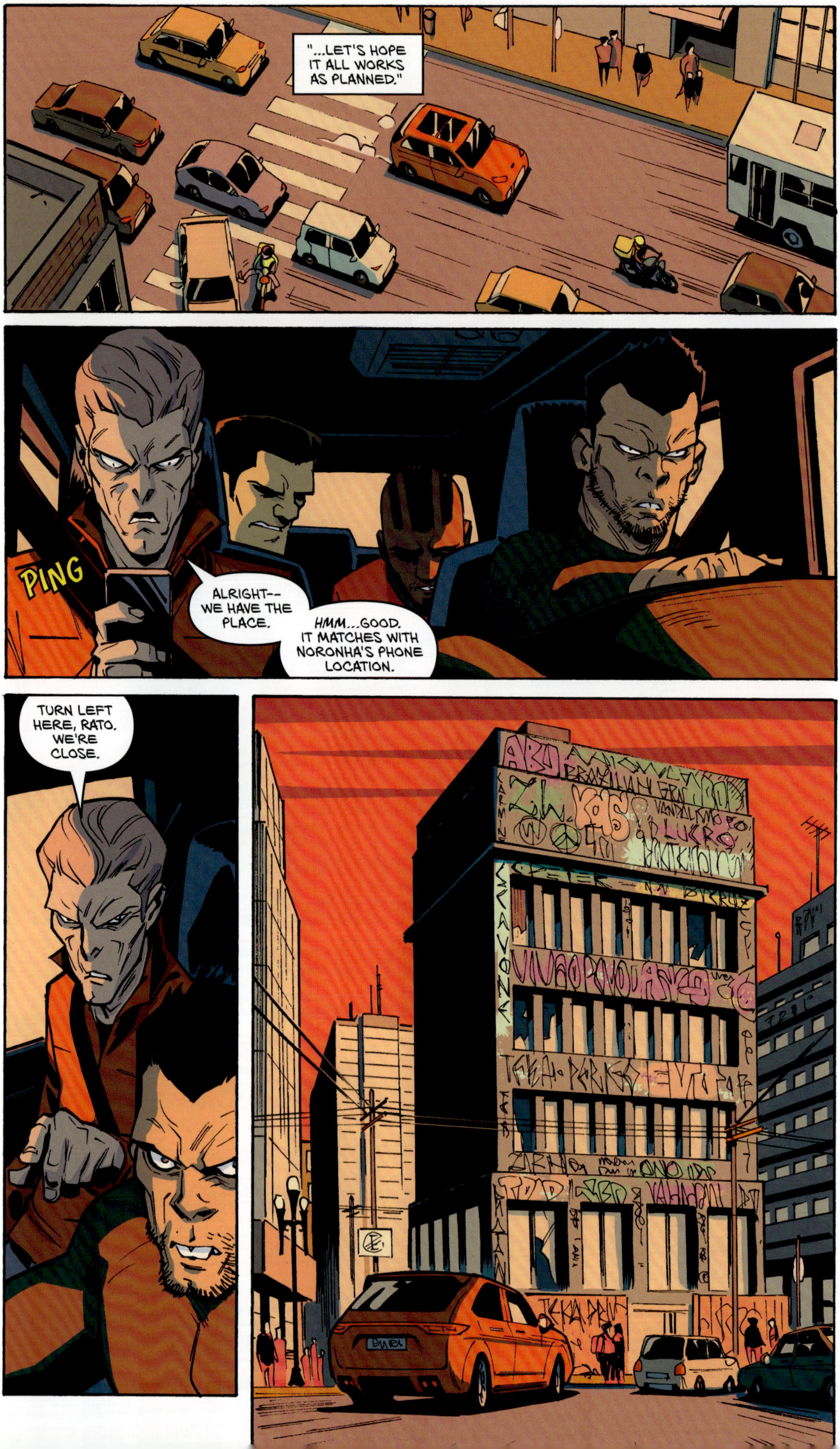
"...LET'S HOPE IT ALL WORKS AS PLANNED."
PING
ALRIGHT-- WE HAVE THE PLACE.
HMM...GOOD. IT MATCHES WITH NORONHA'S PHONE LOCATION.
TURN LEFT HERE, RATO. WE'RE CLOSE.

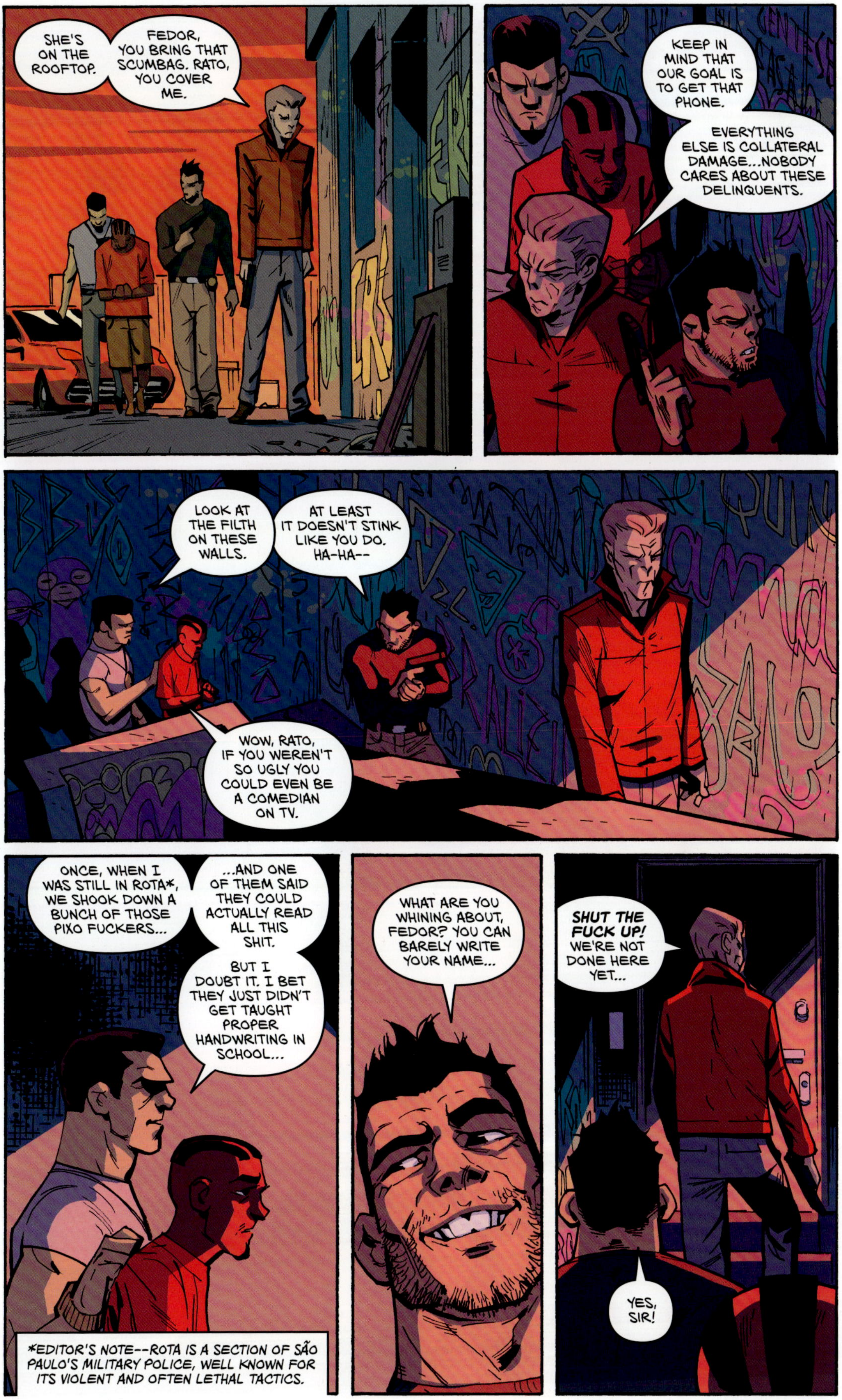
SHE'S ON THE ROOFTOP.
FEDOR, YOU BRING THAT SCUMBAG. RATO, YOU COVER ME.
KEEP IN MIND THAT OUR GOAL IS TO GET THAT PHONE.
EVERYTHING ELSE IS COLLATERAL DAMAGE...NOBODY CARES ABOUT THESE DELINQUENTS.
LOOK AT THE FILTH ON THESE WALLS.
AT LEAST IT DOESN'T STINK LIKE YOU DO. HA-HA--
WOW, RATO, IF YOU WEREN'T SO UGLY YOU COULD EVEN BE A COMEDIAN ON TV.
ONCE, WHEN I WAS STILL IN ROTA*, WE SHOOK DOWN A BUNCH OF THOSE PIXO FUCKERS...
...AND ONE OF THEM SAID THEY COULD ACTUALLY READ ALL THIS SHIT.
BUT I DOUBT IT. I BET THEY JUST DIDN'T GET TAUGHT PROPER HANDWRITING IN SCHOOL...
*EDITOR'S NOTE--ROTA IS A SECTION OF SÃO PAULO'S MILITARY POLICE, WELL KNOWN FOR ITS VIOLENT AND OFTEN LETHAL TACTICS.
WHAT ARE YOU WHINING ABOUT, FEDOR? YOU CAN BARELY WRITE YOUR NAME...
SHUT THE FUCK UP! WE'RE NOT DONE HERE YET...
YES, SIR!

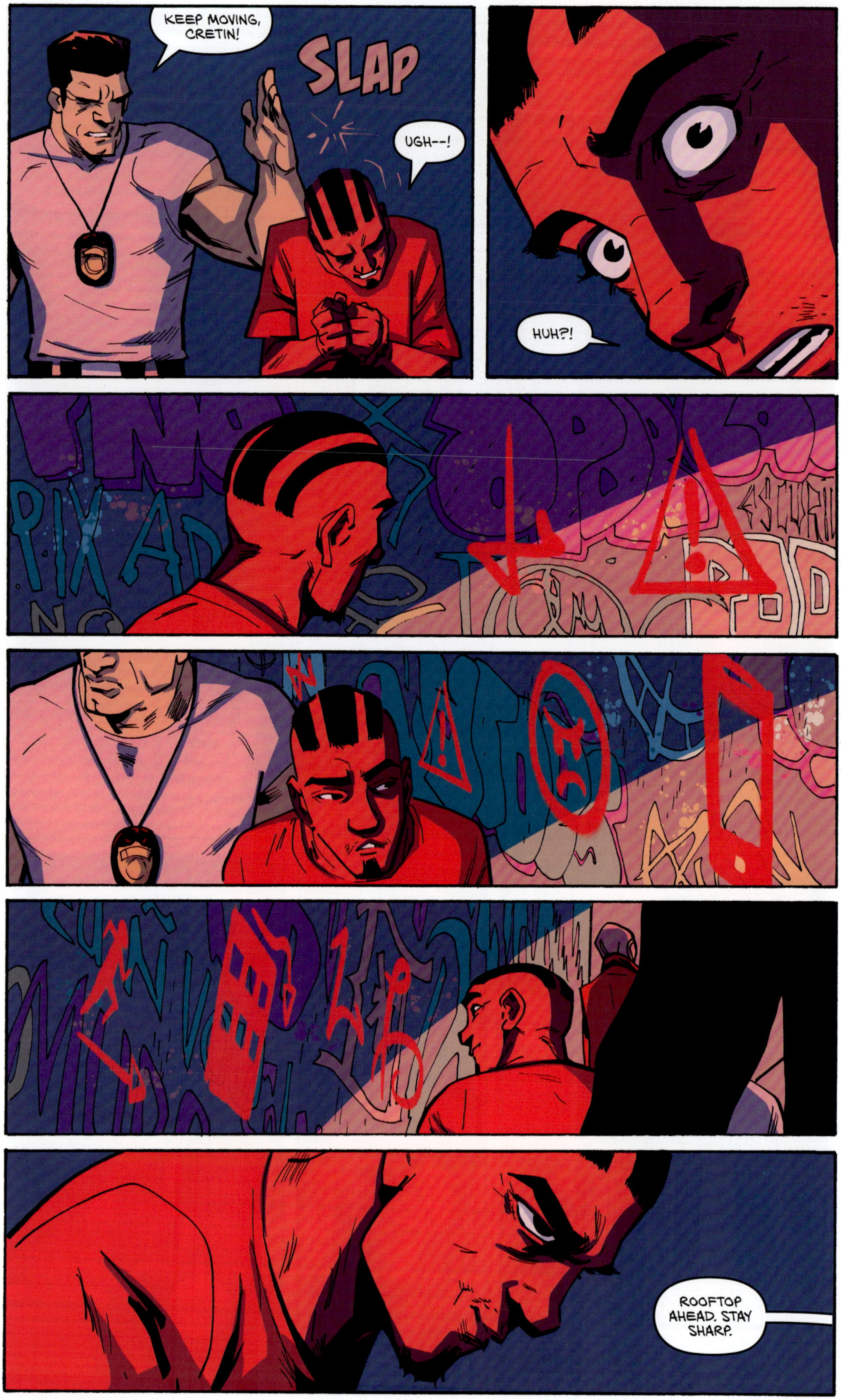
KEEP MOVING, CRETIN!
SLAP
UGH--!
HUH?!
ROOFTOP AHEAD. STAY SHARP.

ONE, TWO...
...GO, RATO!
ALL CLEAR.
ISN'T THAT LUCIANA SUPPOSED TO BE WAITING HERE FOR US, ZÉ?
YES...
...BUT SHE KNOWS WHAT WE'RE REALLY AFTER.

WELL, DIRTBAG... IT SEEMS YOUR GIRL ABANDONED YOU.
BZZZZ BZZZZ
BZZZZ BZZZZ
BZZZZ BZZZZ
SHIT!
SMILE! YOU'RE ON CAMERA

THAT LITTLE SHIT WANTS TO PLAY TRICKS, HUH?
KEEP YOUR EYES OPEN, SHE SHOULDN'T BE FAR!
WHACK
AAARGH!
MOTHER-FUCKER!
BLAM
BLAM
BLAM

I GOT HIM! I GOT--
FUCK...
BLAM BLAM
FOLLOW THEM! GO-- **JUMP!**
ER... I HAVE A BAD KNEE, ZÉ.
HUMPH
SO TAKE THE FUCKING **STAIRS!**
GODDAMMIT! WE FELL FOR IT LIKE SUCKERS...
KLANK

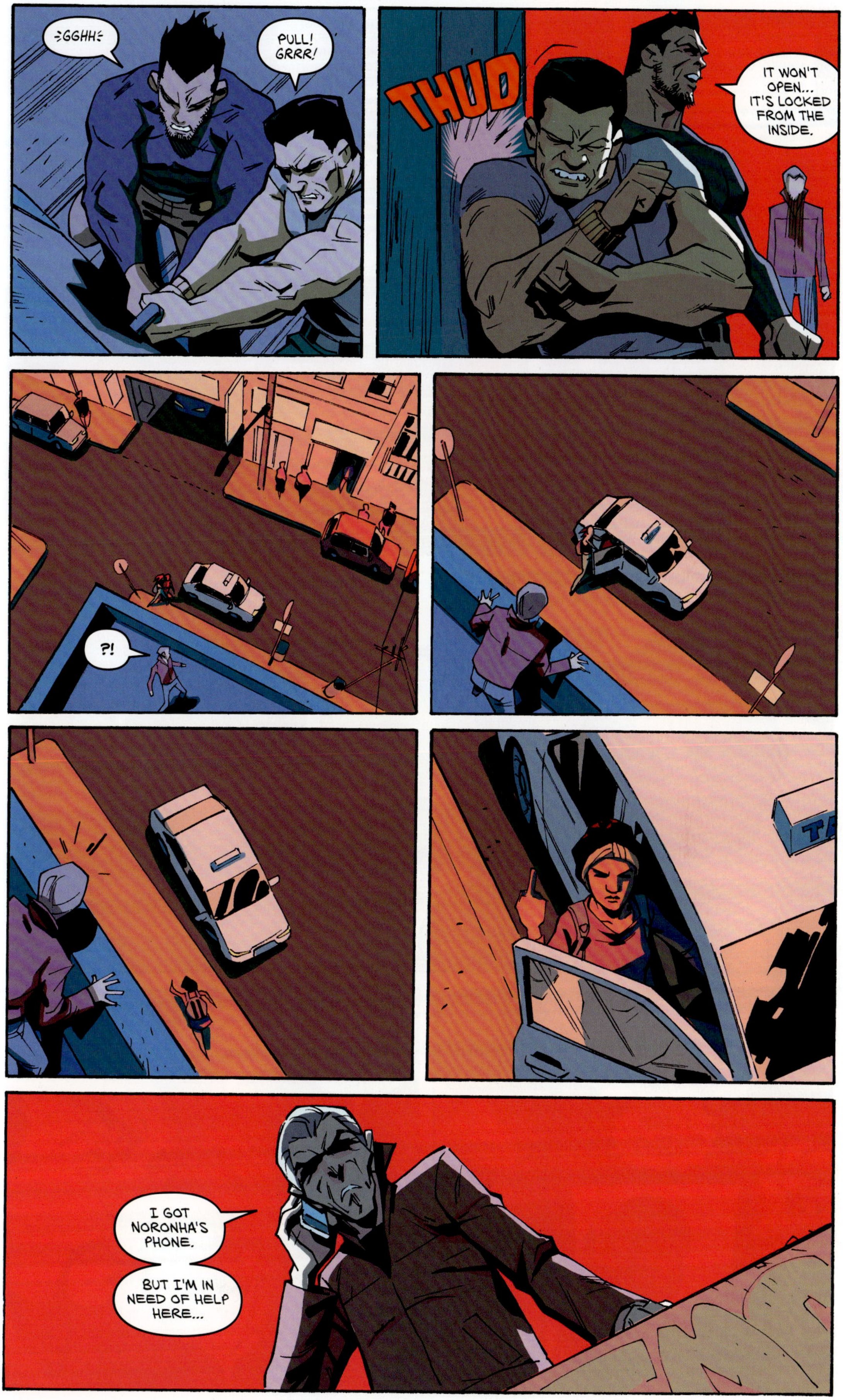
GGHH
PULL! GRRR!
THUD
IT WON'T OPEN... IT'S LOCKED FROM THE INSIDE.
?!
TA
I GOT NORONHA'S PHONE.
BUT I'M IN NEED OF HELP HERE...

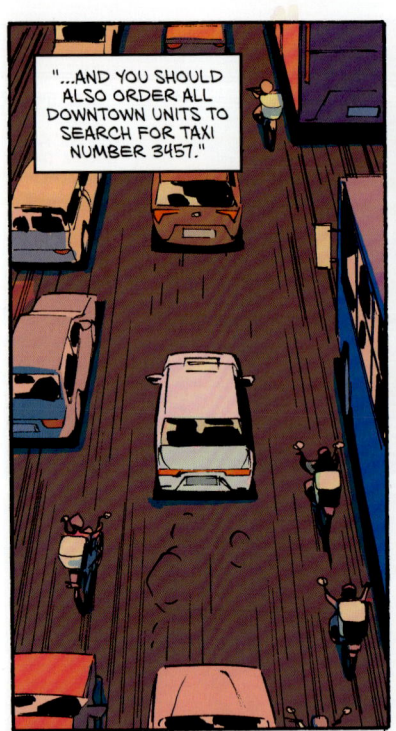

"...AND YOU SHOULD ALSO ORDER ALL DOWNTOWN UNITS TO SEARCH FOR TAXI NUMBER 3457."

OUCH--MY LEG! I'M FUCKED! I WON'T BE ABLE TO WORK ANYMORE...

EASY, LECO, EASY--THE WORST IS OVER.

HE'S BLEEDING A LOT.

MAKE A TOURNIQUET WITH THIS.

HEY--WATCH OUT FOR THE UPHOLSTERY! I HAD THE CAR CLEANED TODAY.

ATTENTION, CAR 3457 ≶BZZT≶ 3457. QTC...

MILITARY POLICE ARE ON THE HUNT FOR YOUR PASSENGERS. ≶BZZT≶ THREE PASSENGERS, ONE INJURED.

PLEASE INFORM QTI. ≶BZZT≶

WHA--?

DON'T EVEN THINK OF ANSWERING IT.

YOU'RE OUTNUMBERED HERE.

THANK YOU, CORPORAL. I DISLOCATED MY SHOULDER TRYING TO OPEN THAT DOOR.
IT COULD BE WORSE. IT WOULD TAKE FIVE GUYS OF YOUR SIZE TO BREAK THAT METAL BAR FROM THE OUTSIDE.
I'M GONNA NEED YOUR RADIO, SERGEANT.
SURE.
BZZT ATTENTION ALL UNITS ON THE HUNT FOR TAXI 3457.
WATCH THE METRO ENTRANCES. DO NOT LET THEM REACH THE METRO! BZZT
I REPEAT BZZT DO NOT LET THEM REACH THE METRO! BZZT
?!
SHIT!
THIS IS UNIT NUMBER--

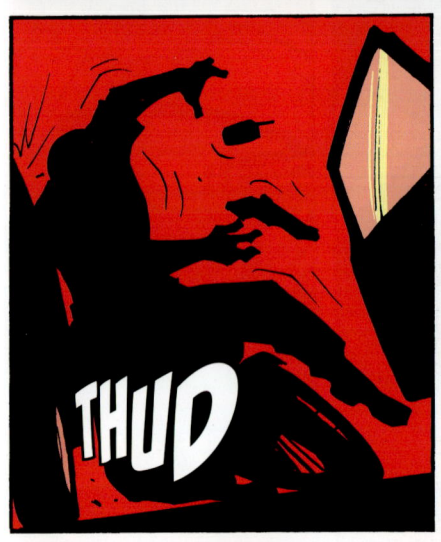

UGH--!

WHAM

THUD

LET'S GO! THE METRO STATION IS RIGHT HERE.

KEEP THE CHANGE, FOR THE UPHOLSTERY...

...YOU CAN CHARGE THE POLICE BIKER FOR THE DOOR.

HEY, WHAT ABOUT MY DOOR?!

AAARGH... MY LEG.

HOLD TIGHT, LECO.

ATTENTION, ALL UNITS! FUGITIVES SIGHTED NEAR THE SÉ METRO STATION!

HEY! WHAT ABOUT MY DOOR?

IT'LL BE SAFER IF WE SPLIT UP. LU, YOU AND LECO TAKE THE METRO. WE'LL MEET AT MY FLAT.

I'LL GIVE ROQUE A HEADS-UP.

FUCK OFF!

YES, OUR NUMBERS HAVE PLATEAUED, BUT WE'RE STILL DRAWING WITH EVERALDO FRANCO.
OUR CHANCES OF GOING TO THE SECOND ROUND ARE STILL GOOD.
IF WE COULD HAVE MORE MEDIA COVERAGE OF THE THREATS AGAINST YOU, THAT'D PUSH US AHEAD.
AND IF WE GET THERE, I'M CERTAIN WE CAN BEAT GOVERNOR GLÓRIA.
WELL, YES...
...BUT IF THE NARRATIVE ISN'T CONVINCING ENOUGH, IT COULD BACKFIRE AND END UP HELPING MY OPPONENTS WHO CLAIM I'M MAKING THIS UP.
WITH JUST A WEEK UNTIL ELECTION DAY, IT COULD TURN THE TIDE AGAINST US.
I'M STARTING TO RECONSIDER IF THAT PRESS CONFERENCE WAS REALLY A WISE MOVE...
ERR, NETO...
...MAYBE THE TIDE HAS **TURNED** AGAIN.

OUCH--!
IT'S DONE! YOU LUCKY GUY! IT WAS ONLY A SCRATCH.
PHEW THANK YOU, LIS.
NOW CALL YOUR MOTHER AND TELL HER AND YOUR SISTER TO GO TO A RELATIVE OR NEIGHBOR'S HOUSE UNTIL IT CALMS DOWN.
SO, LU. DID IT WORK?
WAIT...
CLAK CLAK
CLIK CLIK
...VOILÁ! THE CAMERA SENT THIS PICTURE JUST BEFORE HE SMASHED IT. I ALSO HAVE A BACKUP OF THAT PHONE.
AWESOME! SEND ME THIS PICTURE, PLEASE.
WE'LL NEED ROQUE'S HELP TO FIND OUT WHO THIS GUY IS...

"...BEFORE HE FINDS US."
PING
TOC
HERE IS NORONHA'S FUCKING PHONE. THOSE FUCKERS ESCAPED... THIS TIME.
YOU'RE LATE, ZÉ...
...THAT IDIOT'S PHONE IS THE LEAST OF OUR CONCERNS NOW.

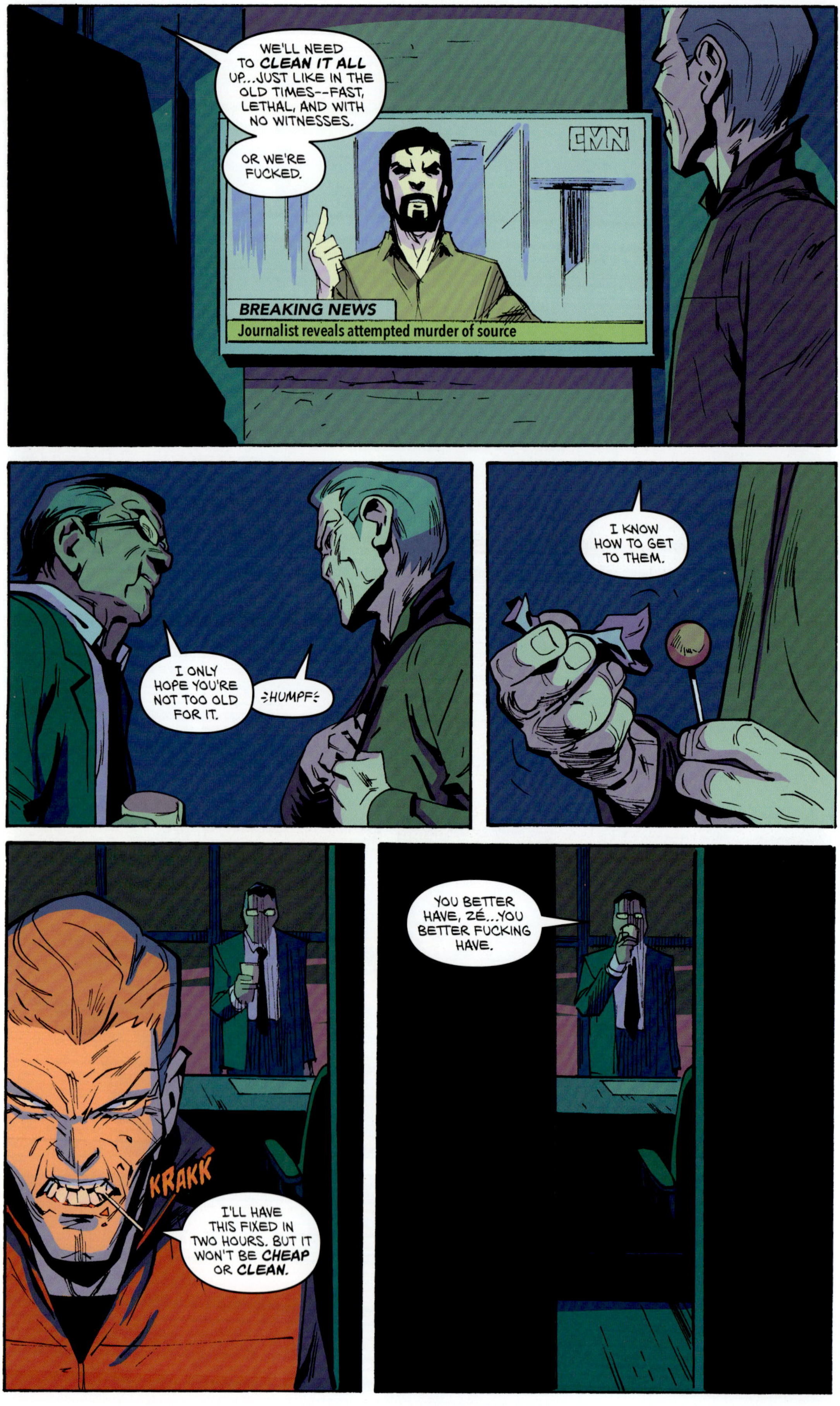
WE'LL NEED TO CLEAN IT ALL UP...JUST LIKE IN THE OLD TIMES--FAST, LETHAL, AND WITH NO WITNESSES.
OR WE'RE FUCKED.
CMN
BREAKING NEWS
Journalist reveals attempted murder of source
I ONLY HOPE YOU'RE NOT TOO OLD FOR IT.
HUMPF
I KNOW HOW TO GET TO THEM.
KRAKK
I'LL HAVE THIS FIXED IN TWO HOURS. BUT IT WON'T BE CHEAP OR CLEAN.
YOU BETTER HAVE, ZÉ...YOU BETTER FUCKING HAVE.

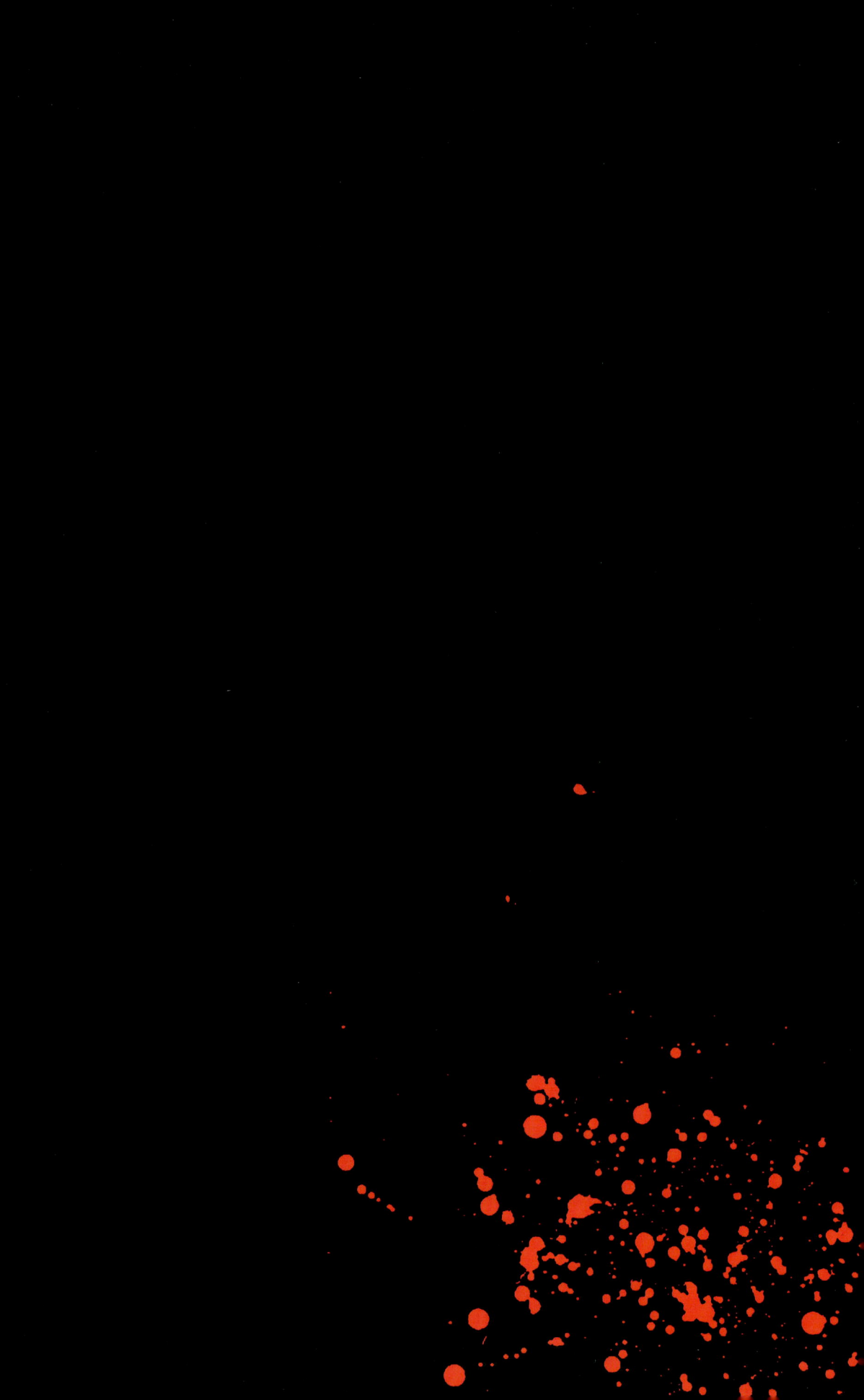

CHAPTER FIVE
SAMBA IN THE DARK

SÃO PAULO, OCTOBER 1979.
BZZZZT
GGAAARGH--
SCREAM, YOU SON OF A BITCH!
BZZZZT
GGH--GASP
SCREEEAM!
KRAK
GGHH--

>COUGH< >COUGH< HA-HA-HA...
...I WON'T GIVE YOU >COUGH< THE PLEASURE. >COUGH<
THEN I'LL HAVE TO BREAK YOUR OTHER ARM--
--YOU WILL NEVER HOLD A PEN AGAIN, YOU SUBVERSIVE MOTHER-FUCKER!
YOU'RE NERVOUS--HA-HA! YOU'RE MORE SCARED THAN ME NOW. >COUGH< YOU'VE REALIZED YOUR DAYS ARE NUMBERED, HAVEN'T YOU?
YOU'RE SCARED YOU'LL HAVE TO PAY FOR IT, >COUGH< THE ONLY THING YOU'VE EVER BEEN GOOD FOR--MAKING PEOPLE SUFFER.
YOU PIECE OF SHIT--I PITY YOU--
BLAM
BLAM
BLAM
KLANK

SON OF A-- -PUFF- -PUFF- BITCH...
THIS ONE DIDN'T SING FOR YOU, ZÉ?
RESPECT YOUR SUPERIORS, DAMN IT!
I DIDN'T ASK FOR YOUR INPUT, RUBÃO.
I-I'M SORRY, CAPTAIN.
BRING A TARP AND TAKE WHAT'S LEFT OF THIS PIECE OF SHIT OUT OF HERE.
YES, SIR.
HUH?
HEY, YOU-- WHAT'RE YOU LOOKING AT?
GET READY, YOU'RE NEXT!
WHEN THE TIME COMES, I WILL CHARGE WITH INTEREST THIS SUFFERING OF MINE, I SWEAR.

SÃO PAULO, 2018.
THAT SCUMBAG'S MOTHER AND SISTER WEREN'T AT HOME, ZÉ.
THEIR NEIGHBORS WOULDN'T TALK... IT SEEMS THEY KNEW WE WERE COMING.
FEDOR ALSO COULDN'T FIND THAT DELINQUENT GIRL AT SANTA IFIGÊNIA.
SO... WHERE SHOULD WE GO NEXT?
I'LL KNOW IN FIVE MINUTES, RATO.
SCHOOL PRINCIPAL
THE MILITARY POLICE'S INTERNAL AFFAIRS?!
THAT'S RIGHT.
IT'S A SHAME TO BRING POLICE MATTERS INTO A SCHOOL ENVIRONMENT, BUT WE HAVE ENOUGH INFORMATION TO SUSPECT THAT ONE OF YOUR TEACHERS MAY BE IN DANGER.
OH? HOW SO?!
THERE WAS AN INCIDENT NEARBY, A FEW DAYS AGO.
ONE OF THE VICTIMS SAID THAT THIS TEACHER SAW EVERYTHING.
DANGEROUS PEOPLE, UNFORTUNATELY... DO YOU KNOW ANYTHING ABOUT IT?
OH MY GOD! WHICH TEACHER?!
I CAN'T REVEAL THAT YET, IT'S CLASSIFIED.
FIRST I'LL NEED ACCESS TO ALL THE SCHOOL'S TEACHER FILES. I NEED TO CHECK IF MY INFORMATION MATCHES. IT'S A VERY SERIOUS CASE, MA'AM.

SURE!
BUT WOULDN'T IT BE EASIER TO GET THIS INFORMATION FROM THE EDUCATION SECRETARY'S OFFICE?
THEY HAVE ALL THE FILES-- I BET THEY'RE EVEN MORE UP TO DATE.
ERR--YES. BUT UNFORTUNATELY THERE HAVE BEEN LEAKS FROM THAT DEPARTMENT BEFORE.
THIS IS WHY I HAVE TO ASK YOU FOR ABSOLUTE SECRECY IN THIS MATTER UNTIL IT'S ALL SOLVED.
AS YOU WISH.
THANK YOU, MA'AM.
EXCUSE ME, PRINCIPAL.
PAULO'S PARENTS ARE WAITING FOR YOU.
AH, GREAT!
SIR, DO YOU MIND STAYING HERE FOR A FEW MINUTES? I DON'T WANT TO LEAVE THESE PARENTS WAITING. THEIR SON'S CASE IS VERY URGENT.
TAKE YOUR TIME, MA'AM. I'LL STAY HERE.
AH... THERE YOU ARE--
--LISA.

MINUTES LATER.
PUFF I'M SORRY FOR THE DELAY, OFFICER...
HUH--?! OFFICER?
HASN'T THAT JOURNALIST RESPONDED YET, LIS?
FOR THE UMPTEENTH TIME, LECO-- NOT YET.
HE SAID HE'S CHECKING WITH ALL OF HIS CONTACTS AND WILL LET US KNOW AS SOON AS HE IDENTIFIES THE GUY.
HE ALSO SAID THAT WE OBVIOUSLY NEED TO BE VERY CAREFUL.
SO LET'S GO TO THE REPUBLICA'S POINT. OUR FRIENDS THERE CAN HELP US HIDE.
WE DON'T KNOW IF THAT GUY ISN'T ALREADY LOOKING FOR US THERE.
HE HAS BOTH OF YOUR NAMES AND ALSO KNOWS WE ARE PIXADORES.
YOU CAN BET THEY'LL LOOK FOR US AT THE POINT.
YEAH... DUDU SAID THE POLICE WENT TO HIS STORE TOO--
BZZ BZZ
IT'S HIM--
--HI, ROQUE!

FUCK--
--OKAY. WE'LL SEND IT. THANK YOU--
HE FOUND OUT WHO THAT GUY IS...
...JOSÉ CARLOS ÁVILA DOS SANTOS.
EX-ARMY AND A FORMER MILITARY POLICE OFFICER.
A FAMOUS TORTURER AND KILLER FROM THE MILITARY DICTATORSHIP. ALSO KNOWN AS **ZÉ FOFINHO.**
ROQUE SAID WE SHOULD HIDE OURSELVES AND SEND ALL THE PROOF WE'VE GOT TO HIM NOW.
DIDN'T I TELL YOU?! THE GUY IS A PSYCHOPATH.
TAKE IT EASY, LECO. WE'RE SAFE HERE.
AH, SHIT! WHAT'LL WE DO NOW?!
PLEASE, LECO...
NO, LIS, I MEAN **NOW!**
THEY ALREADY **FOUND US!**
GO, GO, GO!

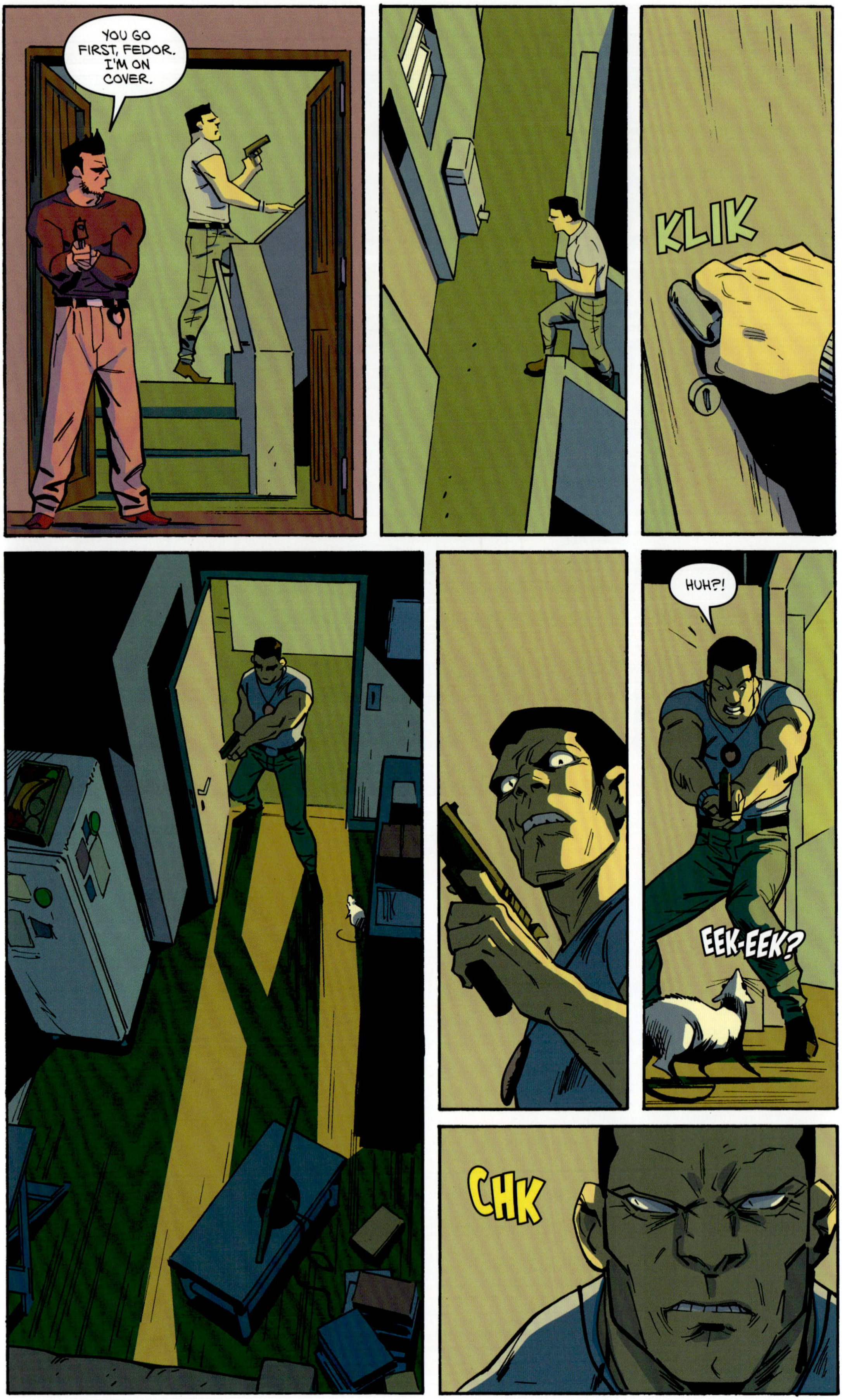
YOU GO FIRST, FEDOR. I'M ON COVER.
KLIK
HUH?!
EEK-EEK?
CHK

FWOOSHH
GACK--!
WHAP
AAARGH...
...AAARGH--
THUD-
KRAK-
THUMP
WHAT THE FUCK, FEDOR?

I FOUND ONE IN THE CORRIDOR.
GOOD CALL, LU!
HOW'S IT GOING, LIS? DID HE ANSWER?
NOT YET. HIS PHONE IS BUSY.
I'LL KEEP TRYING.
HUH?!
THE OTHER GUY'S COMING!
OKAY! GO, HIDE!
HERE, MORE CRUMBS FOR YOU, APOLLO. TAKE CARE!

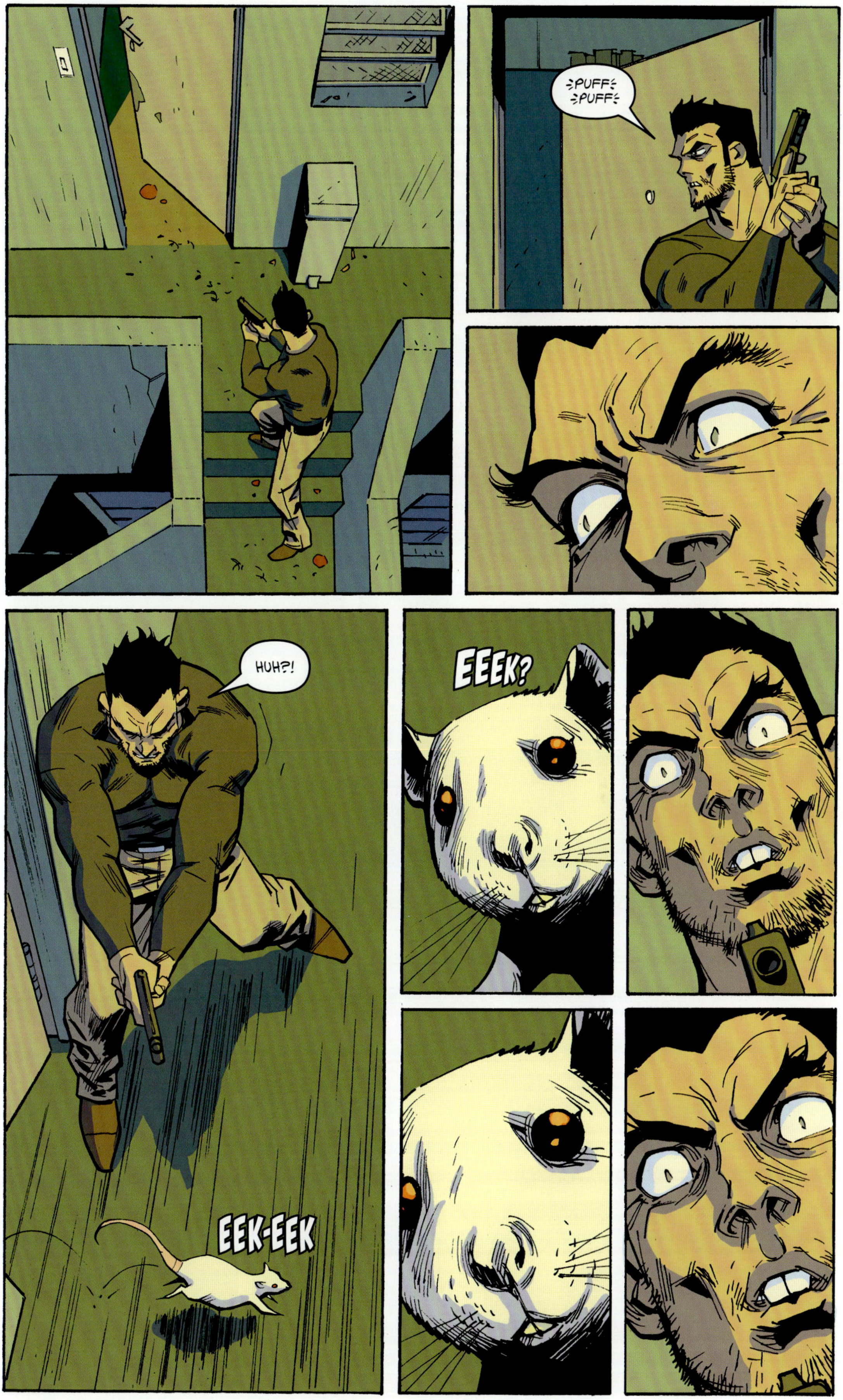

PUFF
PUFF
HUH?!
EEK-EEK
EEEK?

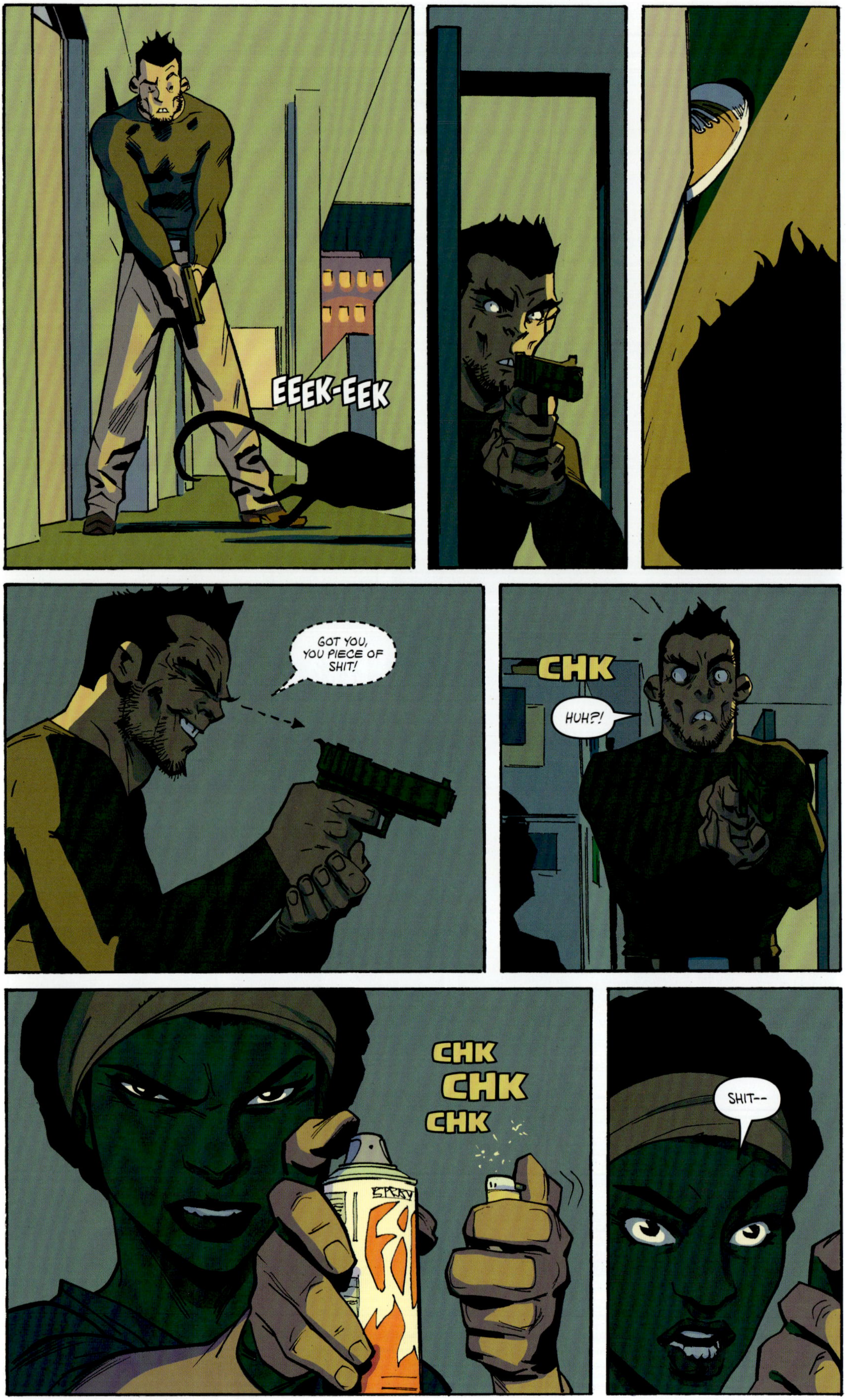
EEEK-EEK
GOT YOU, YOU PIECE OF SHIT!
CHK
HUH?!
CHK
CHK
CHK
SHIT--

FSSSSS
GAAAH!
GET DOWN, LIS!
BLAM
CLONK
GAGH
PHEW THAT WAS CLOSE.
THANKS, LU.

HE'S ALIVE. PHEW
LET'S GET OUT OF HERE NOW!
AGREED! LU, CAN YOU PLEASE CATCH APOLLO FOR ME?
YEAH! I'LL GET THE TINY HERO.
IT'S RINGING THROUGH NOW...
APOLLO!
...C'MON, PICK UP...
APO--
HI, LISA.
LISA?
WELL, WELL, WELL...

...WHERE DO YOU THINK YOU'RE GOING?
THE ONLY WAY YOU'RE LEAVING THIS PLACE IS INSIDE A BODY BAG.
YOU'VE MADE A REAL MESS HERE, HAVEN'T YOU?
AFTER ROBBING A COP IN BROAD DAYLIGHT, NOW YOU'RE BEATING, BURNING-- KILLING THEM?
HE'S ALIVE! AND HE SHOT AT US--
SHUT YOUR FUCKING MOUTH!
I'M THE ONE WHO TALKS HERE!
BUT I WON'T TAKE YOU FIRST.

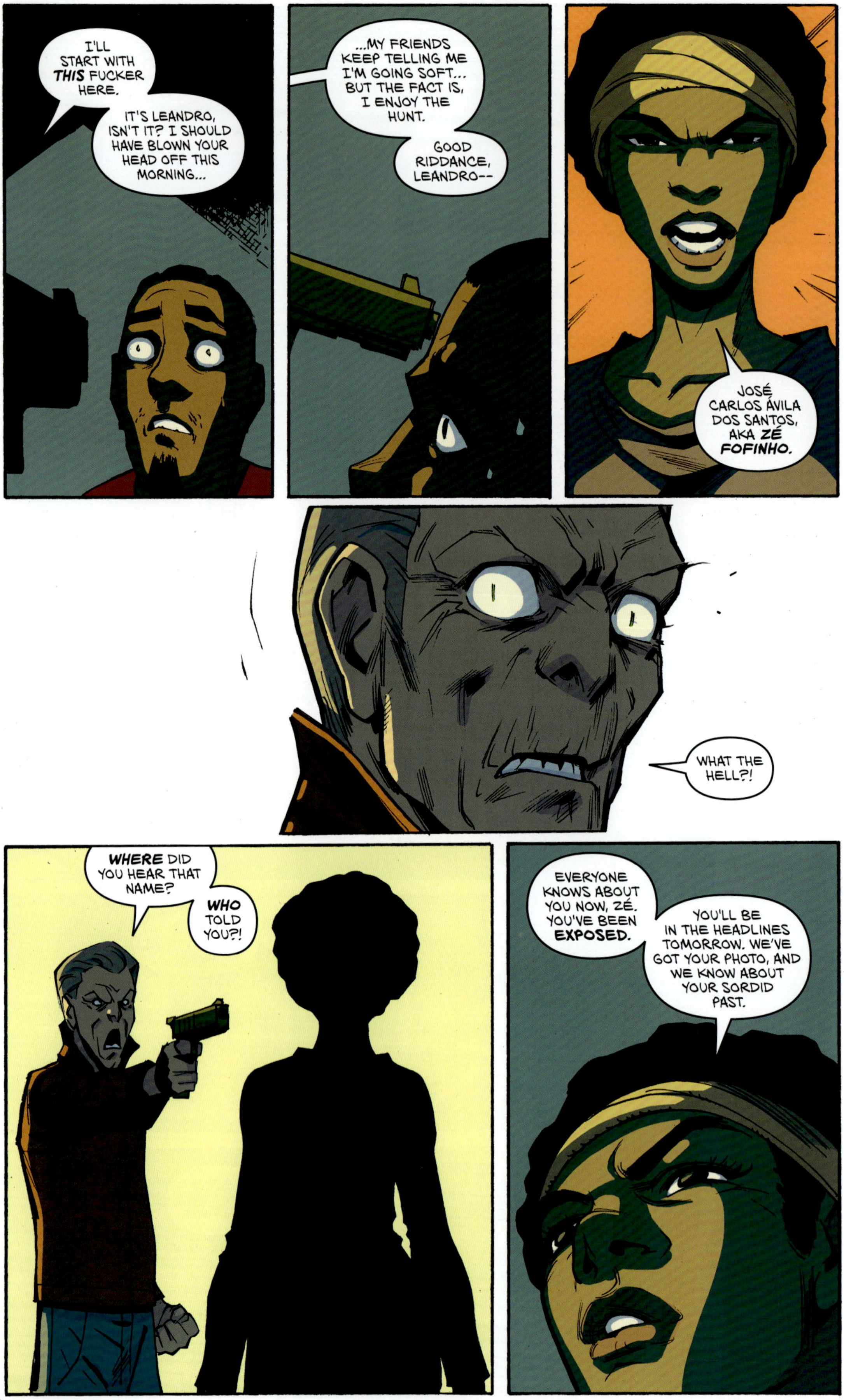

I'LL START WITH **THIS** FUCKER HERE.
IT'S LEANDRO, ISN'T IT? I SHOULD HAVE BLOWN YOUR HEAD OFF THIS MORNING...
...MY FRIENDS KEEP TELLING ME I'M GOING SOFT... BUT THE FACT IS, I ENJOY THE HUNT.
GOOD RIDDANCE, LEANDRO--
JOSÉ CARLOS ÁVILA DOS SANTOS, AKA **ZÉ FOFINHO.**
WHAT THE HELL?!
WHERE DID YOU HEAR THAT NAME?
WHO TOLD YOU?!
EVERYONE KNOWS ABOUT YOU NOW, ZÉ. YOU'VE BEEN **EXPOSED.**
YOU'LL BE IN THE HEADLINES TOMORROW. WE'VE GOT YOUR PHOTO, AND WE KNOW ABOUT YOUR SORDID PAST.

TOMORROW I'LL VANISH INTO THIN AIR, AND YOU WON'T BE ABLE TO DO ANYTHING, BECAUSE YOU'LL BE DEAD--AND THE DEAD CAN'T TALK, YOU KNOW?
I DON'T GIVE A FUCK IF YOU HAVE A PHOTO OF ME, LISA.
PUFF
I KNOW YOU CAN KILL US NOW...THAT'S WHAT YOU'VE ALWAYS DONE, AND NOTHING'S EVER HAPPENED TO YOU BEFORE, HAS IT?
BUT THIS TIME IT WON'T BE SO EASY FOR YOU TO ESCAPE JUSTICE. DO YOU KNOW WHY?
BECAUSE NOW THERE'S A WITNESS ON THE OTHER END OF THIS CALL.
?!
YOU DON'T BELIEVE ME? WHY DON'T YOU SAY HELLO...?
HELLO...?

HE-HELLO... THIS IS ROQUE ALVES, THE JOURNALIST.
I'VE RECORDED IT ALL-- ALL THAT YOU JUST SAID, ZÉ FOFINHO. I ALSO HAVE A COPY OF NORONHA'S PHONE HERE.
IT'S OVER.
HELLO! HELLO?! WHERE'S LIS?!
DON'T HURT THEM! DO YOU HEAR ME? HELLO--
PUFF PUFF
EXCUSE ME PUFF PUFF LET ME THROUGH!

HELLO?!
HEY, ZÉ! IS IT DONE? HAVE YOU CLEANED IT ALL UP?
NO, ALVARENGA, I HAVEN'T. RATO AND FEDOR ARE DOWN. WE CAN BLAME IT ALL ON THEM.
I'M GETTING OUT NOW. I THINK I MIGHT'VE ALSO BEEN EXPOSED.
HMPH
HELLO? HELLO?
ALVARENGA?!
BEEP BEEP BEEP
GHHH
FUCK!
THUD
HEY, RUBÃO. IT'S ZÉ HERE.
I'M BURNED...YES, A NEW SOCIAL NUMBER AND PASSPORT.
DID ALVARENGA CALL YOU?
NO, NOTHING. OF COURSE, I DO TRUST YOU...SEE YOU TOMORROW.

THE STORY OF THE MYSTERIOUS THREATS AGAINST THE POLITICIAN NETO HAS REACHED AN END.
THE PLOT TO KILL THE CANDIDATE FOR GOVERNOR WAS UNVEILED TODAY BY THE JOURNALIST ROQUE ALVES, WHO HAD ACCESS TO THE PHONE MESSAGES OF ONE OF THE SUSPECTS.
POLICE AND MILITARY OFFICERS ARE AMONG THE SUSPECTS, WITH THE MASTERMIND OF THE PLOT RUMORED TO BE A HIGH-RANKING MEMBER OF THE STATE GOVERNMENT.
ONE OF THEM, AN INFAMOUS TORTURER FROM THE MILITARY DICTATORSHIP, JOSÉ CARLOS ÁVILA DOS SANTOS, KNOWN AS ZÉ FOFINHO, IS STILL ON THE RUN.
NETO, WHO'S **MOVED AHEAD** TO SECOND IN THE POLLS, SPOKE ABOUT THESE DEVELOPMENTS EARLIER.
IT'S A SHAME THAT WE HAVE SITUATIONS LIKE THESE IN OUR DEMOCRACY.
I CAN ONLY THANK THE PRESS AND ESPECIALLY THE ANONYMOUS INFORMANTS WHO, EVEN WHILE BEING PERSECUTED AND ATTACKED...
...BRAVELY SPREAD THE TRUTH ON THE CITY'S WALLS.
WOOHOO!
FANCY ANOTHER BEER?
YEAH, SURE!
SO, BABE-- AREN'T YOU AFRAID THAT ZÉ FOFINHO'S STILL OUT THERE? IF HE SHOWS AGAIN...
NO, LU. I THINK THE BIGGEST FEAR OF PEOPLE LIKE HIM IS BEING RECOGNIZED, CAUGHT, AND FINALLY PUNISHED FOR ALL THE SUFFERING THEY CAUSED...

"...AND DEEP INSIDE I THINK THIS TIME, HE WON'T ESCAPE."
ARE YOU SURE YOU DON'T WANT A RIDE ACROSS THE BORDER, ZÉ? I CAN LET YOU OUT IN *CIUDAD DEL ESTE*.
THERE'S NO NEED, RUBÃO. I'LL GET THERE MY OWN WAY.
I ALSO NEED TO VISIT SOME FRIENDS AND EXCHANGE SOME CASH IN *FOZ DO IGUAÇU*.
CAN YOU PULL OVER HERE, RUBÃO? I NEED TO TAKE A LEAK.
HOLD ON FOR A BIT, ZÉ, THERE'S A GAS STATION LESS THAN 10 KM AHEAD.
NO, BETTER NOT. MY FACE MUST BE EVERYWHERE BY NOW.
WELL... IT'S YOUR CALL.
THANKS, IT WON'T TAKE LONG.
ZIPP
AAHHH...
I'M SORRY ABOUT THIS, ZÉ... IT'S NOTHING PERSONAL.

WEEKS LATER...
EVEN DECADES AFTER THE RE-DEMOCRATIZATION OF BRAZIL, THE TRUTH IS STILL EXPENSIVE HERE.
Governor-elect promises to keep campaign pledge of reforming Military Polic
LU, LECO, AND I GOT LUCKY, BUT IT'S STILL RARE FOR JUSTICE TO PREVAIL HERE.
GOOD MORNING, MR. TIÃO!
GOOD MORNING, TEACHER!
TO MOST PEOPLE, THE BRAZILIAN GOVERNMENT ONLY SHOWS ITSELF AS AN UNPUNISHABLE AND VIOLENT FACE IN UNIFORM.
DID YOU SEE THAT NORONHA WAS IN ON THIS PLOT TO KILL NETO? HIS TEXT MESSAGES ARE THE MAIN PROOF!
YES! IT SEEMS THIS TIME WE'LL ACTUALLY GET SOME JUSTICE, WON'T WE?
I HOPE SO! BUT I'M NOT SO SURE... APPARENTLY HE'S ON THE RUN.
I KNEW I'D SEEN THIS TORTURER BEFORE. HE CAME HERE A FEW WEEKS AGO, LOOKING FOR YOU. BUT I SWEAR I DIDN'T SAY ANYTHING.
AH... THANK YOU, MR. TIÃO!
ER... DID YOU HAVE ANYTHING TO DO WITH ALL THIS?
WE ALL DID. EVEN YOU, WHO HAD THE COURAGE TO RECORD NORONHA'S COWARDICE THAT DAY.
SEE YOU LATER, MR. TIÃO!
SEE YOU, TEACHER. HAVE A GOOD CLASS!
THIS IS WHY THE BEST WAY TO RESIST IS TO BE VIGILANT, ALWAYS IN SEARCH OF THE TRUTH...
...AND TO MAKE USE OF OUR GREATEST STRENGTH AS BRAZILIANS-- COURAGE.
THE END.

COVER GALLERY

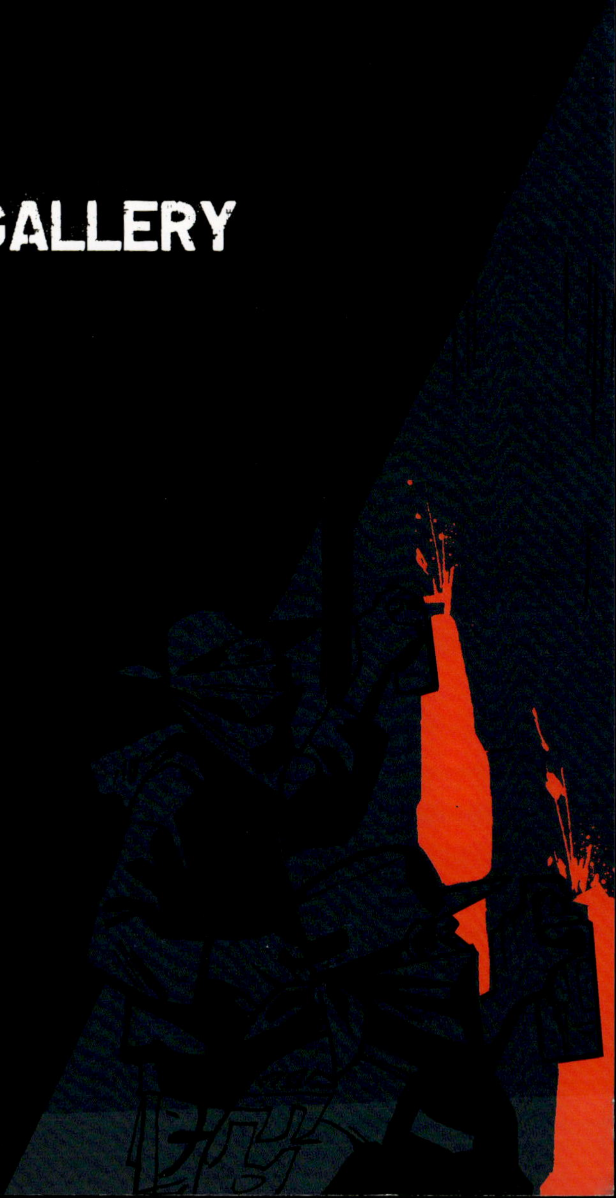

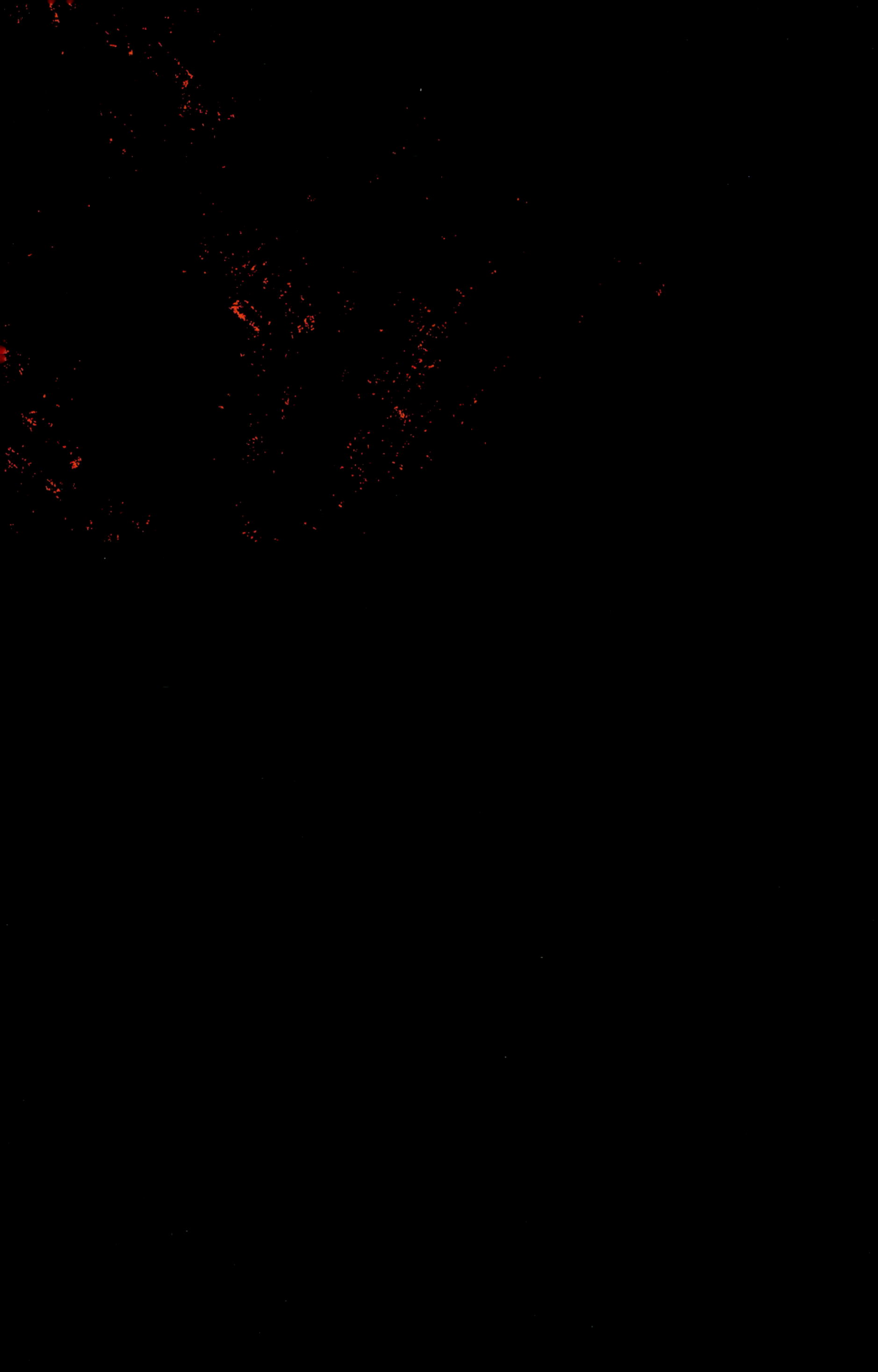

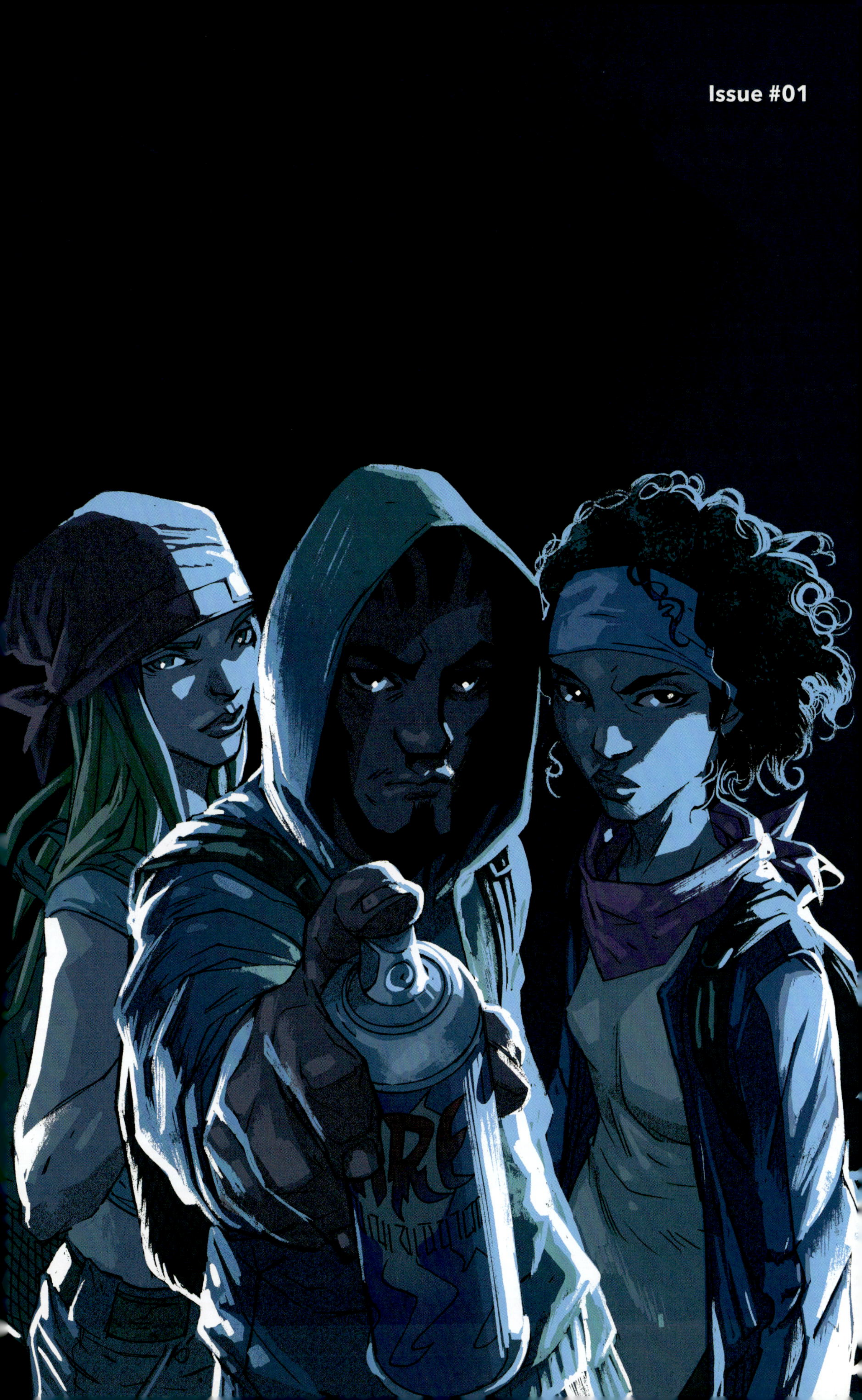
Issue #01

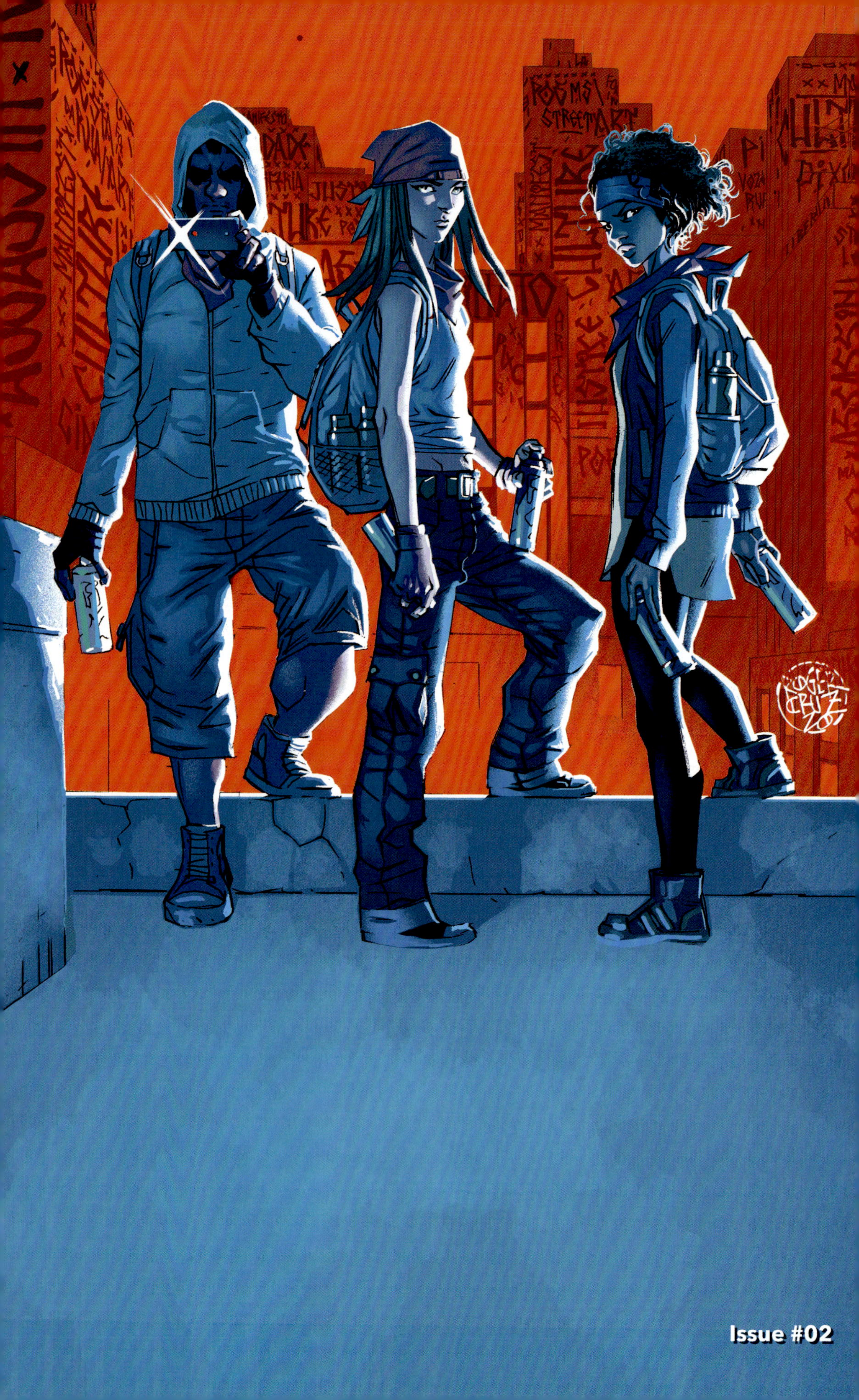
Issue #02

Issue #03

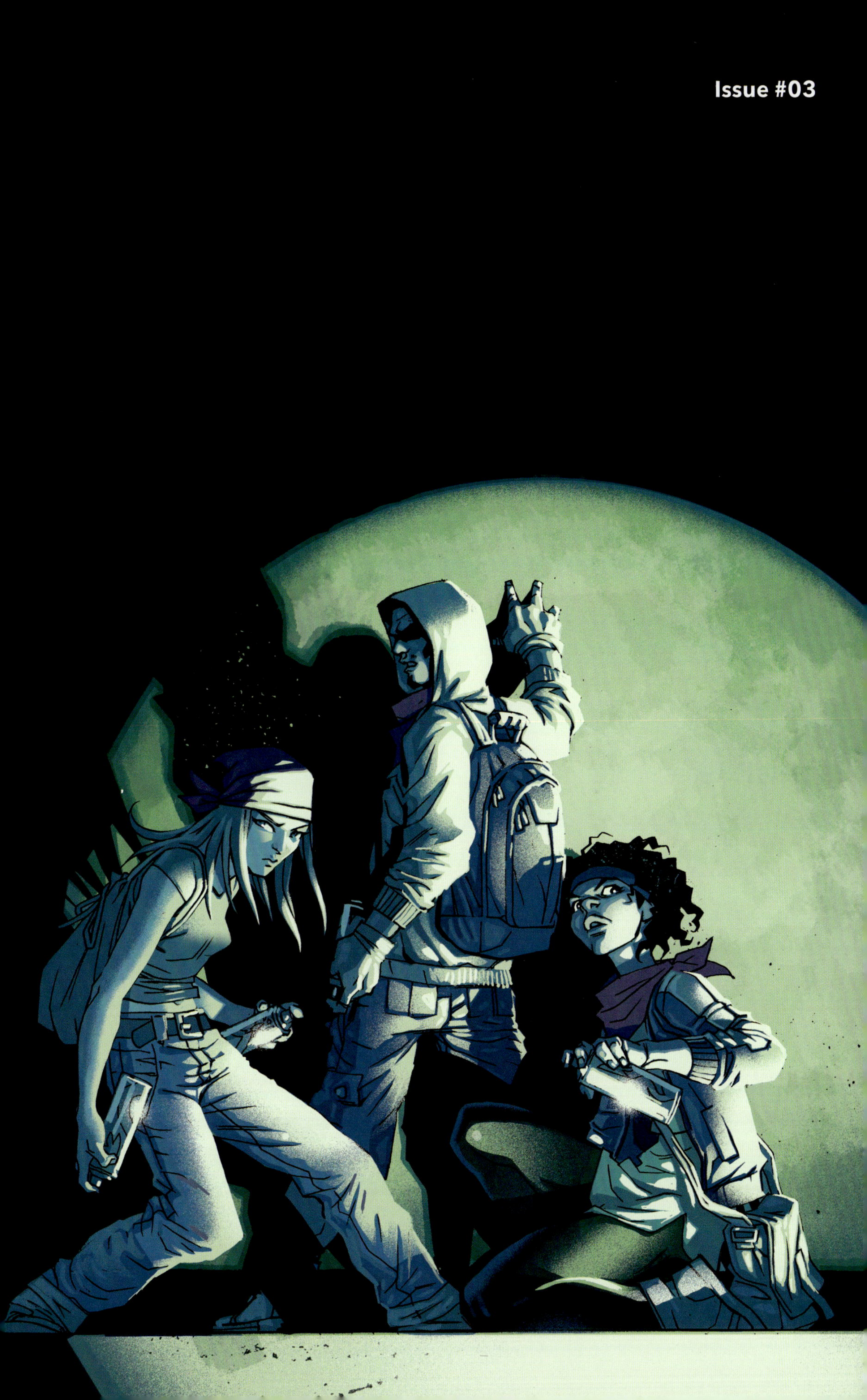

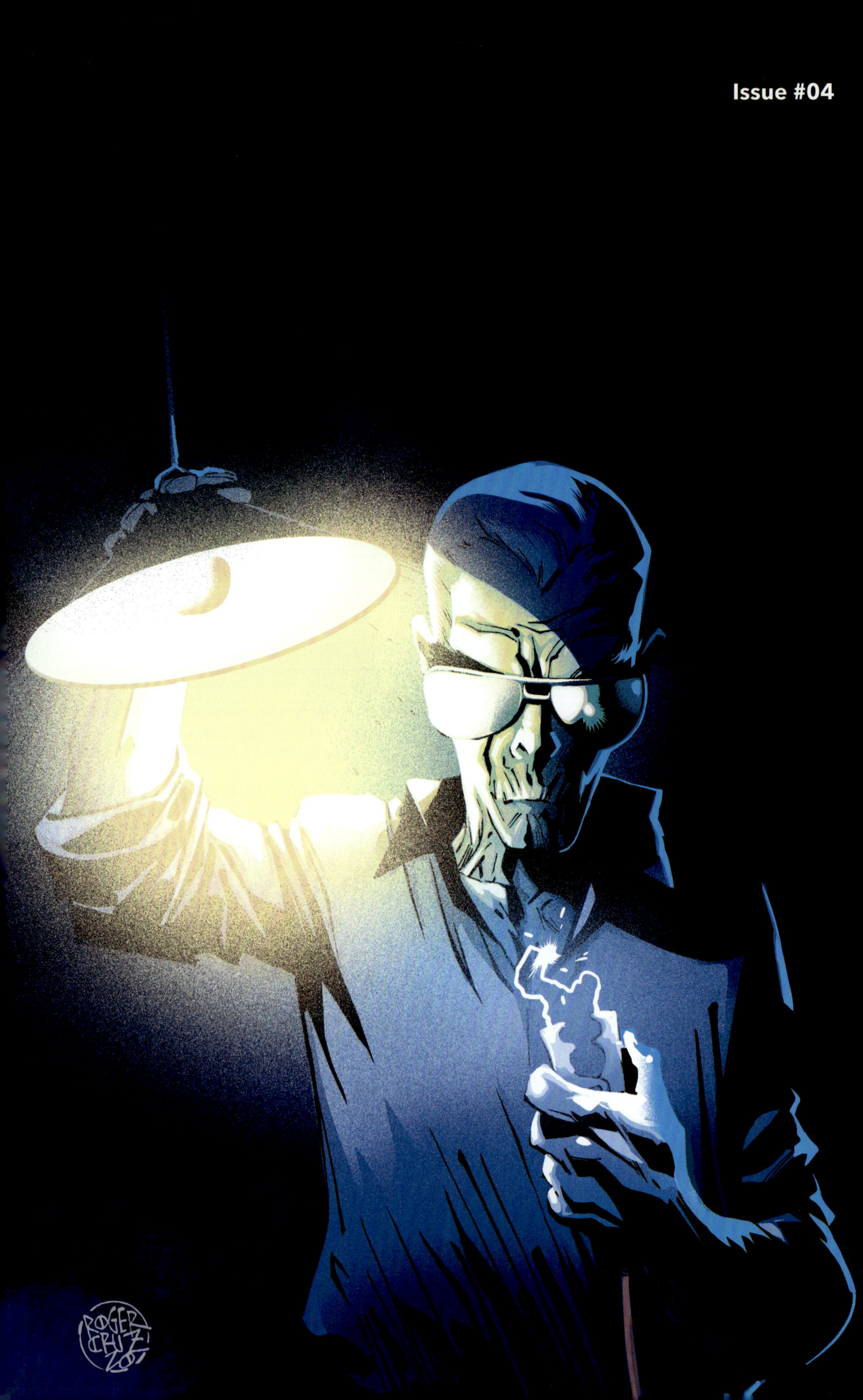
Issue #04

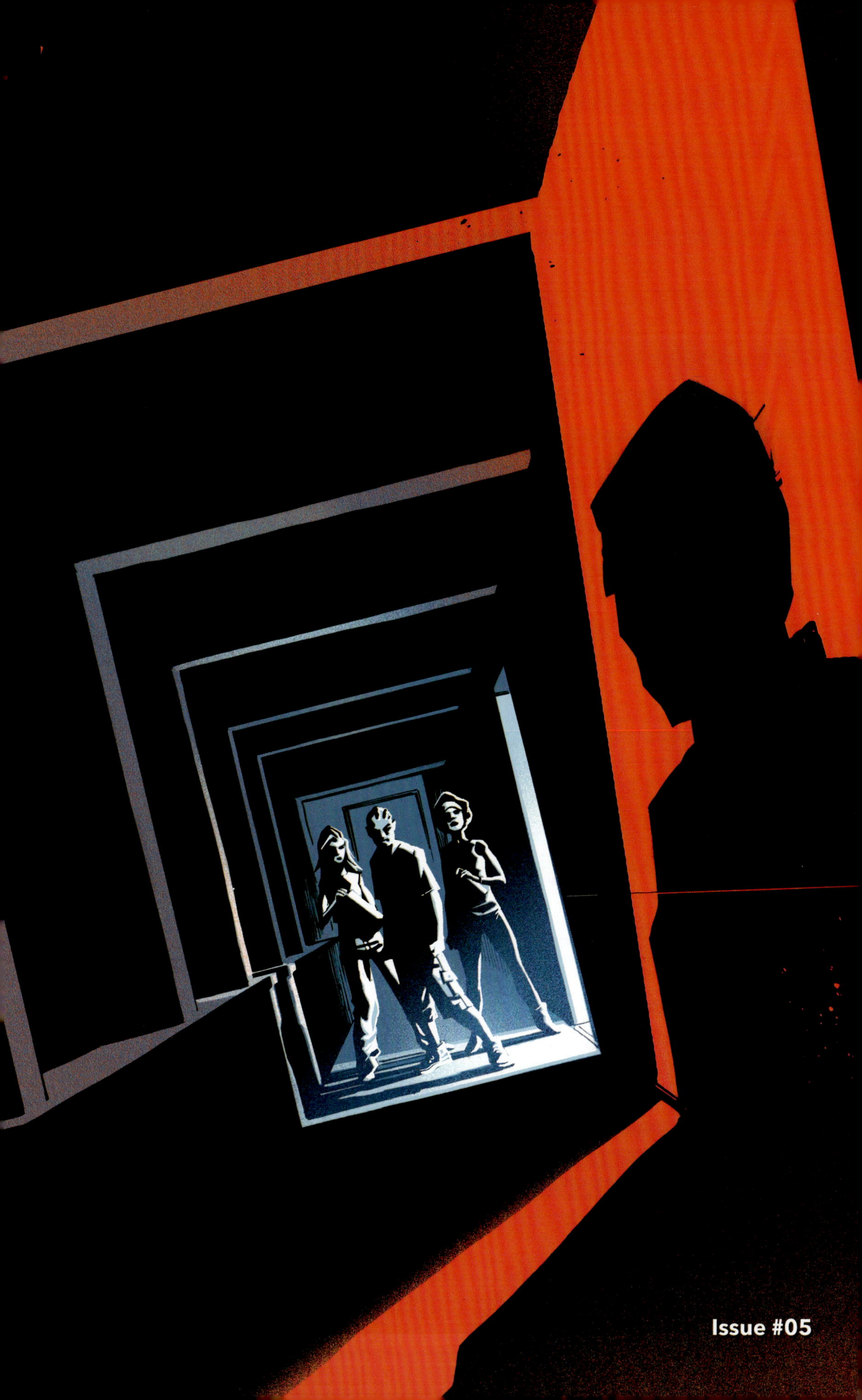
Issue #05

EXTRAS

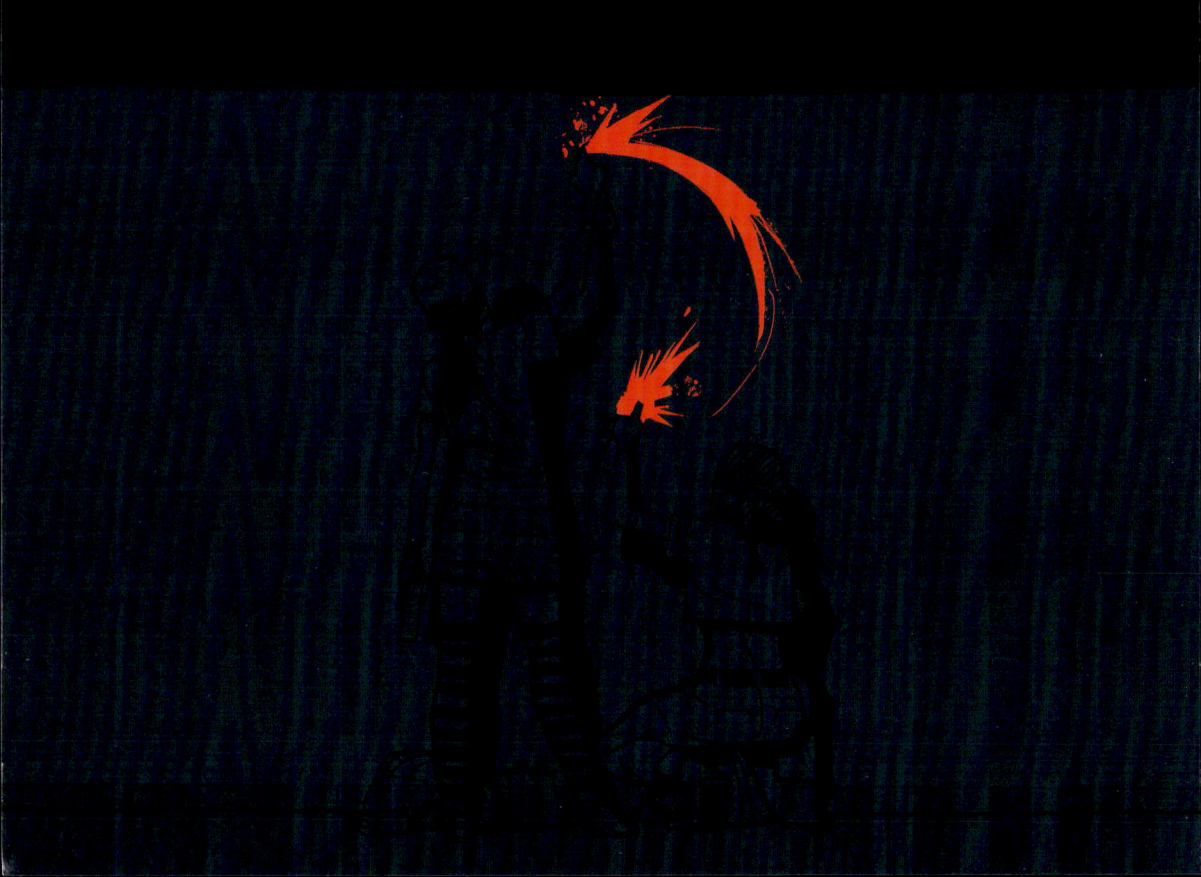

CHARACTER CONCEPTS

Lis, **Lu**, and **Leco** original concepts by **Rafael Albuquerque.**

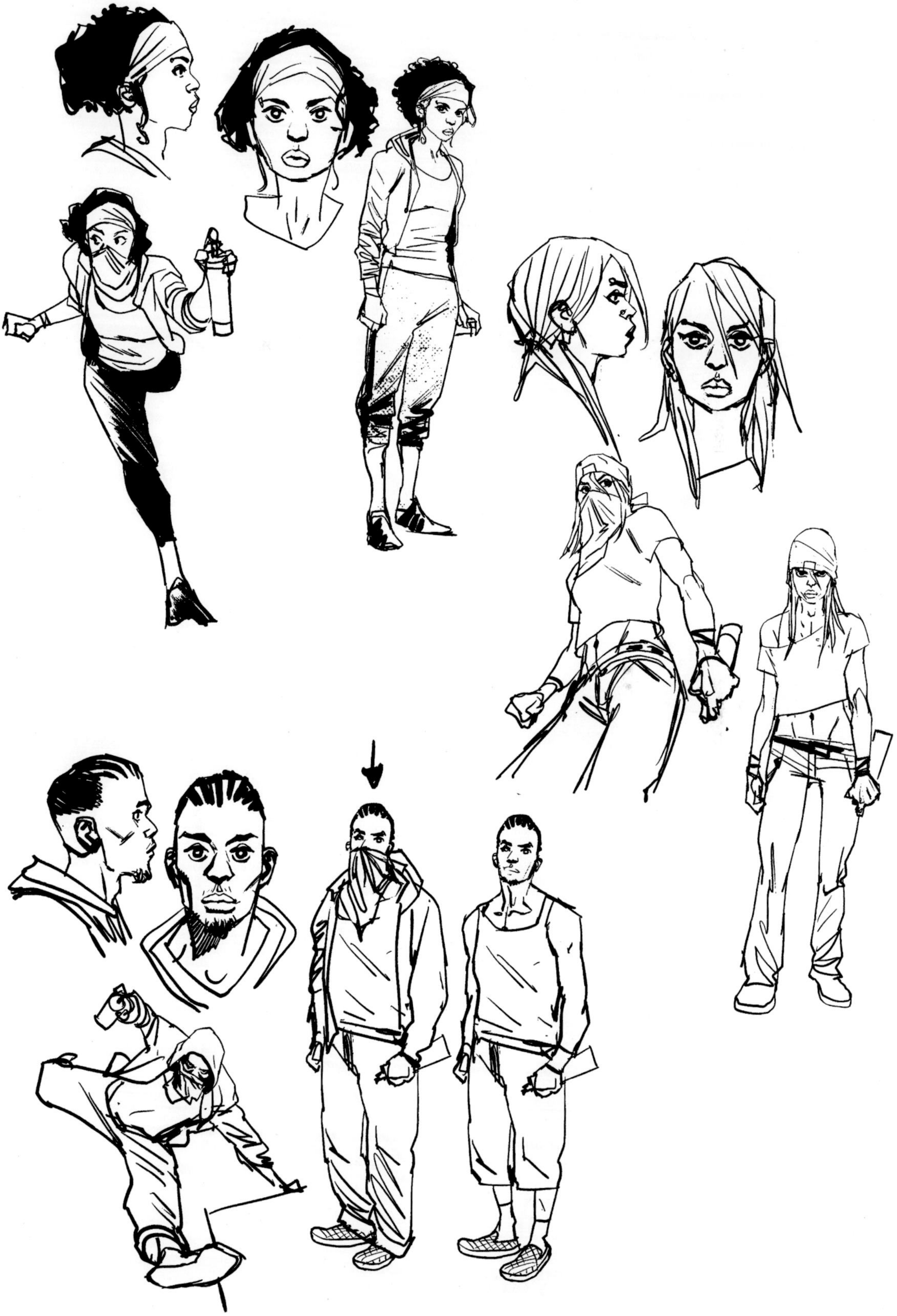

CHARACTER STUDIES

Lis, **Lu**, and **Leco** character studies with their respective pixo tags, by **Roger Cruz.**

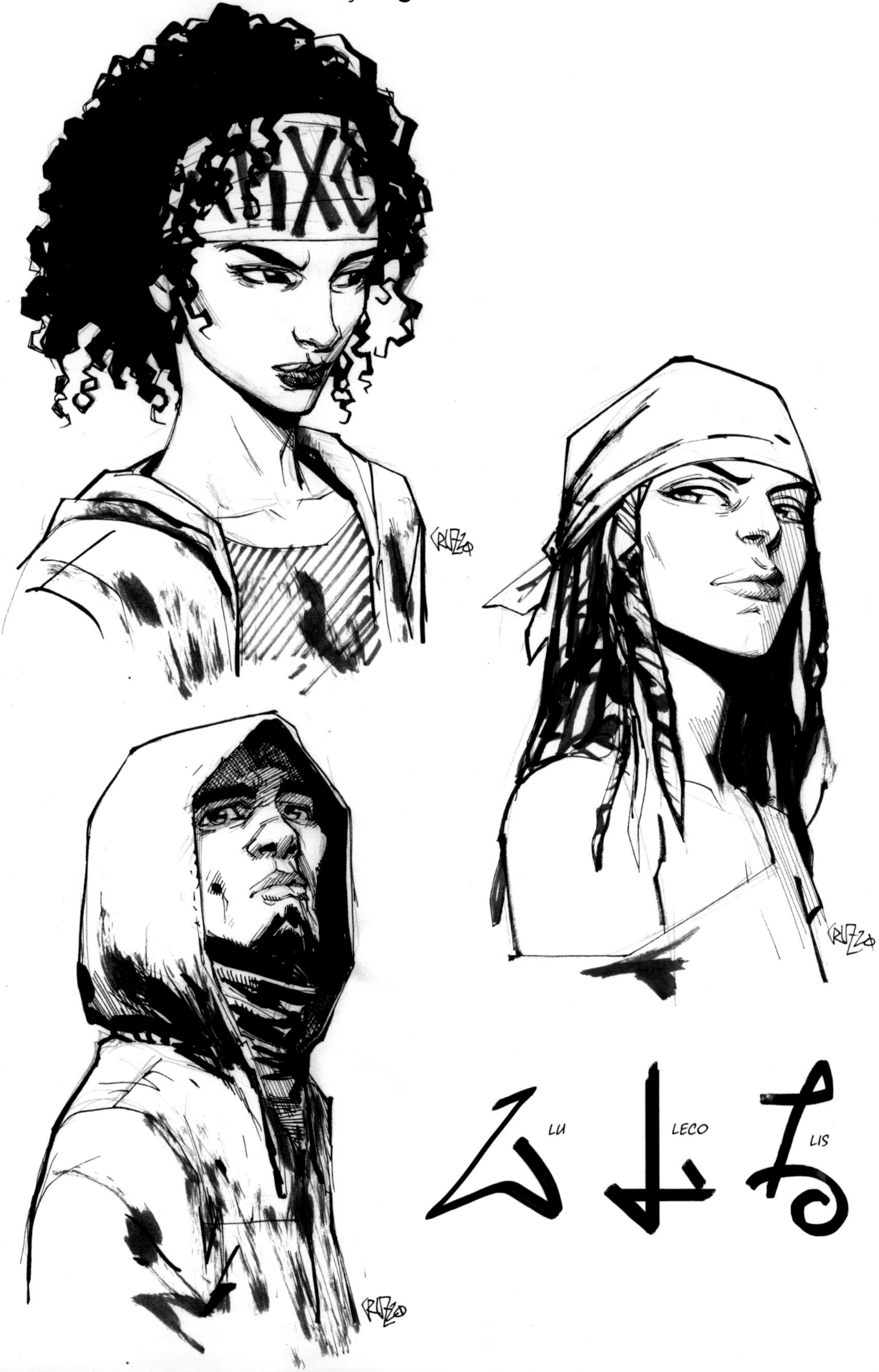
LU
LECO
LIS

CHARACTER STUDIES

More studies of **Lis**, **Lu**, and **Leco** by **Roger Cruz.**

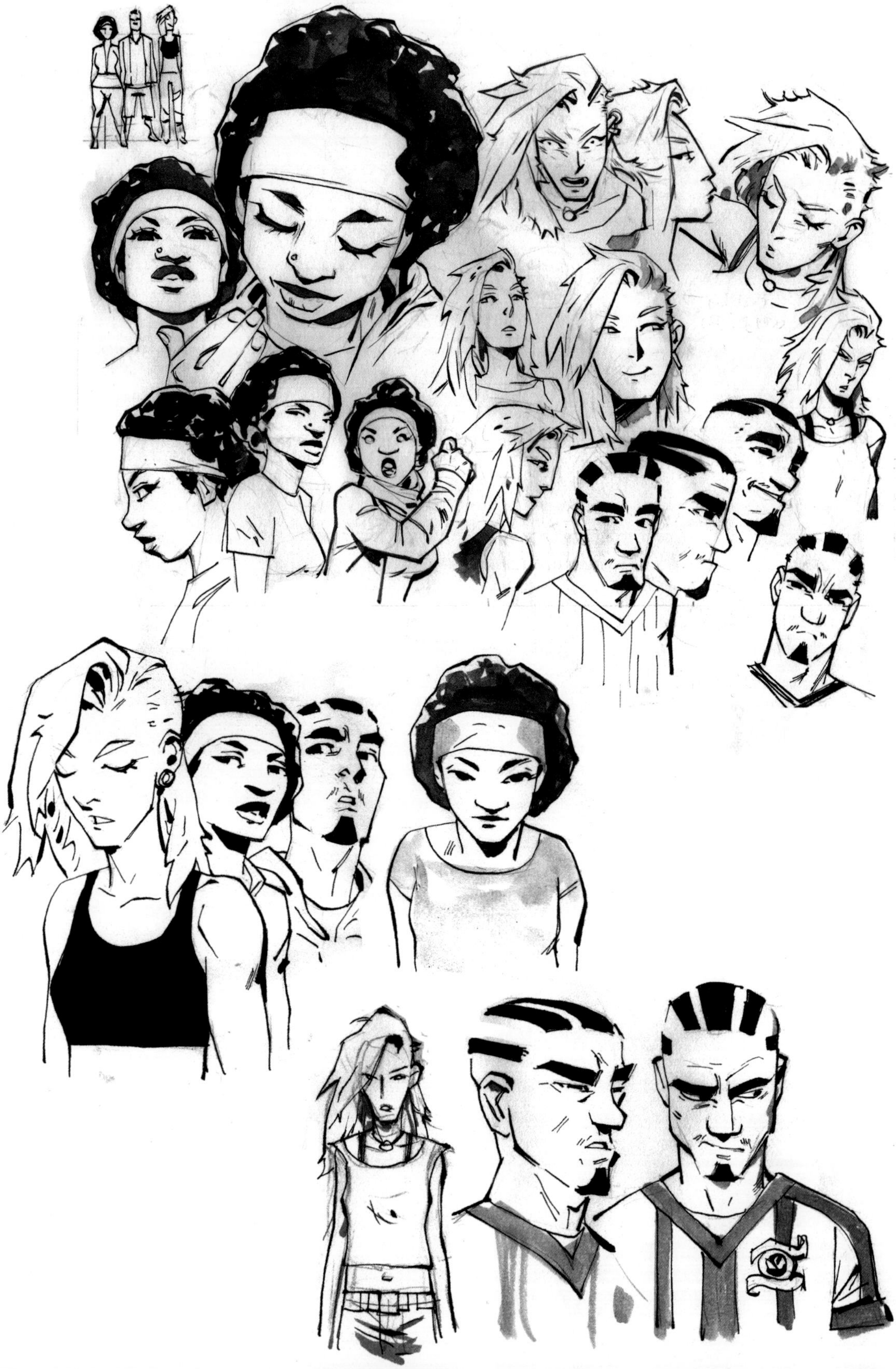

CHARACTER STUDIES

Some preliminary studies of **Zé Fofinho** (*left*) alongside his final look, by **Roger Cruz.**

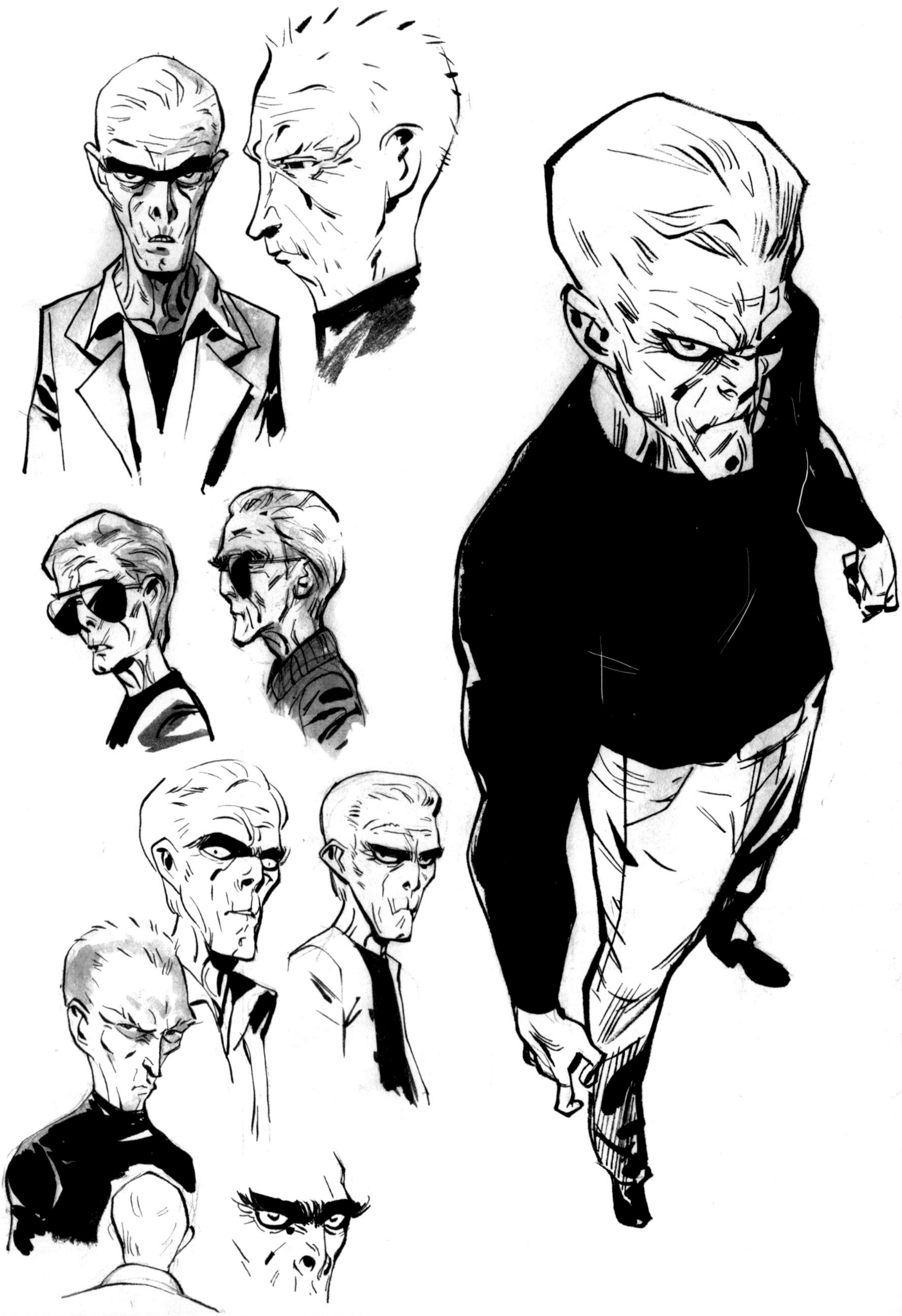

CHARACTER STUDIES

First studies of **Noronha**, **Rato**, and **Fedor** by **Roger Cruz.**

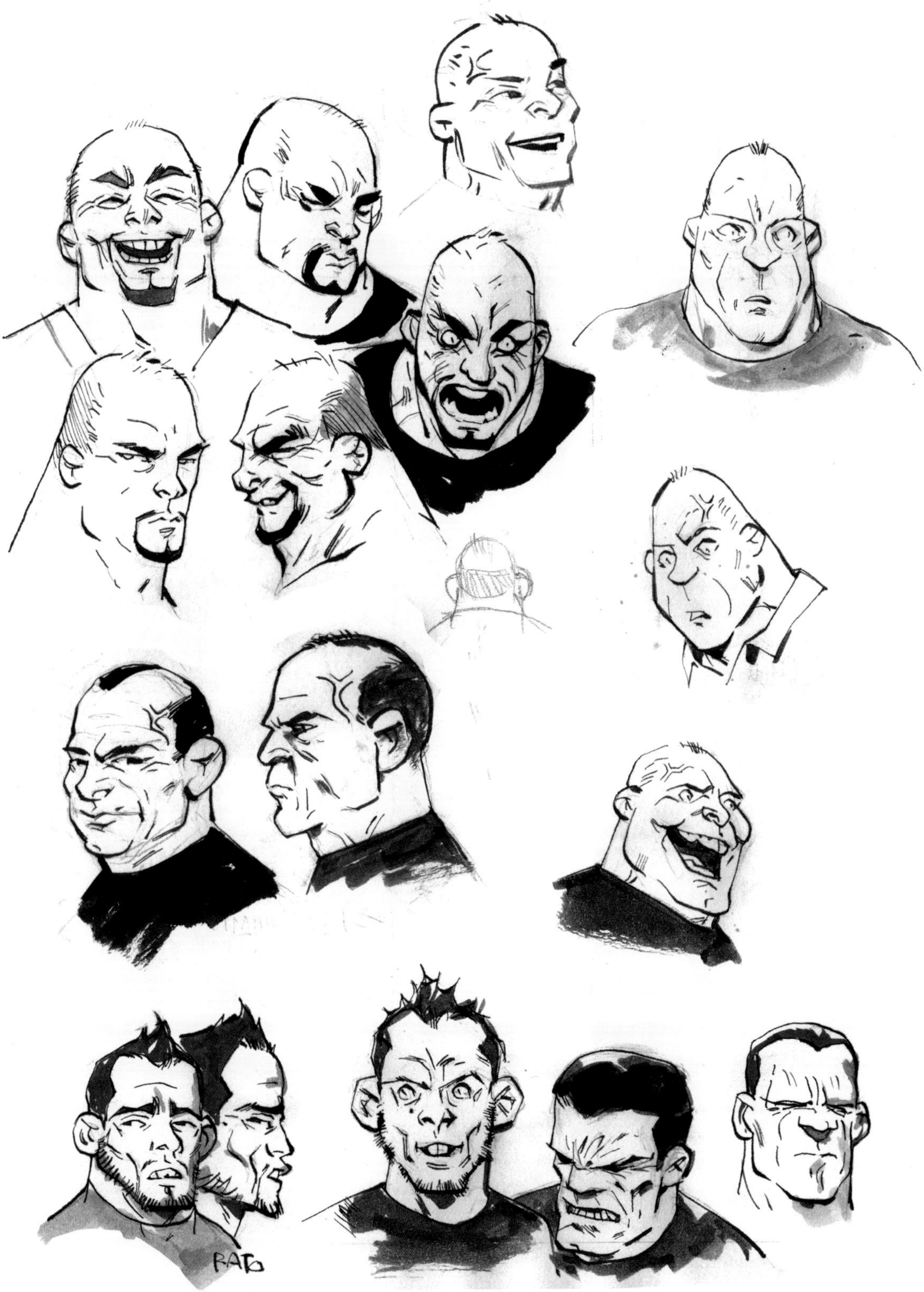
RATO

THE COLORING OF A COMIC PAGE

The first step in **Cris Peter's** work process is to mark the elements on the page using **base colors** (*left*), followed by the **ambient colors** (*bottom left*). Then, the final touch is done with the **lighting colors** (*below*), adding shadows and light to the final art.

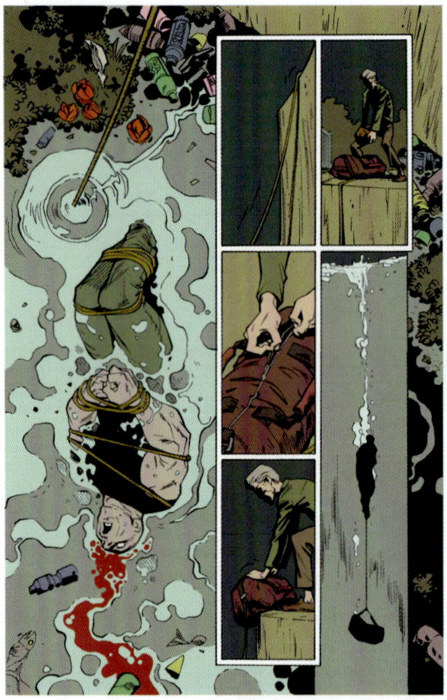

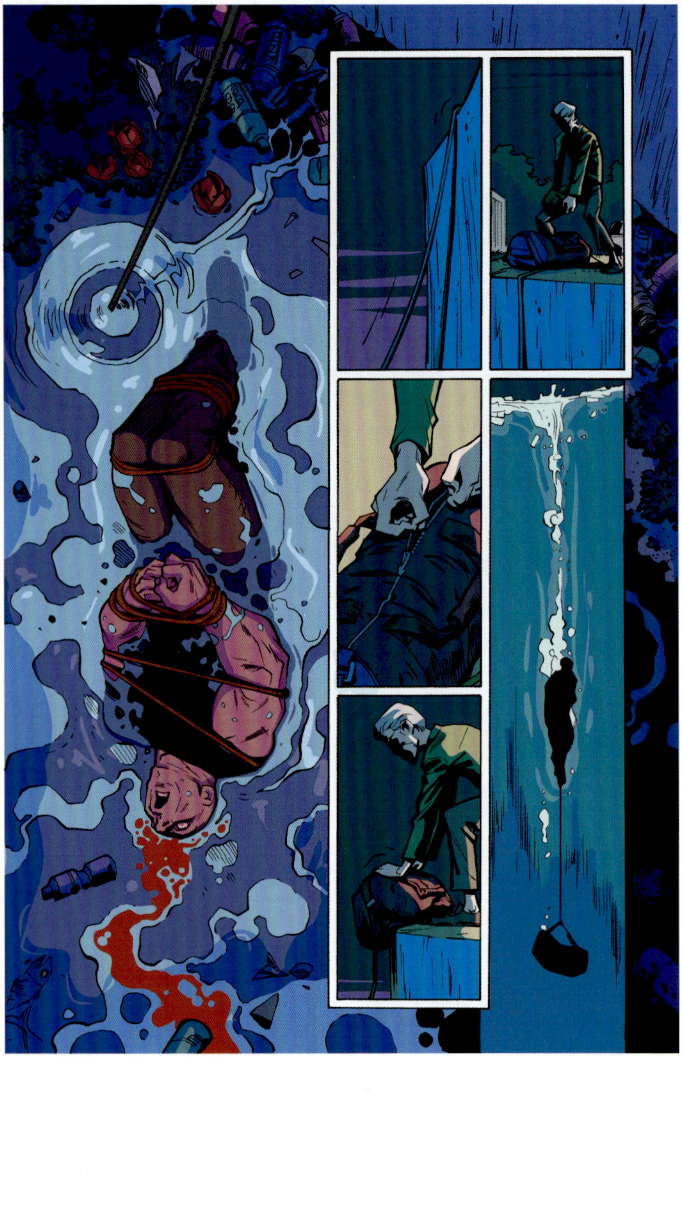

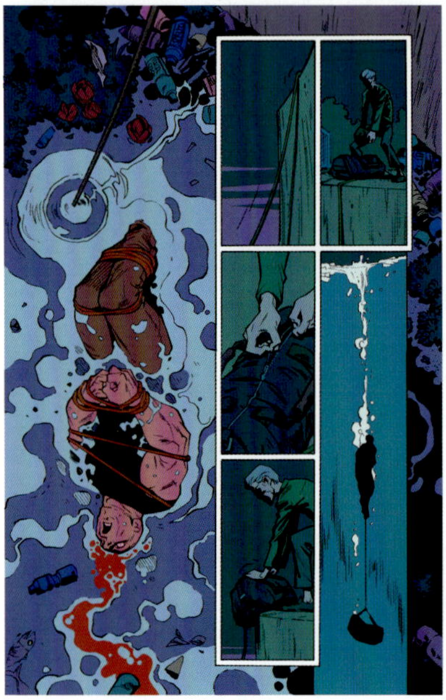

ABOUT THE CREATORS

RAFAEL SCAVONE started writing comics in 2014. His main work includes **Wonder Woman**, **All-Star Batman**, and Mark Millar's **Hit-Girl**. In 2017 he adapted the popular Neil Gaiman tale **A Study in Emerald**. Rafael's latest works are **Hidden Society**, for Dark Horse Comics, and **Funny Creek**, for Comixology.

rafaelscavone.com @scavone @rafaelscavone

RAFAEL ALBUQUERQUE is an Eisner, Harvey, and Inkpot Award winner for the **New York Times** bestseller **American Vampire**. He has been working for major publishers since 2005. As well as his work on **Hidden Society**, **All-Star Batman**, **Batgirl**, **Huck**, and **Ei8ht**, he has adapted the Neil Gaiman tale **A Study in Emerald** and Mark Millar's **Hit-Girl**.

rafaelalbuquerque.com @rafaalbuquerque @rafaelalbuquerque81

ROGER CRUZ has been drawing comics for the US market since 1994. He's known for **X-Men**, **X-Men First Class**, **X-Force**, **Generation X**, **Darkness**, **Spider-Man**, **Doctor Strange**, **Ghost Rider**, **Hulk**, and **10th Muse**, among many other titles for Marvel and Image. In Brazil he published **Os fabulosos**, **A irmandade bege**, and the award-winning comics **Xampu** and **Quaisqualigundum**.

rogercruzcomics.com @rogercruzbr @rogercruzart

CRIS PETER is a comic book colorist who has worked on more than two hundred titles for DC Comics, Marvel, Image, Dark Horse, and many other publishers. She was nominated for Best Coloring at the 2012 Eisner Awards for her work on **Casanova**. She also colored **Petals**, a young readers' book nominated in 2019. Her most recent works are **Collapser** and **Shadow of the Batgirl**, both published by DC Comics.

crispeterdigitalcolors.com @coloristdiaries

BERNARDO BRICE is a comic book letterer based in Santiago, Chile. Lettering credits include **DOTA 2** and **Artifact** (Valve Corporation), **Adora and the Distance** and **Funny Creek** (Comixology Originals), **Hidden Society** (Dark Horse Comics) and **La Voz de M.A.Y.O.: Tata Rambo** (Image Comics), among others, along with other comics anthologies and graphic novels published in English and Spanish.

bardoner.com @bernardobri

FELIX HORNE is a freelance comic book editor and facilitator, with over a decade of experience working in the comics industry. They have worked on comics published by Image Comics and Comixology.

bisbiserka.com

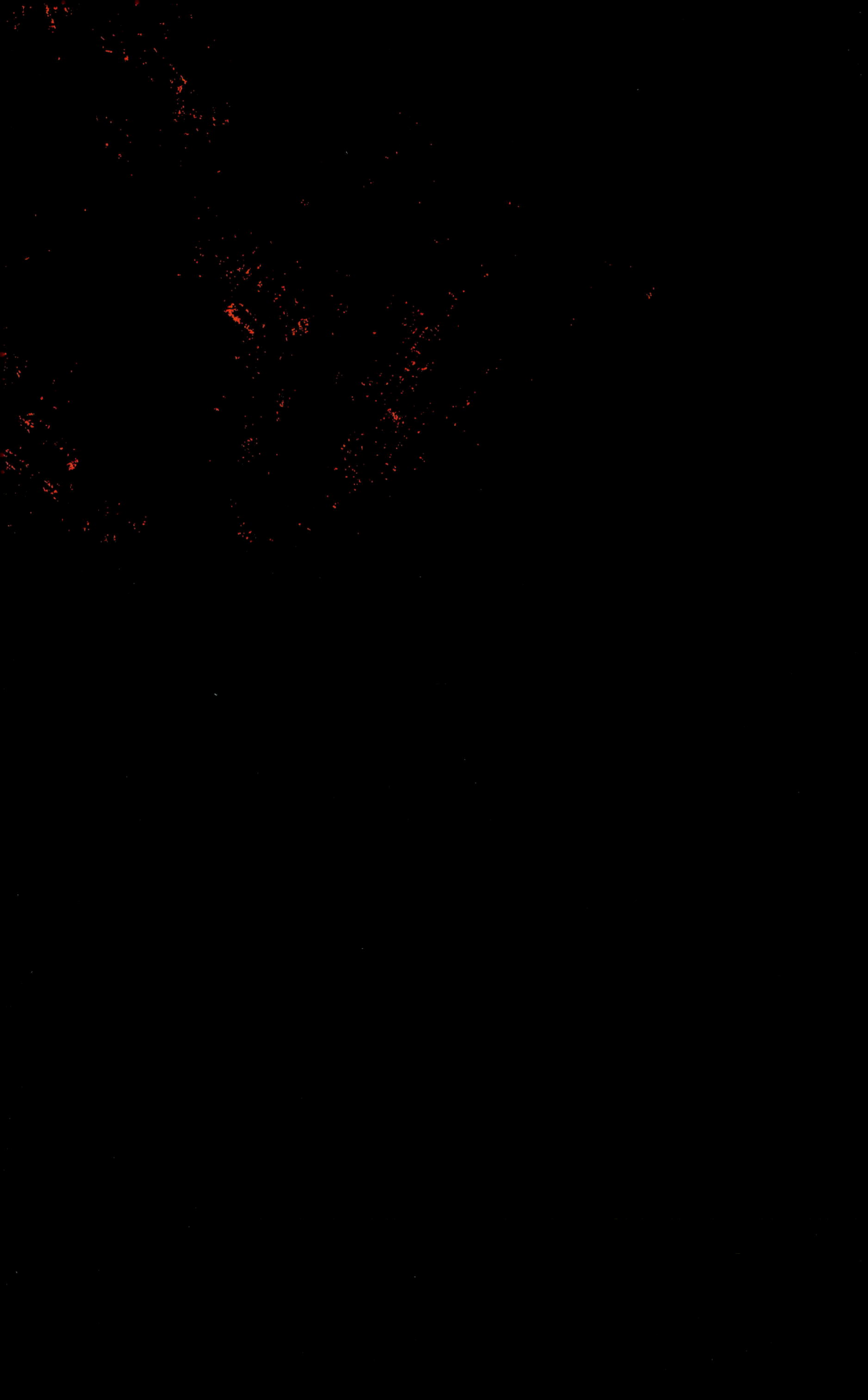

COMIXOLOGY COMES TO DARK HORSE BOOKS!

AFTERLIFT
Chip Zdarsky, Jason Loo, Paris Alleyne, Aditya Bidikar
US $19.99/CAN $25.99
ISBN: 978-1-50672-440-9

BREAKLANDS
Justin Jordan, Tyasseta, Sarah Stern
US $19.99/CAN $25.99
ISBN: 978-1-50672-441-6

YOUTH
Curt Pires, Alex Diotto, Dee Cunniffe
US $19.99/CAN $25.99
ISBN: 978-1-50672-461-4

THE BLACK GHOST
Monica Gallagher, Alex Segura, Marco Finnegan, George Kambadai, Ellie Wright
US $19.99/CAN $25.99
ISBN: 978-1-50672-446-1

THE PRIDE OMNIBUS
Joe Glass, Cem Iroz, Hector Barros, Jacopo Camagni, Ryan Cody, Mark Dale, and others
US $29.99/CAN $39.99
ISBN: 978-1-50672-447-8

STONE STAR VOLUME 1: FIGHT OR FLIGHT
Jim Zub, Max Dunbar, Espen Grundetjern
US $19.99/CAN $25.99
ISBN: 978-1-50672-458-4

LOST ON PLANET EARTH
Magdalene Visaggio, Claudia Aguirre
US $19.99/CAN $25.99
ISBN: 978-1-50672-456-0

DELVER
MK Reed, Spike C. Trotman, Clive Hawken
US $19.99/CAN $25.99
ISBN: 978-1-50672-452-2

DRACULA: SON OF THE DRAGON
Mark Sable, Salgood Sam
US $19.99/CAN $25.99
ISBN: 978-1-50672-442-3

TREMOR DOSE
Michael Conrad, Noah Bailey
US $19.99/CAN $25.99
ISBN: 978-1-50672-460-7

THE DARK
Mark Sable, Kristian Donaldson, Lee Loughridge
US $19.99/CAN $25.99
ISBN: 978-1-50672-459-1

CREMA
Johnnie Christmas, Dante Luiz, Ryan Ferrier
US $19.99/CAN $25.99
ISBN: 978-1-50672-603-8

SNOW ANGELS VOLUME 1
Jeff Lemire, Jock
US $19.99/CAN $25.99
ISBN: 978-1-50672-648-9

SNOW ANGELS VOLUME 2
Jeff Lemire, Jock
US $19.99/CAN $25.99
ISBN: 978-1-50672-649-6

SNOW ANGELS LIBRARY EDITION
Jeff Lemire, Jock
US $19.99/CAN $25.99
ISBN: 978-1-50672-648-9

THE ALL-NIGHTER
Chip Zdarsky, Jason Loo, Paris Aditya
US $19.99/CAN $25.99
ISBN: 978-1-50672-804-9

ADORA AND THE DISTANCE
Marc Bernardin, Ariela Kristantina, Jessica Kholinne
US $14.99/CAN $19.99
ISBN: 978-1-50672-450-8

WE ONLY KILL EACH OTHER
Stephanie Phillips, Peter Krause, Ellie Wright
US $19.99/CAN $25.99
ISBN: 978-1-50672-808-7

THE STONE KING
Kel McDonald, Tyler Crook
US $19.99/CAN $25.99
ISBN: 978-1-50672-448-5

LIEBESTRASSE
Greg Lockard, Tim Fish, Hector Barros
US $19.99/CAN $25.99
ISBN: 978-1-50672-455-3

EDEN
Matt Arnold, Riccardo Burchielli
US $22.99/CAN $29.99
ISBN: 978-1-50673-090-5

ASTONISHING TIMES
Frank Barbiere with Arris Quinones, Ruairi Coleman, Lauren Affe, Taylor Esposito
US $22.99/CAN $29.99
ISBN: 978-1-50673-083-7

WE HAVE DEMONS
Scott Snyder, Greg Capullo
US $19.99/CAN $25.99
ISBN: 978-1-50672-833-9

EDGEWORLD
Chuck Austen, Patrick Olliffe
US $19.99/CAN $25.99
ISBN: 978-1-50672-834-6

ELEPHANTMEN 2261 OMNIBUS VOLUME 1
Richard Starkings, Axel Medellin
US $24.99/CAN $33.99
ISBN: 978-1-50673-540-5

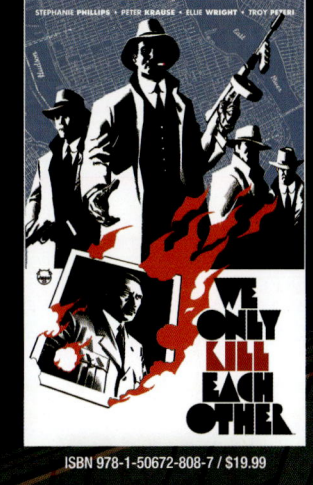

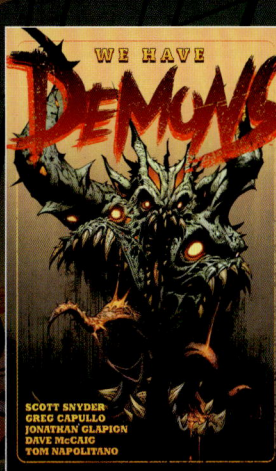

ISBN 978-1-50672-808-7 / $19.99

ISBN 978-1-50672-833-9 / $19.99

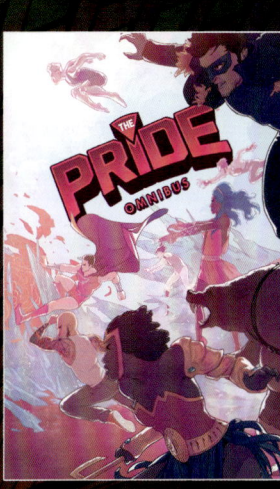

ISBN 978-1-50672-447-8 / $29.99

AVAILABLE AT YOUR LOCAL COMICS SHOP OR BOOKSTORE
To find a comics shop near you, visit comicshoplocator.com For more information or to order direct, visit darkhorse.com

Afterlift™ © 2021 Zdarsco, Inc. & Jason Loo. The Black Ghost © 2021 Alex Segura, Monica Gallagher, and George Kambadais. Breaklands™ © 2021 Justin Jordan and Albertus Tyasseta. The Pride™ 2018, 2021 Joseph Glass, Gavin Mitchell and Cem Iroz. Stone Star™ © 2019, 2021 Jim Zub and Max Zunbar. Youth™ © 2021 Curt Pires, Alex Diotto, Dee Cunniffe. Dracula: Son of the Dragon™ © 2020, 2021 Mark Sable and Salgood Sam.Tremor Dose™ © 2019, 2021 Michael W. Conrad and Noah Bailey. The Dark™ © 2019, 2021 Mark Sable & Kristian Donaldson. Delver © 2019, 2021 C. Spike Trotman, MK Reed, and Clive Hawken. Lost on Planet Earth™ © 2020, 2021 Magdalene Visaggio and Claudia Aguirre. Crema™ © 2020, 2021 Johnnie Christmas. Snow Angels™ © 2021, 2022 Jeff Lemire and Jock. The Allnighter™ © 2020, 2022 Zdarsco, Inc. & Jason Loo. Adora and the Distance™ Volume One © 2021, 2022 Marc Bernardin and Ariela Kristantina. We Only Kill Each Other™ © 2021, 2022 Stephanie Phillips and Peter Krause. The Stone King © 2018, 2021, 2022 Kel McDonald and Tyler Crook. Liebestrasse™ © 2021, 2022 Greg Expectations, LLC, and Timothy Poisson. Eden © 2021, 2022 Matthew Arnold and Darkling Entertainment Inc. Astonishing Times™ © 2021, 2022 Barbiere, Quinones, and Coleman. We Have Demons™ © 2021, 2022 Scott Snyder and Greg Capullo. Edgeworld™ © 2021, 2022 Wimzi, Inc. Elephantmen 2261™ © 2019, 2023 Richard Starkings. "ComiXology" and the ComiXology logos are registered trademarks of ComiXology. Dark Horse Books® and the Dark Horse logo are registered trademarks of Dark Horse Comics LLC. All rights reserved. (BL5108)

COMIXOLOGY ORIGINALS

DARK HORSE BOOKS